The Laura Black Scottsdale Mysteries

Books by

B A Trimmer

~~~~

The Laura Black

Scottsdale Mystery Series

Scottsdale Heat

Scottsdale Squeeze

Scottsdale Sizzle

Scottsdale Scorcher

Scottsdale Sting

Scottsdale Shuffle

Scottsdale Shadow

Scottsdale Secret

Scottsdale Silence

Scottsdale Scandal

Scottsdale Sleuth

~~~~

The Aloha Lagoon

Mystery Series

Hula Homicide

Homicide Honeymoon

Scottsdale Secret

Scottsdale Secret

B A TRIMMER

Editors: 'Andi' Anderson and Kimberly Mathews

Composite cover art and design by Janet Holmes using images under license from Shutterstock.com and Depositphotos.com.

ISBN: 978-1-951052-13-3
Saguaro Sky Media Co.
070124pb

E-mail the author at LauraBlackScottsdale@gmail.com
Follow at www.facebook.com/ScottsdaleSeries

*Thanks to Katie Hilbert
for her wonderful story ideas.*

Thanks also to Bonnie Costilow,
Barbara Hackel, Diana Hepner,
Jeanette Ellmer, Millie Knight,
Gail Shillito, and
Tony Tumminello

Scottsdale Secret

Introduction

If you've never read a Laura Black Scottsdale mystery, you may want to start with *Scottsdale Heat,* the first book in the series. If you'd instead start with this book, here are a few of the key people in the story:

Laura Black – A Scottsdale native with a degree in philosophy from Arizona State University. After a few years as a bartender, she now works as an investigator in a Scottsdale law firm. She wants to make the world better, but she also has bills to pay.

Sophia Rodriguez – Laura's best friend works as the receptionist and paralegal in the law office. Sophie's a former California surfer chick and a free spirit who enjoys dating multiple men.

Gina Rondinelli – Laura's other best friend. She's a former Scottsdale police detective and the law firm's senior investigator. She has a strict moral code and likes playing by the rules.

Leonard Shapiro – Head of the law firm and Laura's boss. He has few morals, loose ethics, and no people skills, but with the help of Laura, Sophie, and Gina, he usually wins his cases.

Anthony "Tough Tony" DiCenzo – Head of the local crime family. He likes Laura and almost thinks of her as a daughter. Through various adventures over the past year, he owes Laura several favors.

Maximilian Bettencourt – Laura's boyfriend and number two man in the local crime family. Before coming to Scottsdale, he was a secret operative for the U.S. government, mainly working in Eastern Europe. For Laura's safety, they need to keep their relationship a secret.

Gabriella – A former government operative from somewhere in Eastern Europe. She currently works as a bodyguard for Tony and Max. She takes pleasure in hurting and killing men.

Danielle Ortega – Laura's friend and the head of a rival crime organization. Her father is Escobar Salazar, the ruthless leader of an international drug cartel called the Black Death.

Milo and Snake – Sophie's main boyfriends. Milo works as a mid-level minion for Tough Tony DiCenzo. Snake is currently the backup quarterback for the Arizona Cardinals.

Grandma Peckham – Laura's longtime neighbor. She's recently become engaged to a man named Grandpa Bob.

Andrew "Jet" Kramer – Gina's current boyfriend. They met at the law office when Jet was a client. He got his nickname back when he was a Navy SEAL.

The Cougars – A group of wealthy, sexy, and fashionable women who like to troll the clubs of Scottsdale looking for athletic younger men for hook-up relationships. Through a series of adventures, Laura, Sophie, and Gina have become unofficial members of their group.

Elle – One of the Cougars. She lives in a beautiful house in North Scottsdale and recently began dating Lenny.

Prologue

"Well," Max said, looking at me with a tired smile. "You did say you wanted us to spend more quality time together."

"That's true," I replied. My throat was dry, and it was getting hard to talk. "But being handcuffed and staked down in the middle of the Sonoran Desert wasn't exactly what I had in mind for a romantic getaway."

"When I took you to Vail, it was only supposed to be for a fun vacation weekend. I'm sorry it's led to this."

"Vail wasn't so bad," I said. "At least I learned how to ski. That was fun. Plus, we got to sip champagne in a hot tub, in the snow. I loved that part."

"It wasn't too cold? You looked half-frozen, standing on the roof in only your bikini. You were shivering so hard I could hear your teeth chatter."

"Yeah, it was cold. I've never had ice in my hair like that before. But we were together, and it was so romantic."

We sat in the dirt of the open desert. The sun was high in the cloudless sky, and only the faintest trace of a warm breeze stirred the air. Two vultures lazily circled the sky over our heads, hoping they'd soon get a meal.

Our cuffed hands were chained to metal rods that had been solidly pounded into the soil. Our attacker had gone, leaving us to slowly die of exposure.

As I thought about how we'd gotten here, it was hard to believe it'd been less than a week since we'd left Arizona for our weekend ski vacation…

Chapter One

Surprisingly, the ski trip to Colorado had started out okay. Max met me at my apartment Friday morning, and we loaded up my luggage in one of his black SUVs.

Milo was driving, and Gabriella was acting as our bodyguard. Actually, I was amazed she was with us at all since she'd been shot only three days before in Nevada by a vicious killer named Jonathan LaRose.

The drive from my apartment to the Scottsdale Airpark wasn't very long, but that's when my intuition started to warn me that something crappy was going to happen.

It had nothing to do with what would occur over the next week. It was instead over something silly -- skiing.

When I'd first told Max I wanted a weekend in the snow, he suggested we go to Vail. I'd been there once before, in the summer, and I'd loved it.

A weekend in Vail had sounded perfect. Well, it did until he also asked if I wanted to learn to ski.

I'd lived in Scottsdale all my life. Honestly, snow skiing was pretty much at the bottom of my bucket list, along with learning to hang glide off a cliff and scuba diving in a shark cage.

But Max had seemed so eager when he asked me, I knew I couldn't say no without disappointing him. Now that I'd agreed to do the skiing thing, there was nothing to do except go through with it.

When we got to the airport, Milo drove us out to a small white corporate jet parked outside a large hangar. When I looked at Max, he seemed to know what I was thinking.

"No," he said. "It's not Tony's jet. We usually lease a plane when we travel. It's easier for Gabriella to bring her gear along this way. If we tried to fly commercial out of Sky Harbor, that would be, um, difficult."

I could understand that. In addition to the things a woman usually puts in her bag, Gabriella kept an Uzi submachine gun and several magazines of ammunition in hers. I knew she also carried a military fighting knife and something that looked suspiciously like a hand grenade.

As Max and Milo loaded the bags onto the jet, I asked Milo if he'd be skiing with us.

"Me?" he asked, a horrible look contorting his face. "Skiing? No. I'll be going with you to Vail, but I don't ski. I won't be able to do anything more than drive the car and sit in the lodge with Gabriella."

I looked at Max, and he seemed to read my thoughts again.

"I usually go skiing with Gabriella," he said. "But no matter how bravely she talks, I don't think she'll be up for skiing for at least a week, maybe two."

Gabriella came up to us, looking annoyed. "The doctors did good job of patching me up. They want me to sit in chair for two weeks, but that's not how I heal. When I get shot, I like to go back to field as soon as possible. If I sit, it takes longer for everything to get better. But no, I won't be able to go skiing on this trip. I tell Max to bring along someone else to be with on mountain, but he say no."

"I think we'll be okay," Max said. "Things are pretty quiet, and only a few trusted people have any idea where we're going. I don't think anyone's going to bother us in Colorado."

Climbing into the plane was a strange experience. I'd never been on a jet this small. Still, with only the four of us as passengers, it seemed relatively roomy and comfortable.

Milo acted as our bartender, and it would have been rude to refuse his offer to pour me an eighteen-year-old Glenlivet scotch, no doubt a gift from Tony. By the time we took off, I'd had a couple of drinks and was starting to feel much better about the trip.

The flight to Colorado was pleasant, and I was able to forget about skiing for a while. It was fun watching as the terrain below went from dry and dusty to green and snowy.

We arrived at the Eagle County Regional Airport about an hour after we took off from the Scottsdale Airpark. As I made my way down the steps from the plane, I was hit by a blast of icy mountain air, a first for me.

As a Scottsdale native, I seldom experience anything colder than the walk-in beer cooler at the QuikTrip convenience store by my house. The frigid Colorado air instantly made my nose tingle and my lungs tighten. These were two interesting and rather unpleasant sensations.

A black SUV was waiting for our group. After all our luggage was loaded in the back and we were all on board, Milo drove us along the scenic route along Interstate 70 to the hotel.

As we headed up the highway toward the Continental

Divide, the hills on both sides of the road gradually rose beside us. Within a few minutes, we were in a broad valley surrounded by high snow-covered mountain peaks. I'd never been in the Colorado mountains in the winter before, and it was an incredible sight.

Vail was as beautiful as I remembered when I'd visited it in the summer. The main village and the ski mountain were on the south side of the valley, just before the road began to climb a steep mountain pass.

The little town was designed to look like a European ski village. The streets were narrow, and cars were only allowed in certain areas.

The hotel was terrific. The décor somehow managed to combine both a Western cowboy vibe and an old-fashioned skiing motif.

Throughout the lobby, a mixture of branding irons and lassos were mixed in with antique wooden skis and bamboo poles. At first, this seemed like a strange mix of themes, but it didn't take me long to get used to it.

One thing about the lobby I immediately loved was the real wood fire, crackling and snapping in the fireplace. It gave the room a warm, pine-scented aroma. I'd never experienced this before, and I knew it would be something I'd miss when we went back home.

Max and I stayed in the Bighorn Suite, which took up three rooms on the top floor. Off the main living area, a balcony overlooked Vail Square, the gondola, and the ski runs on the mountain. Looking out at the steep white slopes made me slightly panicky, but I did my best to keep it in check.

Once we'd settled into our suite, we got ready to rent some skis and head to dinner. Max dug through his luggage and changed into a lemon-yellow ski parka with black trim. The jacket was so bright it was a little hard to look at.

"Nice jacket," I said sarcastically.

"I like to ski in bright colors," he said, ignoring me. "I tend to ski kind of fast, and the jacket helps people see me coming."

We met Milo and Gabriella in the lobby. Max led everyone back outside to a flagstone courtyard in front of the hotel. After the warmth and comfort of the foyer, stepping outside hit me like a cold slap in the face.

When our plane had landed, maybe two hours ago, the sky had been clear and a striking deep blue. But now, clouds were rolling in, and there was a humid tinge to the air.

Max and Gabriella agreed that it smelled like it was about to snow. I wasn't sure how someone could smell snow, but I took their word on this one.

We walked down a narrow pedestrian street to a ski shop where they fitted me for boots, poles, and skis. The boots seemed to fit rather tightly, but I was assured this was how it was supposed to be.

I would have loved browsing through all the colorful jackets, gloves, and hats in the shop, but I could tell Max was more in the mood for dinner than shopping. I didn't want to be the problem child of the group, so we took off.

Dinner was at a very romantic Italian restaurant. Walking in, the aromas of oregano and roasted garlic reminded me a little of Frankie Z's. However, here, the fragrance of the food was mixed in with the Christmas tree scent from another pine log fire.

Max and I were seated at a table in the corner while Gabriella and Milo were against the wall, three tables away. They looked like any other couple on a date. The only difference was that Gabriella kept scanning the room for problems, and her open black bag sat in the middle of the table.

"Well," Max said as we sipped our glasses of Chianti and waited for the dinners to arrive. "Is this what you had in mind for a vacation in the snow?"

"It's wonderful," I said as I reached out to hold his hand. "The village is beautiful, and the hotel is perfect."

"It's not too chilly?"

"I won't lie. It's freezing here," I said with a laugh. "But I'll manage. I'm glad I got an actual ski outfit. The jacket seems good for the cold. I'll wear the snow pants tomorrow, and I should be good for whatever happens."

"How about the altitude?" he asked. "We're up over eight thousand feet here."

"I'm noticing that. I can't even walk across the parking lot before I start to lose my breath."

"Unfortunately, we won't be here long enough for you to get used to it. But we'll take it slow."

"So, um, we're skiing tomorrow?"

"Yes. I've set you up with an instructor at the ski school, and she'll get you going."

"Really?" I asked. "I assumed you'd want to teach me yourself."

"Not this time. There are some things you need a professional for. She'll go over the basics and make sure you can get down the hill in one piece. You'll be able to learn at your own pace, but you'll learn how to ski the right way."

"What about you?"

"While you're learning how to turn your skis on the snow, I'll use the morning to ski the back bowls. After a few hours of that, I'll welcome spending the afternoon going down some groomed slopes with you."

"It sounds like you'll be sore tomorrow night," I said with a grin.

"Yes, I know," he said with a playful smile. "But the hotel has a nice hot tub on the roof. As far as I remember, it has a great view of the village and the mountain. Although, I won't be able to guarantee that it'll snow while we're sitting in it."

"Right, I guess I might have mentioned watching people sitting in hot tubs on the Travel Channel, huh?"

"Only five or six times," he said with a sweet grin. "You said sitting in a hot tub while it was snowing looked magical. I'm not sure about anything mystical happening, but once you get into the water, it feels great and helps work out the kinks after a long day of skiing."

I squeezed his hand and looked into his gorgeous eyes. "Thank you for bringing me. I know it's expensive and was a lot of work to arrange everything."

"Don't worry about it," he said. "I'm glad we'll be able to spend a quiet weekend by ourselves before things start to get busy back in Arizona."

An hour later, after we'd finished sipping our after-dinner coffees, we all walked the five minutes back to the hotel. By the time we arrived, it had started to snow.

I was fascinated watching it fall and was a little disappointed we'd arrived back at the hotel so quickly. After the ski shop, I was in the mood to look around the town and maybe visit some of the other stores.

Once we made it back to the room, I unpacked my things and hung everything in the closet. I was starting to entertain some naughty thoughts about Max. Unfortunately, he had other plans.

"Vacation or no," he said. "I'm going to need to call in for the daily wrap-up meeting. You're welcome to stay here, if you promise to be good."

He gave me a look that told me he knew what I was thinking. The last time I'd stayed with him for one of these meetings, I hadn't exactly behaved myself.

"Well," I said. "If you're going to be on the phone for the next hour, I'll go back down and walk around. It's so beautiful here. I'd like to watch the snow and explore the village."

"Alright, I'll have Milo go with you."

"I'll be fine. I don't need a babysitter to walk the streets of a fancy resort town."

Max gave me a look, like he was going to argue about it, but then sighed in defeat.

"Fine," he said. "Keep your phone with you in case something comes up. And try to find your way back here sometime tonight?"

"Alright, if I have to," I said as I smiled and hugged him.

I dressed in my red ski coat, the gloves, and my new hat. I was still wearing my new boots, which had been advertised as being ideal for the snow.

Bundled up against the cold, I kissed Max and took the elevator down to the lobby. In addition to the fireplace, the hotel had a fun-looking bar, but I wanted to go outside and explore.

I stepped back out onto the street. Even though I'd braced myself, taking in the first lungful of frozen air was still a shock.

It seemed to be a step colder than when we'd been out for dinner, only a little while ago. I'd tried to be brave around Max earlier in the day, but it was freaking cold here.

Fortunately, for curious tourists like me, there was a giant thermometer on the side of the hotel. I looked at it, and the dial was pointed to fourteen degrees.

Damn, that still sounds like something from a science fiction movie.

I randomly picked a direction and walked past several cute shops and restaurants. It was snowing harder than before, and the flakes were huge. I caught a couple of them on my glove, and they were beautiful.

I'd read about snow in school as a kid. I'd even played in it when Sophie and I had gone Christmas shopping in Flagstaff, but this was the first time I'd been outside when it was actually falling out of the sky.

The wind was calm, so the snow floated to the ground very slowly. The streets were lit by thousands of tiny white Christmas lights wrapped around the trees and strung overhead.

It made everything look like a magical village in a snow globe. It was beautiful, and for the first time, I could see why people would put up with the cold to live in a place like this.

Even though it was getting late, most of the shops were

still open. I was surprised by how crowded many of the stores were.

I walked into one of the larger shops and looked around. Seeing the prices on the winter wear reminded me that I needed to call Sophie and thank her again for helping me find my ski outfit.

Thinking of Sophie made me wonder what she was up to. I knew she was supposed to be going out with Snake, who was currently the second-string quarterback for the Arizona Cardinals. Still, her plans were always fluid when it came to dating.

I went back outside and walked toward the mountain. After a few minutes, I came to the gondola. Even though it wasn't running, it was brightly lit and seemed rather imposing.

I sent Sophie a selfie with the falling snow and the ski lift in the background, along with a text asking how she was doing. Rather than texting me back, she called.

"Hey, girlfriend," she said. "How's Vail? Is it as beautiful as the pictures on the internet?"

"It's even better. I feel like I'm walking through some little ski village in the Bavarian Alps."

"Really? Have you ever been to Bavaria?"

"That's not the point."

"It looks cold there."

"I've never been anywhere this cold in my life. It's even colder than the time we went to Flagstaff. If you imagine the freezer in your kitchen, but take out all the food and make the freezer the size of a city, that's what it's like here."

"How's the outfit doing? Is it keeping you warm?"

"So far, so good. Thanks again for finding the thrift store.

It was a real lifesaver. I'm still dreading the skiing tomorrow, but at least I should be warm while doing it. But my face is freezing out here. I should have worn the balaclava. I'm going to head back to the hotel in a few minutes. Weren't you going out with Snake tonight?"

"Well, we had dinner, then hung out at his place for a while. But there's a game on Sunday, and the team's on a nine o'clock curfew. Right now, I'm driving back to my place."

"How's he doing with being the official backup quarterback? Do you think he'll get a chance to play on Sunday?"

"He didn't like it at first, but now he's starting to warm up to it. He's thinking about the ten-thousand-dollar bonus he'll get for every play he's in. If he can play a quarter of the game, that'll be like a hundred thousand dollars. If he can throw for a touchdown, it's even more."

"Damn, we're in the wrong business."

"True that, but he's also starting to get a little cocky. I think I liked him better when he didn't have a prayer of playing."

"What's Gina up to? Is she out with Jet again?"

"Yup, and from the way she talked, she'll probably be with him all weekend."

"Well, I'm glad she found someone. Hopefully, it lasts longer than the guy from the gym. The fact that Jet's an ex-Navy SEAL should help."

"Yeah, some of the other guys she's tried to date freaked out a little when they learned she used to be a police detective. I don't know how long Jet will be around, but I think Gina's determined to use him as hard as she can for as long as they're together."

"Isn't he still a client?"

"Nah. Gina wrapped up the work on his assignment yesterday. Not that she seemed overly concerned about hooking up with him, even when he was a client."

"I guess maybe we're bad examples when it comes to picking out who to date?"

"Maybe," she said, "but I'm not going to worry about it, and I'm glad to see that Gina's happy."

"Me too. She deserves it. Is anything else going on? What about Lenny? Is he going to see Elle again this weekend?"

"Don't remind me," Sophie groaned. "He spent the afternoon asking Gina and me more of his awkward personal questions. Now that they're starting to date, he's worried that he's going to do something stupid and blow it."

"It's a valid concern," I said. "Lenny's pretty inept with women. But do you really think they're actually dating? That still doesn't seem like Elle's style. I know she said she was looking for something more than a quick fling, but I can't see Lenny as anyone's long-term."

"Well, Lenny thinks they're dating. We'll have to ask Elle about it next time we see her. Oh, and speaking of Lenny, don't forget you have an assignment waiting for you when you come in on Monday. The client will be here for a meeting at nine. I assume Lenny'll want you around for that."

"I remember. Any idea what it's about?"

"Honestly, I'm not sure what it is. I only glanced through the folder when Lenny put it on my desk this morning. It's pretty big. He wanted you to study the information before the meeting. It's something about an insurance scam."

"That's something new for us," I mused.

"Yeah, Lenny said he'd picked up a new insurance company as a client, and this must be it. Don't forget, I told him you're sick in bed. He probably wouldn't appreciate it if he found out you were skiing in Vail all weekend."

"I won't forget, and I'll be there. I know you were teasing me about the assignment. Still, I seriously hope this one doesn't have anything to do with taking pictures of naked people. I hate that part of the job. I even had a dream about doing that the other night."

"The assignment sounds pretty harmless," Sophie said. "Actually, it sounds kind of boring. Be glad you don't have to investigate insurance scams for a living."

"I hope I'm not too sore on Monday after a weekend of skiing."

"I hope you aren't laid up in some hospital. Remember that time in Italy when you broke your leg?"

"Shut up," I said. "Damn, I'm glad I'm almost back at the hotel. My face is starting to go numb."

While hurrying into the hotel, I turned the corner and ran into a guy. He'd just been standing there looking at the hotel entrance, like he was waiting for someone to come out.

It was entirely my fault. I had my head down to protect my face from the cold and wasn't paying attention.

"Sorry," I said as I bounced off him.

He gave me a look that was both surprised and angry, like he knew who I was and was pissed that I'd run into him. I focused on his face to see if I recognized him.

He was an ordinary-looking guy. He was of average height and weight and was somewhere in his late forties.

He had short dark hair, dark eyes, a three-day-old beard, and looked like anyone else, except for a nasty scar under his left eye. He was wearing a blueberry-colored Helly Hanson jacket and jet-black ski pants.

"Sorry," I said again, then scooted into the hotel. The blast of warm pine-scented air in the lobby felt terrific. I immediately headed toward the fireplace to take the chill off my face.

"What was that?" Sophie asked.

"Oh, I wasn't paying attention and ran into a guy. The hotel has a big stone fireplace in the lobby, and it smells wonderful. I'm warming myself in front of it right now. I can see why people who live in the snow have them."

"What's Milo up to?"

"I think he's somewhere here at the hotel. I doubt he'll get too far from Max tonight, and I think he'll be on guard duty later. But if he hasn't gone to sleep yet, he'd probably like to hear from you."

"I'll give him a call. Snake is nice and all, but I'm starting to miss my Pooh Bear."

"Pooh Bear?"

"I can't help it. He's so cuddly."

"Well, I wouldn't call him Pooh Bear in front of anyone, especially anyone he works with. That's the sort of name that can stick with you for years."

"I suppose. Good luck skiing tomorrow. Don't break anything important. And don't slam into a tree. Oh, and make sure not to ski off a cliff."

"Shut up," I said. "You're not helping my anxiety about this."

"You'll do fine. Who knows, you might even like it. Besides, Milo, Max, and Gabriella will all be there. What could go wrong?"

I hung up with Sophie and took the elevator to the top floor. Gabriella was sitting on a couch near the elevator, which had a view of the entire hallway. As usual, her black bag was next to her.

"Hey," I said. "How are you feeling? I'm not sure I could travel so soon after being shot. The healing process must be uncomfortable."

She looked down at her side, where I knew she still had large bandages covering both the entry and exit wounds. She then looked back at me and shrugged her shoulders.

"It's not so bad. Jonathan shoot me with medium caliber bullet, probably nine millimeter, but fortunately, he used solid core round. The bullet passed through muscle and skin. I've had worse. As long as I don't get into fight with anyone for a day or two, it will be okay."

"You don't have to sit here all night, I hope."

"Only until midnight. Milo will cover until seven-thirty. Then I'll be back. I do not expect trouble tonight. All should be good."

I wished Gabriella a quiet night, then used my keycard to get back into the room. Max was in the process of finishing up the meeting, so I used the time to strip out of my cold-weather gear. I noticed a bottle of champagne in an iced cooler and two acrylic flutes sitting on the table next to it.

"How was exploring?" he asked after he hung up.

"It's so beautiful here," I said as I walked up and wrapped my arms around him. Max used the opportunity to bend down and give me a wonderful, slow kiss.

"You got us champagne?" I asked during a pause in kissing.

"I noticed that it's snowing and the wind is calm. It sounds like the conditions you described that produce the magical hot tub results. I know we haven't been skiing yet, but would you like to try it? Unless someone else has been watching the Travel Channel, we'll probably have the hot tub to ourselves tonight. If you like it, we can use it again tomorrow. You'll probably need it after a day of skiing."

Yes! One more item checked off my bucket list.

"Really?" I asked. "That'd be great." I knew I was smiling gleefully, but I couldn't help it. I guess I'd been looking forward to the hot tub more than I'd let on, even to myself. "Let me put on a swimsuit, and we can head up to the roof."

Max pulled out his phone and called Gabriella. "Gabby, we'll be going up to the hot tub in a few minutes. The stairs to the roof are at the end of the hall. Would you mind checking it out?"

The closet conveniently held two terrycloth robes, along with two pairs of slippers. I grabbed a robe and went into the bathroom to change. I would've gotten dressed in the bedroom, but I knew what would happen if I got naked in front of Max, and I wanted to actually make it up to the roof to try out the hot tub.

I spent a few minutes in front of the mirror. I'd eaten a big dinner, so it took me some time to decide between the one-piece and the two-piece suits. But after that fashion decision, it wasn't long before I was ready to go.

We left our room wearing the robes and slippers. I was carrying the glasses, and Max had the champagne bottle.

Gabriella was coming down the stairway from the roof and had snowflakes stuck to her long black hair. Looking at us in our robes, she gave us a strange little half-smile. I still didn't know her well enough to know for sure, but I think the smile meant she thought we were crazy.

"There are no people on roof," she reported, the smile getting bigger. "This is not surprising. It is snowing and very cold. It reminds me of winters in Minsk. I think you will have privacy."

Gabriella walked back towards her couch while we climbed the stairs. At the top was a door with a yellow and black sign.

Caution: Icy and Windy Conditions may Exist.

Max opened the door, and we stepped through. As before, I took in the first blast of icy air with the usual shock as my lungs tightened in the cold.

There was a giant dial thermometer on the wall. I quickly glanced at it and saw that the temperature had dropped down to nine degrees.

You've got to be kidding me. I don't know if I could ever get used to this.

The hot tub was a dozen steps from the door, near the edge of the roof. Next to it was a rack for the bathrobes, a place for the slippers, and a raised wooden bench for getting dressed and undressed.

The tub itself was huge. I could see eight or ten people being able to sit comfortably in it at once. I was a little disappointed that it wasn't bubbling like the hot tub on the Travel Channel, but the water must have been hot, as clouds of steam were coming off the surface.

Next to the bench was a stainless-steel box the size of a small refrigerator; the sign on the front read: *Towel Warmer.* I quickly walked to the robe rack, hands in my pockets, trying to stay warm.

Judging the distance from the rack to the stairs that led into the hot tub, I slipped off the robe and instantly regretted it. Standing on a rooftop, in Vail, in November, dressed only in a bikini and slippers, suddenly seemed like a terrible idea.

My entire body was slapped by the cold, and I immediately started to shiver. I was so cold that my teeth chattered together.

Okay, maybe the hot tub isn't going to be so magical.

I quickly kicked off my slippers and made a beeline to the hot tub, leaving footprints in the two inches of snow that had fallen over the last couple of hours. Max was still in his robe, the cold apparently not bothering him at all.

He held out his hand and supported me as I lowered myself into the steamy tub. At first, the water seemed to be too hot. But after being nearly naked in the freezing air, the scalding water was a relief.

As I slowly forced myself down, my body adjusted to the water. It went from scalding, to hot, to perfect.

I sank down until I sat on a bench, and the warm water was up to my shoulders. I'd stopped shivering as soon as I'd gotten about halfway in and began feeling fantastic.

Still in his robe, Max took the wire off the champagne bottle, and there was a soft pop. He poured two glasses and handed one to me.

He then walked over to a dial mounted on the wall next to the towel warmer. "Are you ready?" he asked.

"For what?" I replied.

I was feeling great. I had a glass of champagne, and now I only needed Max beside me. Max turned the knob on the wall, took off his robe, and climbed into the water.

At first, nothing happened. Then, from somewhere

behind the wall, the sound of motors started. There was a sort of grinding and gurgling for several seconds, then water and bubbles began to shoot out from twenty different nozzles scattered under the water's surface.

I happened to have my back against one of the nozzles and was startled for a few seconds. When I realized these were the same bubbles I'd seen on the Travel Channel, I started to enjoy the sensation of the water pounding against my back.

From where we were sitting, I could see down to the village and sort of make out the gondola through the snow. There were lights on some of the trails higher up on the mountain, which gave the view a beautiful glow. The large flakes of snow were still falling, and I again felt like I was in the middle of a gigantic snow globe.

Okay, they were right. This is magical.

Max lifted his glass. "To our weekend in the snow."

We lightly tapped our acrylic flutes together, and I used the occasion to snuggle against him. Max put his arm around me and spent several minutes in a close embrace. The sensation of drinking the chilled champagne was terrific as we sat in the steam and the bubbles.

The parts of my body that stuck out from the water were cold, and the parts below the surface were hot, but they somehow seemed to balance each other out. Snowflakes were landing in our hair, and Max already had a nice dusting of snow on his head.

After about fifteen minutes, the timer on the wall must have run out. There was a click, and the bubbles stopped. Max got out, turned the dial, and filled our glasses again.

After he climbed back in, I used the opportunity to snuggle against him again. He, in turn, started kissing me.

"How long do you usually stay in here?" I asked after the timer ran out again. "I'm starting to get really hot."

"If you get too warm, just sit on the top part of the tub. With your upper body exposed to the cold, you can control your core temperature."

I did as he suggested and climbed to the top edge. My body immediately started to give off clouds of steam, and I quickly felt better.

Sitting like this was an unusual sensation. I felt the bite of the cold air against my skin, but I'd been so warm it actually felt good.

With only my legs still in the water, the ends of my hair started to freeze, but overall, the effect was quite comfortable. I knew it was going to be hard to describe to Sophie precisely what this was like.

By the third time the timer ran down, we knew it was time to head back to the room. Max climbed out first, then helped me to scramble out as well.

I quickly realized how exposed I was to the elements, walking in a bikini through almost three inches of snow. It didn't take long before I felt the cold air begin to bite at my exposed flesh.

"Oh my God, oh my God," I moaned as my teeth started to chatter. "It's so freaking cold out here."

So much for magical.

Max opened the towel warmer and pulled out a hot bath sheet. He wrapped it around me like a cape, and it took the edge off.

He gave me another hot towel, and I used it to more or less dry off my legs and arms. I quickly gathered up my bathrobe and slippers since I was wrapped in the towel and didn't want to take it off to put on the robe.

"Let's get back inside before the rest of my hair freezes," I said.

We opened the door and went down the stairs the best as we could. Max had somehow gotten his slippers and robe back on while I was still holding mine, bunched up in a ball.

Gabriella watched us as we made it to the warm air of the hotel hallway, and she again smiled indulgently at us.

"How was hot tub?" she asked.

"It was great," I said, although my teeth were still chattering, making it hard to talk. For some reason, Gabriella's smile only got wider.

"I'm taking a shower," I said once we'd returned to the room. "I need to melt the ice out of my hair."

I went into the bathroom, quickly stripped off the wet bikini, and stepped into the oversized shower. I adjusted the water until it was perfect. I enjoyed the sensation of the hot water spraying against my body for a few seconds before realizing I wasn't alone.

"I thought you might want some company," Max said from behind me.

"How'd you know?" I asked as I turned and gave him a wet hug. "I know I've already told you, but thank you for bringing me."

"Even though I'm making you learn to ski?"

"Um, you can tell I'm a little nervous about that, huh?"

"You mean the way you ball your hand into a fist whenever we talk about it?"

"I do? Really?"

"You know," he said, his arms feeling very protective as they wrapped around me, "you don't have to go skiing if you don't want to. I only suggested it because we're here, and I thought you might like it."

"No, I'll give it a try. Who knows, it might become my new favorite sport."

As long as I don't smash into a tree or fall off a cliff.

"Would you mind if we don't talk about skiing anymore tonight?" I asked. "The less I think about it, the better I'll do."

"Okay," he said as he bent down and kissed me softly. "Maybe we could do something to take your mind off it for a while."

"Really? What do you have in mind?"

Max bent down and kissed me again. This time it was a little more urgent, and his tongue flicked against my lips. My heart started pounding, and I actually did forget about skiing.

"Okay," I said as I started kissing him back. "That'll do it."

Chapter Two

I woke the following day to the smell of coffee. I sat up and watched as Max poured two cups. As he walked to the bed and handed one to me, he flashed me his beautiful smile.

"Why are you so perky?" I asked, still too tired for my eyes to focus properly. I looked out the window to see a rosy glow over the mountains. "What time is it?"

"It's not too early. I thought I'd let you sleep in a bit."

"Thanks," I said as I carefully sipped the hot coffee. "What's the schedule for today?"

"We're going down with Gabriella for a light breakfast at seven-thirty. We'll then come back to the room and get dressed for the mountain. You have a lesson set up at the ski school from nine until noon."

"I can learn to ski in three hours?"

"Pretty much. Then, if you like it, we can spend the afternoon skiing together."

"And, if I hate it?"

"Then we can spend the afternoon going through the village. I doubt if you got a chance to see everything last night."

"So, I get an afternoon of either skiing or shopping?" I asked. "Can I pick now?"

"Wait until the lesson's over. Then we'll do whatever you want."

After breakfast, we returned to the room and started putting on our ski equipment. I was doing okay with the ski socks and the snow pants, but when it came to the boots, I had a hard time getting them on.

"How do you get your feet into these things?" I asked. "I know I got them on last night at the ski shop, but I had help."

"Pull out the tongue as far as it will go, and you'll be able to slip your foot in. Then, slam the heel on the floor a couple of times. That'll give you enough room to be able to buckle it up."

I did as he said and was eventually able to get them on. I then put on the jacket, the balaclava, the helmet, the goggles, and the gloves.

This was the first time I'd had on the entire outfit since I'd bought it. My jacket and ski pants were blood red, and the back of the coat had a giant spider embroidered on it.

After I finished, I glanced at myself in the mirror. I had to admit, I certainly *looked* like a skier.

I looked over at Max. In addition to his bright yellow parka, he wore black ski pants and a black helmet.

Well, it'll be easy for Gabriella to spot us, even from the bottom of the hill.

We walked out of the room, and Gabriella followed us as I clomped down the hall to the elevator. I couldn't tell for sure, but I think she cracked a smile at the way I was trying to walk in the boots.

At first, I felt a little strange getting out of the elevator and stomping across the hotel lobby. However, several people were also dressed for skiing and were clomping and stamping through the hotel the same way I was. Well, maybe they weren't stomping as loudly, but it was pretty close.

We stepped outside into a beautiful day. The snow had stopped falling, and the morning sun was peeking out from behind some big fluffy clouds. It was still bitterly cold, and the wind had started to pick up, but other than that, it seemed like a good day to learn to ski.

Our skis were stored in a rack next to the hotel. Max took both pairs of skis, and I grabbed the poles. With Gabriella trailing a few paces behind us, we started toward the ski school.

The village streets were a buzz of motion and activity as hundreds of people streamed towards the mountain. I was amazed at the variety of colors of the skis and the ski outfits. Apparently, the louder the colors, the better they fit in.

I was still having a hard time walking in the big stiff boots and was grateful the ski school was only two hundred yards or so from the hotel. As we walked, Max didn't seem to be troubled by his boots. In fact, he looked rather graceful as we walked through the village.

"Hey," I said, a little annoyed. "How can you be so nimble in your boots? I'm walking like Frankenstein in these things."

"I've had more practice," he said. "Don't worry. You'll get used to them in a few hours."

We arrived at the ski school and found the instructor, a short, perky woman named Nellie. She had a broad smile and long blonde hair tied up in a thick braid. After we'd made introductions, Max pulled me aside.

"Have fun," he said. "I'll be back around noon, then we can grab some lunch. Until then, I'll be on the other side of the mountain. Gabriella will be nearby in case something comes up. Milo will be back on duty after lunch. Everyone will have their phones on. Call if you need anything."

"I'll be fine," I said as I kissed him. "See you in a few hours."

Nellie turned out to be a great teacher, and I quickly realized Max was right. I was much more comfortable learning from an instructor than I would have been from him.

I didn't need to impress Nellie with how fast I picked everything up. I also wasn't worried about disappointing her if I didn't like it.

Within the first hour, she'd taught me how to put on my skis and then how to take them off again. How to fall and how to get up.

Next, she showed me how to use a soft-rubber moving-sidewalk to go up the gentle slope of what she called the bunny hill. She then spent an hour teaching me how to do what she called wedge turns and how to bring myself to a stop.

"Well," she said after I'd pretty much figured out how to do the turns. "You're looking good. Would you like to try a lift?"

What? Are you serious? God, no.

"Lift?" I asked. "You mean like a chairlift? Do you think I'm ready for that?"

"You'll do fine," she said as she pointed to a short

chairlift on the far side of the bunny hill. "That's a beginner's lift, and it'll be perfect for you."

We took the lift, and fortunately, getting on and off wasn't as bad as I'd feared. But the most surprising thing was how much fun skiing was. Once I started to go fast enough to do the turns Nellie had been teaching me, I seemed to find a rhythm.

"You've got it," Nellie called out from behind me as I skied down the hill. "Make a wide turn to the left, then one to the right. Use your turns to control your speed. Go as fast as you feel comfortable. I'll be behind you the whole way."

In less than three minutes, I'd made it to the bottom of the little hill, and I felt great.

"Oh my God," I squealed out. "I thought I would hate that, but it was a blast. Can we do it again?"

"Sure, we still have almost an hour before the lesson ends. We can get in several more runs."

It turned out I was able to ski down the bunny hill five more times before noon. When the lesson was over, I felt I had mastered the beginner's hill and was ready for something more intense.

We made it back to the ski school, where everyone was waiting. Max and Gabriella clapped as I used the ski stop I'd learned to come to a halt three feet in front of them. Nellie stopped next to me, and we took off our skis.

"We watched as you came down the hill from the top of the lift," Max said. "It seems like you've gotten the basics pretty much down."

"Nellie's a great teacher," I said as I turned and thanked her for giving me such a good lesson.

"It was my pleasure," she said. "You picked it up quickly. Come back tomorrow if you'd like, and we can work on some advanced turns."

I thanked her again, and she scampered off.

"Well," Max said. "What's it going to be for the afternoon? Skiing or shopping?"

"Skiing," I said with a wide smile. "Definitely skiing. That was a blast. I can't wait to go on something harder."

I then looked up at the main mountain, where the slopes looked even steeper than they had the day before. "Um, but not too much harder, at least not to start."

"I know the perfect run for you," Max said.

We had a quick meeting to plan out the afternoon. Gabriella would stay in the village with her phone on while Max and I were on the mountain. We tentatively planned to meet back at the hotel at five, or whenever my legs gave out.

We walked to the gondola and got in line. I was feeling a strange mix of apprehension and excitement as I wondered what it would be like to go down a real Colorado ski hill.

The ride up in the gondola was a hoot. The views of the village and the surrounding mountains were breathtaking as we quickly climbed to the top of the resort.

When we got off the gondola, I was surprised that there was a huge ski lodge at the top of the hill. The main entrance was maybe thirty yards from where we'd gotten off.

"Do they always have a ski lodge at the top of the mountain?" I asked. "I thought it would be on the bottom of the hill."

"Actually, it's common to have them on the top of the mountain as well as the base. I like this one in particular because it has a great restaurant. Are you ready for lunch?"

As soon as he mentioned food, I realized I was starving. "Yes, lunch sounds great. Then we'll go skiing?"

"From here," Max said with a laugh, "the only way back to the hotel is down a ski slope. Anything from a green beginner run to a black double-diamond expert."

"Good. I suppose we'll need to start out on a beginner, but who knows where we'll be by the time we leave."

The ski lodge was a lot bigger on the inside than it looked from the outside. Every time we turned a corner, there was a big fireplace with a cheerful fire. It was getting to the point where I knew I wouldn't ever be able to see a fireplace again without thinking of Colorado.

After a bathroom break, Max led me to a lovely-looking bistro. When the hostess asked if we'd like to sit inside or out, I was surprised that anyone would want to sit outside in the cold.

But when I looked at where she was pointing, several groups were out on the patio. The sun had come out, and many of them seemed to be warming their faces in the bright light.

Max, knowing me well, asked for an inside table. "The wind's starting to blow out there," he said as we were seated. "But someday, we'll need to sit outside and do lunch. On a nice day, it's sort of like your hot tub experience."

"Eating lunch on the top of a mountain is magical?" I asked.

"I wouldn't go as far as magical, but on a nice day, it can be a lot of fun. Maybe next time."

We sat at a table for four, and I used the extra chair to stash my gear. Although the equipment had kept me toasty warm all morning, it was nice to have it off.

After lunch, we trekked back outside and put on our skis. Even this tiny amount of effort made my heart pound and left me trying to catch my breath. Max looked over at me and smiled.

"We're at an altitude of over ten thousand feet," he said. "There's not a lot of air up here. We'll take it slow until we descend to the oxygen."

Max took off and led me to the top of a wide groomed slope. It was steeper than the bunny hill, but it still looked manageable.

"Well?" he asked as I stopped next to him.

"It looks perfect. Wish me luck."

I took off down the slope, and it felt great. The trail must have been fifty yards wide, and the snow was completely smooth.

I was able to make my turns as wide or as tight as I wanted to. I only felt out of control a couple of times, but I was able to make another turn, which seemed to slow me down again.

The slope seemed to go on forever. By the time we'd gotten to where it stopped, my legs were burning, and my heart was pounding. Max did a fancy sliding stop next to where I was standing.

"How are you doing?" he asked.

"Hold on," I gasped at him as I tried to catch my breath. "I'll need a minute."

We stood close together on the slope, and after two or three minutes, my lungs and legs gradually began to recover.

"Well?" he asked when I could breathe again. "How was your first real ski slope?"

"That was amazing," I said. "It was so big and wide, I almost felt like I could blast down the mountain."

"Really? Do you think you're ready for blasting?"

"Maybe," I said as I looked around for the lifts. I was ready to go back up and try something more challenging. "Where's the gondola?"

Max gave me a puzzled look, then started laughing. "We're not even halfway down," he said. "We still have a lot of skiing to do before we get to the base. But it sounds like you're ready for something slightly steeper."

"Yes, but, you know, not too steep. It's my first day, and I'm still learning here."

He led me to the top of another run. It looked slightly steeper and a bit narrower than the last one. I knew it would be more of a challenge, but I was looking forward to it.

Max used his ski pole to point to a big yellow warning sign: *Caution: Trees Don't Move.*

"What's that about?" I asked.

"There're a few trees in the middle of the slope, about halfway down. They help give the trail some challenge and variety, but you'd be surprised how many people run into them."

"Oh."

Sophie's words from the night before echoed in my ears. *Don't slam into a tree.* I knew I'd have to be careful. If I actually did hurt myself by crashing into a tree, she'd never let me live it down.

Max led the way down the slope. Even though it was steeper than the last trail, it still felt great.

Once again, I found myself slightly out of control a few times. I had to purposefully slow myself for the last little bit, but overall, I felt like I was flying.

The trail flattened out for about fifteen yards before the last plunge down to the village. Max did one of his sliding stops next to a sign that was stretched partway across the trail. This one read: *Caution: Slow Skiers Ahead.*

The view from this point was beautiful. You could see most of the village along with the broad valley and the snowy mountain peaks in the distance.

The sky had cleared entirely, and the sun was brightly shining. If it weren't for the wind, which seemed to be blowing even harder down here, it would have been a perfect weather day for skiing.

"We're almost at the bottom," Max said. "You can see the gondola, and there's our hotel."

"Good," I said, still trying to catch my breath. "I'd like to go up again, but maybe we could take a small break before we get back on the lift?"

"Sounds like a plan," he said. He pulled out his phone and called Gabriella. "Gabby, we're almost down. We're going to grab a coffee before we head back up. I trust you and Milo have been keeping yourselves entertained?"

Before she could answer, I heard the strangest noise. It sounded like a bumblebee and a loud snap, both at the same time.

A snapping bumblebee?

I was going to ask Max what sort of mountain insect made that sound. I could tell he also heard it because his head shot up. Even through his goggles, I could see his eyes were opened wide in surprise.

"Head to the trees, *now!*" he barked out and pointed to

the trees to our left.

What?

"Don't think, *move!*" he shouted, since I was still standing there, wondering why he was yelling at me.

The snapping bumblebee sound flew by us again. By now, I'd started to ski across the trail, toward the trees. Max took my arm and helped me go faster.

We quickly got to the first of the trees, but as soon as we left the trail, the snow wasn't packed down, and it became tough to ski in. I couldn't turn, and I'd slowed to a walking speed.

Max was somehow still able to navigate, and he headed to a big tree. He half dragged me behind him and made me stand behind it.

"Don't move," Max said. He then moved to another big tree, maybe five yards away.

Max still had his phone out, and he put it up to his ear. "Gabby, are you still there? There's a sniper on us. Roughly a thousand yards away. Most likely from one of the condos on the other side of the highway."

A sniper? Oh crap.

Max briefly paused as he listened to Gabriella.

"My guess is the tall, dark brown one with the red trim and the green roof," Max said. "It's at about the same elevation as we are and has the widest view of this part of the mountain. If I was setting up, that's where I'd be. Fortunately, the wind's playing havoc with his aim."

There was the snapping bumblebee sound again, followed by a loud cracking *thump*. Pieces of the tree trunk Max was hiding behind flew out in all directions.

I looked over and could see he was concentrating. When

Max heard the dull crack of a rifle in the distance, he got back on the phone and corrected himself.

"Gabby, the distance is about nine hundred yards. Across the highway is the only place he can be. You and Milo check it out. We'll stay under cover until you give us the all-clear."

We both stood against our tree trunks, waiting for something to happen. I was breathing hard, and my throat had gone dry, but this time, it was from fear rather than the altitude.

Why the hell is a sniper shooting at us? I'm having a hard enough time learning to ski without this.

"These are aspen trees," Max said in his steady voice. I think he was trying to calm me. "Unfortunately, they don't have leaves this time of year and won't offer a lot of cover. Evergreens would be better, but this is the wrong part of the mountain for those."

Even as he said the words, there was a loud *thump* sound as another part of the tree trunk Max was hiding behind splintered and flew out over the snow. A second later, we again heard the crack of the rifle. But the sound seemed somewhat muted, like it was a long way off.

"Stay behind the thickest part of the trunk," he said in his calm voice, almost like he was teaching a class on how not to be shot by a sniper.

"Make sure you don't let any part of your body peek out. If he can see it, he can shoot it. He might even try to shoot through the tree to get at us, so stay as centered as you can. But if he's where I think he is, we'll be relatively safe here."

We stood behind our trees for three or four minutes. My heart was pounding, and I couldn't catch my breath. No doubt, it was a combination of terror and the lack of oxygen.

As we waited, everything became quiet and peaceful.

The shooter had stopped shooting, either because he'd packed up and left or because we weren't giving him a good target.

While we were hiding, a couple of advanced skiers shot past us as they skied down the mountain. As I watched them disappear down the slope, I had a disturbing thought.

"Hey," I said. "Both Milo and Gabriella are going after the shooter. But what if the bad guys left one or two behind to come after us on the ground? There could be someone behind us on skis or a couple of guys at the base, waiting for us if we happen to make it to the bottom."

"Maybe, but snipers typically act alone."

"Yeah, okay, but what if he's not alone? What if his primary purpose was to make us take cover and stay put, so someone waiting here in the trees could take us out?"

"Okay, it's possible," Max admitted. "What's the plan?"

"Well, we need to move, but not in a direction they'd expect. What happens if we keep going through the trees? They wouldn't expect that."

"True, but we have no idea what's through the trees. We could find ourselves at the top of a cliff."

"Or going onto a ski slope that takes us to the bottom in a different direction," I said. "I don't think we have a choice."

"Alright," Max said. "Through the trees. Just remember, you'll only have three seconds between the time you show yourself and the time the bullet hits. That's how long we'll have to find new cover."

"There's a big tree about ten feet ahead of you," I said, pointing with my pole. "If you push off, you can be behind it in about three seconds. While you're moving to your new tree, I'll ski to the one you're behind now. We can leapfrog like that all the way across the mountain. I'll ski in the tracks you've already made, so my skis should go the right way."

"That should work," Max said. "He can't target both of us at the same time. My only concern is that you're not used to skiing in this unpacked powder. If you fall, you'll make yourself an easy target."

"Then I'll try not to fall," I snapped out, sounding slightly more upset than I'd meant to.

I then spent a minute positioning my skis so they were pointed at Max's tree. "Sorry," I said. "I'm still not used to being shot at. Are you ready?"

"On three," he said. "One... Two... Three."

I pushed off with my poles and slid towards Max's tree. I'd made it about halfway when my skis started to go in the wrong direction.

I tried to remember how Max had turned in this snow, but it was no use. I came to a stop on the wrong side of the tree trunk and had made myself an irresistible target.

"Get to the other side!" Max called out.

"What? Ya think?" I yelled back at him as I scrambled to get out of the shooter's line of sight.

There was the snapping bumblebee sound and a loud *crack* as splinters of the tree trunk I was now hiding behind flew out over the snow.

"Are you okay?" Max asked.

"I'm good," I panted out. "I think I'm getting the hang of this deep snow. Let's keep going."

"Okay," Max called out. "You come to my tree, and I'll head to the next one. On three again. One... Two... Three."

We both moved at the same instant and this time, I made it to the next tree without incident. We waited about a minute, then did it again.

Fortunately, the shooting had stopped. Either the shooter had left his nest, or we'd moved to a part of the mountain where he couldn't see us.

We continued to hop from tree to tree for another five minutes before the trees abruptly stopped. We found ourselves standing on the side of another ski trail. This one was very steep and very narrow.

"Wow," I said, briefly forgetting about the sniper. "Um, this trail might be a challenge for my first day."

"It's an expert slope," Max said as he looked it over. "Fortunately, we're only about a hundred yards from the base. There aren't any trees, but there are a few rocks. Ski across the trail, do a tight turn, then ski across again. Keep doing that, and you'll be able to make it down."

"I'm not so sure this is going to work," I said as my eyes were fixed on the slope. It only seemed to get steeper and narrower as I looked at it.

Max saw how scared I was, and his voice softened. "Do what you can. If you can't control your speed, fall backward and sit down on the snow. You'll slide all the way to the bottom. Try to avoid the rocks."

"That doesn't sound very safe."

"No, but your alternative is to take off your skis and try to walk down."

I thought about it for a second. "We don't have time for that. I'll ski it."

While Max waited on the side of the trail, I carefully inched my way to the middle of the narrow strip of snow. I looked down the steep slope and knew this wasn't going to end well.

"Do your best," Max called out. "But remember to sit when you start going too fast. Make sure to sit on the snow, not on the back of your skis. Otherwise, you'll turn into a missile."

I gave myself a gentle push and immediately started going too fast. I made one turn, which seemed to help, but when I tried to make another turn, I found my skis were pointed directly down the hill.

In a panic, I tried to turn my skis so I'd again be going across the trail, but it was already too late. I picked up speed incredibly fast. I briefly turned into a screaming starfish as I flailed about, trying to turn my skis.

"Sit down," I heard Max call out. I sat back and to the side, then felt my ass start to slide on the snow. My top half quickly traded places with my feet, and I found myself sliding down the mountain, head-first, at an incredible speed.

Crap, Sophie was right. I'm going to kill myself.

As I continued to slide faster, I thrashed out with my hands and poles, trying to stay more or less in the middle of the slope and away from the trees on either side. I saw a big rock rapidly approaching and kicked out with my feet to try to steer around it.

I missed the rock but instead hit a hard mound of snow with a rough thump. This caused me to start to spin, and I more or less spun the rest of the way to the bottom of the slope.

I stopped with a jolt as I crashed into an orange mesh fence that had been stretched across the end of the trail, ten yards before I would've slid into a parking lot. Once I stopped moving, I felt around to see if anything was broken. I had snow under my coat and in my helmet but didn't seem to be injured.

I sat upright and looked up the mountain. Max was still in the trees, watching me slide. Now that I'd come to a stop, he took off and skied down the hill.

Even in my dazed condition, I marveled at how he kept his skis tightly together as he made turn after quick turn. His knees smoothly pistoned up and down while his head stayed steady, his arms and shoulders always pointing directly downhill.

How does he do that?

Within about thirty seconds, he slid to a stop, directly beside me.

"How is it that you do everything so well?" I asked.

"I hardly do everything well, but I've been skiing most of my life. Are you okay?"

"I think so. But help me up. I've had enough skiing for today."

Max's phone started to buzz. It was Gabriella.

"You were right," I heard her say through the phone. "Shooter was on top floor of brown building. Room seven-one-five."

"Are you sure?" Max asked.

"You need to ask if I'm sure?" she asked with some snark in her voice. "I can smell the powder. I knock on door and said I was housekeeping, but room is quiet. I doubt it is still occupied. I heard five rounds. I would never stay in same position after firing five rounds."

"Alright," Max said. "What's your situation?"

"I am currently at end of hallway in case someone comes out. Milo is checking roof. I doubt anyone is there, but it would be my secondary firing position. Milo will then go outside to look for anyone leaving building. I will wait for you to arrive before I do anything else."

"Thanks, Gabby," Max said. "We'll be there as soon as we can." He then looked at me. "Time to go."

We stashed our skis and poles on a rack in front of a ski shop, and then we were able to wave down a taxi. As we drove through the narrow streets, Max called and got an update from Milo.

He reported that he was continuing to look for the sniper. So far, he hadn't seen the shooter or anything out of the ordinary.

We pulled up to a tall brown condominium building. Max directed the taxi driver to park on the far side, next to a back entrance.

Max handed him a fifty and asked him to wait as we scooted out of the taxi. We then went inside as quickly as our ski boots would let us. Milo met us in the lobby and discreetly passed a semiautomatic pistol to Max.

"Boss," he said, "I'm glad to see you're both okay. No one's come in or out since I got here. I just talked to Gabriella. She says the room's still quiet."

"Alright," Max said. "Did you check the stairwell?"

"I walked down it after I checked the roof. Nobody was there except for some kids."

"Good, there's a taxi waiting outside. Get the SUV, bring it here, and park as close as you can to the back entrance. Call me when you get here, and we'll come down."

Max and I took the elevator up to the seventh floor. When the door slid open, we saw Gabriella standing down the hallway.

She was eyeing the elevator, and her hand was in her black bag. She relaxed when she saw it was us.

"Anything?" Max asked as we clomped down the hallway. Our ski boots made it impossible to be quiet.

"Still no sounds from room," she said. "I believe he is gone."

"Let's make sure." He looked at me. "Stay back until we find out what's going on in there."

Max stood against the door, and Gabriella stood beside him. Her Uzi was now out of the bag. At a nod from Max, he put his shoulder to the door, and it popped open. He took a step in, and Gabriella smoothly came in after him, scanning the room with her Uzi.

"Clear," Max said. "Let's check the bedroom."

I was still standing in the hallway, looking into the living room, when Max stuck his head out of the bedroom. "The condo's clear."

I walked in and pulled off my ski gear. I then dropped everything onto the kitchen table and went to the bedroom.

Gabriela was out on the balcony, looking at a chair that had been set up next to a small end table. I looked out over the village and toward the mountain.

I made a guess as to where we'd been standing while the guy was shooting at us. The spot must have been at least a half-mile away. I was surprised anyone would think they could accurately shoot something at that range.

Max walked up and saw me looking at the mountain.

"Don't be fooled by the distance. For a trained sniper, this is an easy shot. If the wind hadn't been blowing as hard as it was, we wouldn't have been so lucky."

"He was set up here," Gabriella said, looking down at the chair and pointing toward the end table. "He must have fired his five rounds, then packed up and left."

"That's what I would have done," Max said. "He set up to fire at us as we skied down the slope. From this angle, he likely lost us once we got fully into the trees.

Max headed back to the living room, and Gabriella followed. They were already talking about what to do next.

"Hold on a minute," I said as I stood in the bedroom doorway. "Before we take off, let me look around."

Max gave me a nod that said he'd let me do my thing, but not to be too long about it. He then went back to discussing strategy with Gabriella.

I went to the balcony and looked at the chair the shooter had used. I lifted the cushion and bent down to look for stray hairs. Finding nothing, I went back to the bedroom.

From the layout of the place, it looked like it was a rental unit that was currently unoccupied. The room was neat, and the bed hadn't been slept in.

I opened the drawers in both the dresser and the nightstand without finding anything. I opened the closet, but it was also clean.

I got down on my hands and knees and looked under the dresser and the bed. As I was about to stand up, I saw something shiny.

"Hey," I called out to Max, "I found a shell casing."

They both returned, and Max joined me on the floor, looking under the bed.

"It was sloppy to leave a casing," he said. "A trained sniper never leaves brass for the enemy to find."

"It's several feet from where he was sitting on the

balcony to the bed," I said. "If it rolled here, he might not have had time to look for it before he left."

I looked up at Gabriella. "See if you can find a pencil or a thin stick or something."

Max got up and helped her look around the condo. Gabriella found a pen in a small desk in the corner of the room and handed it to me.

I slid the pointed end of the pen into the casing, then stood up and handed it to Max. He looked at it for a moment, held it close to his nose, and sniffed it.

"Recently fired," he said. He looked at the casing for a few seconds before a puzzled look appeared on his face. He held it out for Gabriella to see. "What do you make of this?"

"NATO, seven-six-two," she said. "Common sniper cartridge." She then took the pen and looked at the casing more closely. "No, wait, that's three-oh-eight. That's civilian cartridge."

"That's what I thought," Max said. "Well, that cuts the number of people it could be in half. If it was any of our old friends, they'd have military hardware, most likely a fifty caliber. This must somehow be related to Arizona."

Gabriella gave me the pen, and I went to the kitchen, hunting through drawers until I found a plastic sandwich bag. I dropped the casing into it and zipped it shut.

Milo called and said he was at the rear entrance to the condo building. Gabriella led the way as we went down the stairs, all seven floors worth.

I'd been willing to risk the elevator rather than clomp down the stairs in my ski boots. But Gabriella thought the elevator would be an obvious place to stage an ambush. Even as we wound down flight after flight of stairs, Gabriella's hand was in her bag the entire time.

After climbing into the SUV, I popped open the buckles on my boots. Between walking around the condo building and then going down seven flights of stairs, a couple of hot spots were starting to form on my feet.

Max directed Milo to drive to a random parking lot about two miles outside of Vail so we could plan what to do next.

"Well, Gabby?" Max asked as we drove. "Who could it be?"

"The Black Death is still our main threat," she said. "But I have not sensed they are negotiating merely to divert our attention from assassination attempt."

"What about the others?" he asked.

"Other gangs in Phoenix have been quiet for several months, and truce we established last year is still in place. Except for minor occurrences, everyone has operated within their respective boundaries."

"I agree," he said. "I can't see them setting something like this up."

"Besides," Gabriella said, "it makes no sense for any of them to come after us here. Assassination attempt would be much easier in Scottsdale where movements are more predictable, and the shooter would have friendly organization to fall back on."

"So, you're saying there shouldn't be anyone after us at the moment? That was my feeling as well. My only thought is that they might have come after us here because security is softer on a skiing weekend than it is in Arizona."

Max paused, and I could sense him analyzing the

situation. "I thought this trip was a well-guarded secret, but perhaps there's another mole somewhere in our organization."

He seemed to think about it for another moment, then came to a decision.

"Alright," he said, "At this point, it doesn't matter who's shooting at us. Let's do it by the numbers. Milo, call Johnny. Let him know what happened. Then call the pilot and tell him we'll be leaving as soon as we can get there."

Milo looked at Max. "Right, Boss."

"I'll call Tony," Max continued. "This might be part of a larger operation targeting all our top guys. Gabby, stay alert. There's a sniper out there. I wouldn't be surprised if he tries again."

As he said this, I couldn't help but notice the rosy glow on Gabriella's face. Once again, she'd unzipped her bag.

Of course, by now, I sort of expected that from her. The weird part was that her hand was in the bag, and she'd started to stroke her Uzi.

I'd seen her do this before, but it still creeped me out a little. I had no idea what her complete backstory was, but as Max once told me, Gabriella was a complicated woman.

Everyone was on their phone for the next hour, informing the organization what had happened and planning the trip back to Arizona. It felt good to be actively working on a goal.

Max called the hotel to gather up our things. He also described where we'd stashed the skis and poles, what they looked like, and then asked that everything be delivered to our vehicle.

There was a small coffee shop just down from where we'd parked. Max told Milo to get coffee and sandwiches for everyone while we waited for the luggage and skis.

Thirty minutes later, a bellhop from the hotel came driving up to the SUV in a hotel van. As everything was unloaded, I found my bag and pulled out my cross-trainers.

I returned to the SUV, took off the ski boots, and slipped the shoes onto my aching feet. After wearing the tight boots all day, I felt an immediate sense of relief.

When the bellhop was done loading the bags into the back, Max handed him my ski boots. He'd already separated out my rental skis and told the bellhop what shop to return them to.

The bellhop was about to grumble about it. Still, when Max handed him a hundred-dollar bill, the guy immediately perked up and became much more polite.

"Yes, sir," he said eagerly before hopping into his van and speeding back to the village.

Within a few minutes, we were loaded and ready to go. I knew everyone was eager to return to Arizona, but I'd been thinking about what had happened.

Max and Gabriella didn't have a clue about who the sniper was. The only solid information we had was that he'd used a civilian rifle that took what Max called a three-oh-eight cartridge. I didn't know how rare it was for rifles to use that bullet size, but I knew it was a solid lead that could be tracked down.

"Before we fly out of here," I said, "let's think this through. You're surprised someone came after us with a civilian rifle. You assumed they followed us here from

Scottsdale, but we don't know anything for sure."

"That's true," Max agreed.

"Okay. What if the sniper was already here? What if he went to a gun store and simply bought whatever was handy? If he used a credit card, we might be able to get a name."

"That's possible," Max said. "But then, we couldn't know for sure unless we canvassed all of the gun stores in the area. That could take some time. Even then, if he bought the rifle in Denver or Colorado Springs, we'd never find out where it came from."

"Hey, you have your skills. I have mine. Give me a minute, and I'll narrow down the possibilities."

I could see that Max and Gabriella wanted to return to Scottsdale as soon as possible. Still, I wanted to help unravel this mystery, so I held my ground.

"Here," I said, holding up the phone. "If he bought the rifle within fifty miles of Vail, it was probably at one of these three shops."

Max took the phone, and his eyes scanned down the list.

"My guess would be High Country Arms," I said. "It's not the closest, but the listing says they specialize in tactical and competition arms. Besides, it's in Eagle and on the way to the airport."

"Alright," Max said. "Start your investigation. Let us know how we can help."

Chapter Three

The drive to the small town of Eagle was uneventful. The sun was going down over the high mountains, and the sky in the west had become a dazzling display of bright colors. The lights in the shops and houses started coming on, making everything look like a snowy Christmas card.

We found the gun shop easily enough. It was in a nice-looking group of businesses that all shared a small parking lot.

I asked Milo to drive slowly by the entrance and then park on the far side by a place called the Eagle Diner. I could see that Max and Gabriella were both eager to come in, but I asked everyone to stay in the vehicle.

"From what I can see, only one guy is working," I said. "I'll probably get better answers if I go in by myself."

"Oh, I wouldn't say that," Gabriella murmured. I looked at her, and she was using her big military fighting knife to clean under her fingernails. "I think I could get the answers we need from him."

"But I might be able to do it without resorting to torture," I said.

Gabriella shrugged as if to say suit yourself. Max agreed, and everyone stayed put.

I left my jacket in the SUV, walked into the shop, and

spent a few minutes looking around. As I'd seen from the outside, only one man was working in the store, and I was the only customer.

I was wearing a tight black turtleneck that showed off my body as well as possible. I let him look at me for several minutes while I slowly wandered up and down the aisles in front of the counter. After I was sure he'd noticed me, I went up to him.

"A friend of mine came in within the last few days and bought a competition rifle. One that takes a three-oh-eight cartridge. We're both going to start training for long-distance shooting, and I was hoping to get the same gun."

"Sure," he said. "I know the rifle you're talking about. I sold it to him myself this morning. Your friend was outside waiting for me to open the shop. He bought the rifle along with a pistol."

The man turned and pulled a wicked-looking rifle with a long black barrel from a rack display on the wall. He held it up for me to look at before carefully placing it on a piece of black felt on the counter.

"This is the Bergara B14 BMP. It's the best competition rifle I carry for the three-oh-eight cartridge. It comes standard with a five-round detachable magazine. There are more accurate rifles out there, but they'll set you back three or four thousand dollars. If you pair this rifle with a precision optic, it's a combination that'll win you championships, at least at the competitions around here."

"How much would everything cost if I got the same setup?"

"The rifle's seventeen hundred, and the scope is almost a thousand. With tax, it'll come to a little under three thousand dollars. I know it's expensive, but with rifles and optics, you really do get what you pay for."

"What pistol did he get?"

"It was a nine-millimeter Beretta, the 92X. It's one of the best pistols I sell. It has combat sights, enhanced fire control, and an extended magazine release. I have two more in stock, if you're interested. That model would add another fourteen hundred to the total."

"Okay, but even without the pistol, that's a lot of money. Let's make sure we're talking about the same rifle. Did he pay with a credit card? I could check the name and make sure that way."

"Nope, he paid in cash. Actually, having that much cash in the store spooked me a little. I made a bank run during my lunch hour."

"Oh, no problem. Maybe we can do it from his description. My friend's a sixty-four-year-old accountant, slightly balding with a bit of gray on the sides."

"Huh," the man said. "It might not be the same rifle then. The guy who bought this was probably somewhere in his forties."

"White? Black? Hispanic? Anything unusual about him?"

"No, just your average white guy. Nothing notable about him at all, well, except for the scar."

"Scar?"

"Yeah, he had a big scar under his left eye. I tried not to look at it, but it was sorta hard not to. Most of the cheekbone under the eye was gone. Hard to say what could have done that."

Crap, the man from outside the hotel.

"Um, was this guy wearing a dark blue jacket? Did you see the brand?"

"Well, it was blue, but I didn't see who made it. I'm not into ski fashions. You know the guy?"

"Um, yeah, he's my friend's son. Well, let me go home and see about the finances on the rifle. I'll be back in a few days."

"Okay," he said. "But keep in mind we're running a Thanksgiving special until the end of the month. If you buy the rifle, I'll throw in a free travel case and a box of match-grade cartridges."

"Thanks," I said. "That makes it pretty tempting."

I left the store and hurried back to the SUV, which was still idling on the far side of the parking lot. As I climbed into the backseat, I felt everyone's eyes on me.

"Were you able to learn anything?" Max asked in his sexy, soft voice.

"Um, yes. I know the rifle that was used, a Bergara B14 BMP. He bought it here, and the setup cost him three thousand dollars. He also bought a Beretta 92X pistol for another fourteen hundred. He paid in cash, and I have a description of the guy."

"That is good," Gabriella said. "The Bergara is relatively accurate bolt action civilian rifle made in Spain. It matches with what we know. The pistol would only be effective at short range, but perhaps he felt need for defensive weapon. The man, tell us about him."

"He's a white guy in his late forties, average height and weight. He has dark eyes, short dark hair, and a big scar on his left cheekbone. It's really deep, like something bad happened to him. He was wearing a dark blue Helly Hanson ski parka."

"That's a lot of information," Max said. "I'm surprised the clerk remembered so much about him."

"Well," I said. "I didn't exactly get all of that from the clerk. I sort of ran into this same guy while I was walking around the village last night. The meeting was an accident, and I didn't think anything about it, but it has to be the same guy."

"Where was he when you first saw him?" Max asked carefully. He'd asked the question casually enough, but I could tell his senses had just sprung to alertness.

"He was standing outside the entrance to our hotel. I thought it looked like he was waiting for someone."

Everyone in the car became unnaturally quiet. Max and Gabriella looked at each other and seemed to have a long conversation without speaking. Milo fidgeted uncomfortably.

"Damn," Max said.

I looked at him, wanting more than a *damn*.

"That means he's been watching us for at least eighteen hours," Max said. "He knew where we were staying but waited until we were skiing to try and take me out. Why he would do it through a long-distance shot is a mystery to me. The only good thing is he wasn't after you. Otherwise, he could have taken you outside the hotel. It looks like I've started to get lax in my security."

When we reached the airport, we drove to one of several large hangars. Our jet was waiting outside one of them, and Milo parked the SUV as close as possible to the stairs. We quickly loaded the luggage while Gabriella stood guard, not bothering to hide her Uzi.

As soon as we closed and latched the door, the pilot fired up the engines, and the jet smoothly began to move. We quickly taxied across the tarmac and stopped at the end of the runway.

Several seconds ticked by. I could only suppose the pilot was getting permission from the tower to take off.

I could feel the gathering tension as everyone on the plane thought the same thing. If the sniper still wanted to take us out, this would be his last chance until we got to Scottsdale.

Looking out the window, I felt exposed and vulnerable in the little plane. I started imagining rockets shooting across the sky, hitting the jet underneath the wing, then exploding in a huge fireball.

When the plane finally did start to move, I was still waiting for something horrible to happen. I didn't begin to relax until we had taken off, and the Eagle County airport became small lights far below in the distance.

I then felt the knot in my stomach start to unwind. There was a collective sigh of relief from everyone on the plane. Within a few minutes, we'd reached altitude, and the plane leveled out.

"Milo," Max said. "I don't know about everyone else, but I could use a drink."

Milo poured out three drinks. As usual, when on duty, Gabriella shook her head no.

Max brought my drink over and sat next to me. "Sorry to cut our weekend short, but I'll need to meet with Tony right away when we land. Would you be able to get Sophie or Gina to pick you up at the airport? If not, I'll arrange a car and driver for you."

"Don't worry about our weekend," I said. "Except for almost getting shot, I had a wonderful time. Gina's on a date, but I'll give Sophie a call."

Max went up front to talk strategy with Gabriella. I pulled out my phone and connected it to the plane's WiFi.

"Hey, Sophie," I said when she answered.

"What are you doing calling me?" she asked. "I figured you and Max would be finishing up dinner and about to head to the hot tub for some magic time."

"Sophie, I'm having a really shitty day."

"Again? Seriously? What happened this time? You didn't slam into a tree, did you? Or did you fall off a cliff this time? That would suck if you fell off a cliff. *Oh my God,* don't tell me you broke your leg again. Are you in the hospital? I could come and visit you. Which hospital are you in?"

"I wish it was something simple like a broken leg. When I was skiing with Max, a sniper started shooting at us. He came close to taking us both out."

"Damn, a sniper? For real? Like some guy dressed in a full-body camouflage suit was shooting at you with a high-powered rifle from hundreds of yards away? Seriously? Wow, you really are having a shitty day. How's my Pooh Bear? And why is it so noisy there?"

"Pooh Bear is fine, but we're on the plane heading back to Scottsdale. Max is worried this might be the first move of someone going after the entire group. Would you be able to pick me up from the Scottsdale Airport? If not, it's okay. Max said he'd arrange a car and driver for me."

"It's no problem. I can come up and get you. It'll be fun. I've driven by the airpark a hundred times, but I've never been to the actual airport before."

"I'm not messing anything up tonight, am I?"

"Not a thing. Gina's with Jet, Pooh Bear's with you, and Snake's still on team curfew. I was planning on going out with the Cougars tonight. But I can meet up with them any time between nine-thirty and one. You know, since you're having such a shitty day, you should come out with the girls too. You'll get free drinks, and you can dance with some hot guys. That'll take your mind off being shot at and almost killed."

"Tell you what, come get me, and we can decide what to do then."

"Fair enough. See you soon."

I disconnected with Sophie as Gabriella came up to me.

"You did good today," she said. "You no panic. Milo wants to make you one more drink before we land."

"Thanks," I said as I set my phone down. "Alright, I could probably use it." I then went to the front of the plane, where the bar had been set up. It seemed like an excellent way to end a crappy day.

The plane landed in Scottsdale, and we quickly taxied to the hangar. Milo had called Sophie and told her where we'd be.

Her yellow Volkswagen convertible was parked just outside the hangar, and she was standing next to it, watching us come in. From her outfit, it looked like I'd caught her right as she was leaving for the club.

Two black SUVs were parked on either side of the entrance to the hangar. A couple of beefy-looking guys in black polos stood next to each vehicle. There weren't any visible weapons, but I didn't doubt each one of them was heavily armed.

After a few minutes, the luggage was unloaded from the

plane, and all of my bags were stuffed in the back seat of Sophie's Volkswagen. While Milo loaded the luggage into the car, Sophie had used the opportunity to sneak in a couple of quick kisses. I'm not sure if it was because Max was nearby and the overall situation was serious, but Milo seemed to go out of his way not to kiss her back.

Before I left, Max pulled me aside. "It's a shame this cut our weekend so short. You were doing great for your first time out. We'll need to set up another ski trip sometime soon."

"Don't worry about it. I understand how serious this is. I'd like to help you figure out who this guy is and find out what's going on."

Max hesitated. "Until we know more about this, I think it's best that you're not too close to the situation. So far, it appears they're only after me or maybe the guys from the group. But at the very least, we know we're dealing with a trained sniper. He may be acting alone, or he may only be the tip of the spear. I don't want you getting caught in the middle of anything."

"Um, hello?" I said. "He was shooting at me too. I think I'm already involved. You say you're going to figure out who it is. How are you going to do that? I'm the only person who's actually seen the guy and knows what he looks like. I think I have a better chance of tracking him down than anyone on your side."

Max hesitated again. "Let me think about it. I know you'd be a valuable resource, but I'm also concerned for your safety. In the meantime, it's been a long day, and I still need to meet with Tony."

"You'll take care of yourself?" I asked.

"I'll take precautions on my side. But just to be safe, you keep your eyes open as well. Until we figure out what's going on, we all need to be in a tight security mode. If you get the sense that anything's wrong, anything at all, give me a call. I'll have some of my guys come to your place and watch over things, or if you prefer, you can stay at the Paradise for the next few days."

"I'll be fine. But yes, I'll let you know if anything comes up."

"It sounds like you've had an exciting day," Sophie said as we drove south on Scottsdale Road toward Old Town.

The top of her convertible was down, and I appreciated the wind on my face. I still wore the turtleneck from earlier in the day and was feeling a bit warm in the mild Arizona evening.

"More like terrifying," I said. "We had to hide behind trees while the guy took shots at us. According to Max, the only thing that saved us was the wind. It was blowing too hard for him to shoot accurately."

"Speaking of terrifying, how was skiing? Are you still a little pissed at Max for making you do that?"

"Actually, the skiing part was great. I was only on skis for a few hours, but I think I could get the hang of it. I would have gotten a chance to ski all afternoon, but the jerk started shooting at us and blew the weekend all to hell. But we did get to spend some time sipping champagne in a hot tub last night."

"Really? How was it? Was it as much fun as they make it look on TV?"

"The actual hot tub part was great. But the process of getting into and out of the tub kind of sucked. They don't mention those pesky little details on the Travel Channel. All they showed were laughing people, sitting in the water and drinking champagne."

"Milo said you got a look at the guy. Did he look familiar? He wasn't one of your old friends, was he?"

"No, I'd never seen him before. I don't think he has anything to do with me. But the guy really doesn't like Max for some reason."

"Are you positive the guy was going after Max and not you? After all, you've pissed off a lot of people over the past couple of years."

"I know I've made some enemies, but I can't see any of them hiring someone to follow me to Colorado just so they could take me out with a sniper rifle. That sounds more like stuff from a spy movie."

"Is Max going to let you look for the guy?"

"Probably not."

"But you're going to do it anyway, aren't you?"

"Duh, of course I am," I laughed. "Someone's trying to kill my boyfriend, and Max thinks I'm just going to sit around in my apartment? All I can think about is tracking down the shooter. I know Max wants to protect me, but I can take care of myself."

"I think it's because he likes you. It's a guy thing."

"Oh, I know," I said. "Look, it's one thing if I get into a jam. Fine, he can come rescue me. But until then, I'll need some room to work. Speaking of that, is Milo alright? He was acting a little weird around you tonight."

"I know. I got some stink-eye when he saw I was going out with the girls tonight. I think he might be picking up an attitude about it. But hey, I'd be glad to spend more time with him. It's not my fault he has to work all the time."

"He didn't say anything about you going out, did he?"

"Oh, he knows better. I told him my rules for dating almost a year ago. If he wants a woman who's completely exclusive, he needs to find someone else."

"Hey, as long as he's good with it," I said.

"So, what do you want to do tonight?" Sophie asked. "I got a text from Jackie right before you landed. The Cougars are moving across the street to the Maya Day and Nightclub. She said they'll be there for an hour or so, and if nothing's going on, they'll move over to the Living Room Lounge. Why don't we both go over and hang out with the girls? A couple of free drinks from some hot guys would probably take the edge off."

"Going out with everyone sounds like a lot of fun. Plus, I'd love to talk with Elle about what's going on with her and Lenny. But honestly, between learning to ski and being shot at, I think I've already had all the excitement I can handle for today. Would you mind dropping me off at my place?"

I woke up the following day, feeling something soft pushing against my face. As my eyes focused, I was vaguely disappointed I wasn't waking up next to Max.

Instead, Marlowe was on the bed, gently putting his paw on my cheek. When he saw my eyes open, he started purring and then rubbed his face against mine.

"Fine," I said as I roused myself. "I'm awake. I'll feed you."

When I'd arrived the night before, he'd been next door at

Grandma Peckham's. I knew he'd been well taken care of, but I also knew he wouldn't leave me alone until I fed him.

I slowly sat up, remembering the skiing trip and the sniper. I got out of bed, stretched, and then shuffled to the kitchen to put on a pot of coffee and make breakfast for my starving cat.

Holding a steaming mug of coffee in my Doctor Who mug, I flopped down on the couch. I needed to help find out what was going on with the sniper, but I also needed to stay out of Max's way, at least at first.

I knew both Max and Tony would have their hands full for the next few days. I didn't want to interfere, but it was like I'd told Sophie, I couldn't sit idle while someone was trying to kill my boyfriend, especially when I was the only person who knew the face of the would-be assassin.

As I sipped my coffee, I reviewed the information I had so far. I knew the model of the rifle used to shoot at us on the mountain, the gun store where the creep had bought the rifle, and that he had purchased a pistol.

I had a used shell casing and a mental image of the guy's face. I tried to come up with a plan, but without any other clues, I was going to find it challenging to make any headway.

I eventually decided to start with the casing. Gina still had several contacts in the forensics lab from her time as a detective with the Scottsdale Police Department. I knew she'd be able to talk someone into looking it over for any additional clues.

My next avenue of attack would be the security cameras at the hotel we'd been staying at in Vail. The guy had probably been standing in front of the hotel entrance for some time before I ran into him. The cameras there likely picked up some good photos of the shooter.

I wasn't sure if Tony had any direct pull over the hotel, but if not, we'd booked the penthouse suite for the weekend. That couldn't have been cheap, and technically, the room was still ours until check-out time this morning. Hopefully, that would give me enough leverage to have them pull the video files.

I also thought I might be able to get some more information from the gun store. The guy had paid cash for the rifle, so there was no credit card I could've used to get his name.

But in thinking about it, I realized he had to give a name for the mandatory firearms background check. Maybe he'd used his real name for that?

The only downside about the gun store idea was that I'd need to be there in person. Even if he still remembered me, I doubted the owner would hand out that kind of information over the phone.

I mentally thumped my head that I hadn't thought to ask about that when I'd had the chance. My lack of clarity in the gun store the day before was likely going to cause me to go back to Vail on Tuesday or Wednesday to do the interview all over again.

If I could come up with a name and a picture of the shooter, I could check out the other hotels in Vail and hopefully learn more details about him. With any luck, I'd be able to pick up his trail after he left Colorado, presumably to head to Scottsdale.

By eleven o'clock, I was starting to get hungry. I didn't have anything in the refrigerator or the cabinets, so I decided to go out. Before leaving the apartment, I made sure to look out the peephole but didn't see any creepy-looking people in the hallway.

When I got to the parking lot, I scanned it for anything suspicious. Knowing I was in the clear, I drove out to the Filiberto's on McDowell Road and got a couple of drive-through carne asada tacos.

I returned to the apartment and set the tacos on the coffee table in front of the couch. I then pulled out a Diet Pepsi from the fridge and started munching.

I was almost through the last one when the theme to *The Love Boat* sang out from my phone. I was surprised but happy to hear Max's ringtone.

"Hey," I said when I answered. "I'm glad you called. I knew you'd be busy, so I wasn't going to bug you today."

"You're right about being busy, but I wanted to check in on you. Is everything still okay over there? Nothing that raises any security concerns?"

"No, things are pretty quiet here," I said. "Going out for tacos this morning has been my only bit of excitement. How are things over there? Is everyone stirred up because of the sniper?"

"You could say that. Tony's pulled in some of our guys and put everything on heightened security. We'll likely have the business offices on lockdown to outsiders. That won't impact the organization until tomorrow when everyone returns to work. Then, it will become more problematic. We also have a golf tournament starting tomorrow at the Blue Palms to add to it. Unfortunately, until we can find out more about what's going on, we're pretty much at a standstill."

"I'll talk with Gina today to see if she can get one of her friends in forensics to look at the shell casing. I was also going to contact the hotel in Vail to see if they'd send over the security videos from Friday night. Um, Tony doesn't own that hotel, does he?"

"No, we don't have any sort of business connection to it. Contacting them for the security videos was on our to-do list as well. But if you'd like to help out, that would be a good one for you to take. You seem to have better people skills than we do regarding this sort of thing. Let me know if anything comes from it."

He paused and seemed to think about it. "You know I appreciate your help," he said, "but I also don't want you getting too close to the shooter. I have heartburn enough dealing with the internal aspects of this. I don't want to start worrying about you as well."

"I know you want me to stay out of it. But somebody's trying to kill you, and I don't think I can completely sit on the sidelines. Look, I'll do my best to stay out of your way, but if I can think of any leads, I'll need to chase them down."

"Keep in mind that this guy appears to be a trained assassin. If you think you've come up with a lead as to where he is, I'd prefer you pass the information on to me. I'll have our guys look into it. No need for you to start kicking down doors."

"Fine," I said, trying not to roll my eyes. "I'll consider that."

"Thank you. Hopefully, things will start to settle out over here one way or another in a few days. Maybe I'll be able to break away for dinner sometime later this week."

"I'd like that. Let me know if you get a free evening, and I'll come over."

I sat on the couch and finished the last taco while thinking about what to do. Besides giving the shell casing to Gina and calling the hotel, I didn't have a clear idea of how I could help figure out who was trying to kill Max.

Gabriella had said that the Black Death was still their main threat, but she didn't think they had anything to do with the assassination attempt. That seemed reasonable, but there was one way to find out for sure.

I pulled out my phone and called Danielle.

I've always had a complicated relationship with Danielle Ortega. At first, I knew her as an office manager for a trucking company, and she quickly became my friend. She got to know Sophie and Gina and became friends with them as well.

This was especially true with Sophie. I think they found their common Mexican heritage and love of the Spanish language something they could quickly bond over.

My friendship with Danielle quickly ended when I found out she was actually the daughter of Escobar Salazar, the vicious worldwide head of the Black Death drug cartel. For this information to stay a secret, Danielle was willing to let me be tortured to death at the hands of a sadistic jerk named Raul. Only luck and some good fortune got me out of that mess before I was seriously injured.

I would have been comfortable knowing Danielle was my enemy, but then there was an uprising in her group. She came to me and asked for my help in saving her life. She said she knew I despised her, but that made her confident she could trust me.

For the next two weeks, I hid Danielle from members of the Black Death who were trying to kill her, and I even helped her take over as head of the group.

Throughout the process, we reestablished a kind of mutual respect. I think it must be similar to the friendships formed between soldiers who go through war together.

It got to the point where it didn't matter if I liked her. I knew I could trust her.

"Hey, Danielle," I said when she answered.

"Laura, how have you been? We need to get together. Hopefully, with something that isn't work-related."

"Actually, that's what I wanted to ask you about. I need to talk with you, and I'd like your advice about something. Are you free for dinner tonight?"

"Sure," she said. "Things are quiet over here, and I have no plans for the evening. Pick a place on the north side of town, and I'll meet you there."

"Carolina's on Cactus Road at six?"

"Perfect," she said. "I love their salsa. See you there."

After I disconnected with Danielle, I went to the fridge, pulled out a Diet Pepsi, and called Gina.

"Hey," I said when she answered. "Sorry to disturb you on a Sunday."

"No worries. Jet and I are at my place watching the Cardinals."

"I didn't realize the game was on already. Has Snake gotten to play yet?"

"He's been in for three plays so far. The regular quarterback had something break in his shoulder pads, and he had to go to the locker room to get it fixed."

"How'd Snake do?"

"Not great. He handed the ball off once for a short gain, then missed on two short passes. The Cardinals had to punt the ball to the other team."

"Still, three plays, that's thirty thousand dollars in bonuses. Not bad for an afternoon's work."

"It's more than we'll ever get from Lenny," Gina said with her great laugh. "How was the skiing trip? I didn't think you were coming back until later tonight."

"Um, it was okay. And you're right. We ended up coming back a little early. I'm starting to work on a side project. I have a three-oh-eight shell casing, and I'd like to learn what I can. Do you still know anyone who could take a look at it?"

"Sure, there are still four or five guys in forensics I could ask. Although, I'd probably have to buy him lunch as a thank you."

"Perfect. Would you mind if I dropped it off today? I'll need the information as soon as I can get it."

"Sure, we'll be here watching the game for at least the next hour and a half."

As I drove to Gina's, I couldn't help but notice what a beautiful day it was. Temperatures were in the mid-seventies, with only a few clouds on the horizon.

I guess I've lived here for so long I've come to assume the weather's pretty much the same everywhere in the country. Visiting the deep freeze that is Colorado in late November made me appreciate Arizona a little bit more.

Gina came to the door wearing red gym shorts and a Cardinals midriff top. She led me into the living room, where Jet was getting up from the couch.

"Hi, Laura," Jet said as he held out his hand. After we shook, I told him to sit back down. I wasn't going to stay long. He promptly did and started watching the game again.

Gina and I walked to her kitchen. She pulled a Diet Pepsi out of the refrigerator and handed it to me.

"Thanks," I said. "Did Snake ever get back in the game?"

"Not yet, but it's halfway through the third, and the Cardinals are up by twenty. If they don't blow the lead, I wouldn't be surprised to see him play at least one series of downs in the fourth quarter."

"That'll make Sophie happy. Is she sitting with the wives and girlfriends again?"

"She's supposed to be," Gina said. "They seem like an odd bunch of women."

"From what Sophie says, they have a strict pecking order based on how much money their man makes. If Snake gets to play more, maybe her standing in the group will improve."

Gina glanced at the living room, then lowered her voice. "You have a shell casing for me?"

I pulled the sandwich bag containing the shiny brass cartridge out of my pocket and handed it to her.

"Are you looking for anything in particular?" she asked.

"DNA, latent prints, anything unique."

"Do you want to tell me about this?"

"Not yet. Like I said, it's only a side project so far."

I was waiting for Gina to start asking a lot of questions, but she shrugged her shoulders instead. "Okay, I'll drop it off before I come into the office tomorrow. Depending on how busy everyone is, you'll have the results in a day or two."

I drove back to my apartment and met Grandma Peckham in the parking lot. From the number of bags in her car, it looked like she was coming back from an afternoon's worth of shopping.

"Well, Laura," she said. "I heard you come in last night. I didn't think you were coming back until later today. I hope nothing went wrong on your skiing trip."

"We'd planned on staying in Colorado until tonight, but a guy started shooting at us, and we ended up coming home a day early."

"That seems to happen to you a lot lately," she said with a shake of her head. "I do hope you're being careful. Maybe you should consider a line of work where people aren't always trying to injure you?"

"I think about it all the time," I said.

"Well, I'm glad you came back as late as you did last night. I had Bob over for dinner. Since I thought you'd be out for the evening, we ended up making a lot of noise."

"So, I take it you and Grandpa Bob made up after your disagreement?"

"We're back on track. Now that he's not going to make me wear his dead wife's ring, I'm good with getting married again."

Rather than stand in the parking lot, we each grabbed a couple of bags from her trunk and walked into the apartment building.

"Have you made any progress on when the wedding will be?" I asked. "I know you were having a hard time finding a date when everyone could make it."

"We've decided to do it next month. Bob's a member at The Scottsdale Barrington, and they had a cancellation for New Year's Eve. The club was all geared up to do a wedding with flowers, caterers, and a photographer. We'll simply take over everything they'd planned for their wedding."

"That should make it simple."

"We're also getting everything at a discount because the people who originally booked the club had already made several deposits. If anyone in our families can make it to the ceremony, that would be lovely. If not, we'll send them pictures."

"That's only about six weeks away. You won't have time to get a dress for either you or the bridesmaids."

"I know. It will upset Megan, but I honestly don't need a new wedding dress when I already have a closet full of gowns. For the bridesmaids, I'll tell everyone to wear a royal blue dress and black shoes. That way, no one will need to buy anything, and the photos should come out pretty well."

"Sounds like a plan."

"I hope you, Sophie, and Gina can make it to the wedding. It always cracks me up when the three of you are together."

"I'm sure everyone will be thrilled to come."

"That invitation goes for your cousin as well. I know she's still new in town. Maybe she can meet a nice man at the wedding." Although," Grandma said as she lowered her voice, "tell her to stick to my side of the family. Bob's side can be a little strange."

Chapter Four

I returned to my apartment and got ready to call the hotel in Vail. I needed to come up with a story that was plausible but also had to be compelling enough so the hotel would send over the security videos.

I briefly thought about telling them the truth and seeing what happened. Unfortunately, I knew from experience that when I tell someone I'm looking for evidence in an attempted murder investigation, they usually get nervous and put up barriers. Plus, I didn't want to say anything that could link criminal activity with Max, even if he was only the intended target.

I called the hotel and was connected with the front desk. I asked to speak with the manager. After waiting for almost two minutes, a man came on the line.

"This is Mr. Barnes," he said in a practiced, professional tone. "How may I assist you?"

"Are you the hotel manager?"

"That is my privilege. How may I help you?"

"My name is Laura Black. We were staying at your hotel this weekend, and I was wondering if you could do me a favor."

"Certainly, madam. What name was the room under?"

Crap. I have no idea.

I knew Max usually used a false name when he traveled, but I couldn't remember what it was. For some reason, the name Anderson seemed right, but I really had no clue.

"Well, the company made the reservations, so it could have been under one of several names. Anderson, perhaps?"

"Ah, yes, you were staying in the Bighorn Suite. We were a little surprised when you checked out yesterday. I hope everything was to your satisfaction."

"Oh my God, yes," I said, putting as much glowing emphasis into it as possible. "The hotel and service were wonderful. We can't wait to come back. But we had a little problem."

"I'm sorry to hear that," he said. "How may I assist you?"

"You see, my ex-husband is rather violent, and I have a restraining order against him. Somebody in our party noticed he was waiting in front of the hotel for me to come out on Friday night. She ran right into him, and it scared her half to death. He's done this sort of thing before, but I've never been able to prove it."

"I see," Mr. Barnes said in a noncommittal way.

"Um, I was wondering, do you have security cameras that cover the outside of the hotel, near the entrance? If so, would you be able to send me a copy? If I can get a video of him waiting for me, I think it would be enough evidence to get him to stop. Worrying about this has been giving me nightmares, and I'd appreciate it more than you know."

I was so proud of my story. It was plausible but not too over the top. I was ninety percent sure he'd go with it. Unfortunately, as soon as he started speaking, I knew it hadn't worked.

"I'm sorry, madam. It's strict hotel policy not to release videos or photographs of our guests. You'll understand that the security video in question will have many of our guests coming and going. However, I do understand your situation. If you can give me a full description of your ex-husband, I will ask our corporate legal department if they can review the video and provide you with a photograph."

"Well, I guess that would work," I said. "Any idea how long something like that will take?"

"I'm afraid corporate legal moves at its own pace. I will prompt them as to the urgency of the situation. I expect we should hear back from them in four to six weeks."

Crap, that doesn't help at all.

"Yes, well, please tell them the importance of this. I don't feel safe knowing he's still stalking me."

I then gave Mr. Barnes my phone number and email address. I also gave him a complete description of the guy I'd run into outside the hotel. He said he'd call back as soon as he had some news.

I made it to Carolina's Mexican a few minutes after six. When I walked in, Danielle was already seated at a booth in the corner.

Roberto, the man who was her bodyguard and current boyfriend, sat alone at a table near the front door. He reminded me of Gabriella in the way he was constantly scanning the room for potential problems. There were also a couple of grim-looking goons at a side table, one with a good view of the room.

Danielle ordered three of their crunchy tacos while I got

my usual shredded-beef machaca burro, smothered in green chili sauce. I then dumped about half a cup of salsa on it.

It was nice being able to sit and simply chat with Danielle. It brought me back to when we'd first gotten to know each other and were merely co-workers in an office.

"Grandma Peckham's getting married on New Year's Eve here in town," I said. "She says you're invited, if you're interested. It won't be a big wedding, but it should be fun."

"Of course, tell her I'd love to come," Danielle said with a broad smile. "Send me the details when you get them. Grandma and I had a couple of afternoons together, and we sat in her living room and drank Appleton Rum and Diet Pepsi. She had a name for those."

"Jamaican Jerks," I said. "I haven't heard the whole story behind them, but it apparently involves her and three local guys she met while on a backpacking trip across the island when she was in college."

"I get the feeling she was pretty wild in her youth. It gives me hope that things in my life will eventually calm down."

When we were mostly done with our dinners, I thought it would be a good time to ask her about what had been bugging me.

"I know we haven't always been friends," I said. "But I know I can trust you. Max and I were on a skiing trip in Vail earlier this weekend. While we were there, a sniper tried to take Max out. From what I've been told, it was only due to some odd circumstances that the sniper didn't succeed. I'm trying to find out who it is and why he's doing it."

Danielle looked a little shocked at the news, then spent a few moments processing the information.

"Laura, first of all, you didn't come out and ask, but as

my friend, I'm telling you we had nothing to do with any sort of assassination attempt on Max."

Thank God for that.

"From what we understand," she continued, "he's due to take over from Tony in the next few weeks, and we have no quarrel with him. We've negotiated an agreement between our two organizations that will benefit both of us. I don't want to return to the war Carlos and Sergio had dragged us into."

I hadn't detected any deception on Danielle's part, and relief flooded through me at the news. I guess I'd been worried that the two gangs would start to go after each other again.

The last time had resulted in Tony being severely wounded and Carlos the Butcher being killed. I never wanted to go through something like that again.

Danielle saw me thinking, and she looked into my eyes. "I've been associated with organizations like Max's for many years. You may not want to hear this, but when there's a change of leadership, the new leader can either be appointed, or he can take control on his own."

"Alright, that makes sense."

"Now, keep in mind I don't know anything for sure, and I'm only making a guess here. Max clearly seems to be Tony's choice, but what if there's someone else in the group who thinks they would make a better leader? If this is the case, taking out Max would be their first logical move in establishing control. If that didn't give them a direct path toward leadership, removing Tony, one way or the other, would be their second."

I considered Danielle's words and felt a sense of dread creep over me. I hadn't considered an internal struggle for power as a possible explanation for what'd been happening. Still, the more I thought about it, the more I realized it was a possibility.

Max had said it himself. No one but a few of his top guys knew he was spending the weekend in Vail.

What if one of these men wanted to seize control, now that Tony was stepping down? I'd never sensed any sort of rebellion within Tony's organization. Still, what did I know about the group's internal politics?

"Trust me," Danielle said. "I'm not telling you anything that Tony and Max aren't already keenly aware of. We heard that Max had been scheduled to take over a month ago, but, for some reason, Tony has hesitated. To the lieutenants in his group, this may have been interpreted as Tony being unsure who to give the group to. Someone with ambition may have seen this as an opportunity."

"How so? Walk me through it?"

"If someone wanted to take Max out, what better way than to simply send an assassin out to where you were staying on vacation? Max would be killed, and the man who'd arranged the hit would have been in Arizona, maybe even standing next to Tony when it happened. It would be the perfect alibi. There could be no way of directly associating the man who set up the contract with the actual deed. He'd be hoping Tony would then have no choice but to hand over the group to him, even if Tony suspected he was involved."

"I hear what you're saying, but I can't imagine anything like that happening in Tony's group. They seem, I don't know, happy."

"You said this happened in Colorado? I imagine only a few people in Tony's organization knew about your trip. I'd start my investigation with them. Keep in mind that it wouldn't be a single person acting alone. He would have needed to have quietly set up a group of followers. But, honestly, if I were you, I wouldn't look too hard. If they sense you're becoming a problem, you might find yourself on the target list."

I quietly nodded to show I understood what she'd said. I then tried to eat the last couple of bites of the burro, but I'd lost my appetite. Danielle saw what I was thinking, and she reached out to hold my hand.

"I sincerely hope I'm wrong," she said. "But these things are sometimes inevitable in our business. Keep in mind that both Tony and Max are bright and resourceful men. They'll likely be able to complete the changeover without further problems."

"I think you already know this, but I'm getting pretty involved with Max. It would break my heart if anything happened to him."

"I'm starting to get that," Danielle said with a nod. "I can see why you'd be attracted to him. He does have a great smile."

After I left the restaurant, I went down a random side street and slowly drove back to my side of town. I mentally tried to refute what Danielle had suggested, but the pieces fit together too perfectly. Besides, I'd seen enough gangster movies over the years to know that the scenario she'd outlined seemed to be a common theme.

I'd gotten to the point where I felt comfortable being around Tony and his staff. Could it be possible that one of his top people was planning his overthrow? If so, Max would be in constant danger, not just from an unknown sniper, but maybe from one of his close coworkers.

I got back to my apartment at about nine-thirty. I then sat on the couch and flipped channels until almost eleven.

I'd been hoping to get another call from Max, but the only time I heard from him was a text I received around ten o'clock. He let me know everything was still good, but he'd likely be busy with meetings and setting up security for the next day or two.

The one bit of good news on the TV was that Snake had played almost the entire fourth quarter of the game and had even thrown a touchdown pass. I knew Sophie would probably be out late, celebrating Snake's good fortune.

The following day, I made it to the office at about eight-thirty. Sophie was at her desk, a large cup of gas station coffee in front of her.

Her computer was on, but she was focused on the Surfline surf reports on her tablet. As I walked through reception, I noticed many of the piles of file folders, which had been stacked on every horizontal surface in the reception area, were now gone.

"Hey, Sophie," I said as I looked around the office. "Where'd all the files go? Are you starting to clean the place up?"

"Yeah, well, it's pretty obvious Lenny isn't going to get me any help with the filing, and I'm starting to lose track of where I've put everything. After you left on Friday, I spent over an hour looking for a file I'd shoved in one of the stacks. That's when I started putting some of the folders away."

"Are you going to file all of them?"

"God, no. I don't want Lenny to think I have a lot of extra time and can do the filing myself. But I want to make sure I know where the main folders are. I'll leave the unimportant ones in a few piles around the office, so Lenny will still know he needs to hire another admin."

"I hope it works. The place seems to run smoother when you have someone to help."

"Speaking of files," Sophie said as she handed me a thick folder. "Here's the one for the assignment today. Lenny wanted you to read it before the meeting."

"There must be forty or fifty pages here," I said as I leafed through the stack of paper.

"Most of it's boilerplate. I guess we'll need to get used to this if we'll be working with an insurance company."

"I saw Lenny's Porsche parked out back. How's he doing today?"

"Well, I don't know how he's doing, but he didn't look so hot. He got in right before you. He didn't say anything. He just went into his office and shut the door."

"Did you go out with the Cougars after you dropped me off Saturday night? Did you get a chance to talk with Elle?"

"Yeah, I caught up with them at The Living Room lounge. When I asked her about it, she said she wasn't sure what she and Lenny were doing yet. I was going to ask her more about it, but then she took off with this basketball player from ASU. The guy was really tall. I'm talking like six foot six."

"Elle isn't sure if they're dating or not? I wonder if Lenny knows how she feels?"

"I don't know," Sophie said, "but I'm not going to tell him anything. He's been enough of an ass while he's been dating Elle. I don't want to be anywhere near him if she breaks it off. Have you heard from Max? Do they know what's going on with the sniper yet?"

"We talked on the phone yesterday. I get the feeling they don't know anything yet."

"Are you still going to run your own investigation?"

"Well, yes, sort of. I gave Gina a shell casing for forensics to look at, and I've been making some phone calls. I also had dinner with Danielle last night. She said her group didn't have anything to do with it."

"I didn't think it did," Sophie said. "Everything seems to have calmed down after she took over. I don't think she'd want to stir things up again, at least, not right away."

"But she did have an interesting take on it. She thinks that maybe someone within Tony's group isn't happy about the decision in favor of Max leading the organization. She says it's possible one of Tony's senior guys is trying to take over. If that's the case, removing Max would be the first logical step."

"It's funny you said that. When I talked to Pooh Bear yesterday, he sort of implied the same thing. He didn't come out and say it, but I think they're doing a quiet internal investigation into all of their top guys."

"I can't believe anyone in the group would do something like that. But honestly, I only know a dozen guys over there by name, and I know nothing of the group's inner workings. I think Max and Tony go out of their way to keep me out of that side of the business."

"It's probably a good idea. The less you know about what's actually going on over there, the better."

"How was the game yesterday?" I asked. "I saw on the news that Snake got to play a lot."

"The game was okay, but I don't think I can stand sitting with the wives anymore."

"What happened? I would've thought things would be

better now that Snake's playing."

"I thought so, too. But it turns out that Snake playing is the problem. The usual backup quarterback's been there for several years, and everyone in the group likes his wife. Now that he's out with an injury, the wife's blaming me for Snake stealing her husband's job."

"She's blaming you? How could she do that?"

"Damned if I know. But every time Snake went in, she glared at me. When Snake threw that touchdown pass in the fourth quarter, she actually started crying. The other wives were all hugging her and telling her that it would be alright. They told her not to worry. Her husband would be back in his rightful place soon. They all looked at me like I was a pile of dog shit they'd stepped in."

"That sucks. How long will it be until the usual backup will be able to play again?"

"They're still thinking four to five weeks, which is the end of the regular season. But seriously, I don't think I want to hang out with the ladies anymore, no matter how much Snake plays."

"You look pretty perky today. I figured this would be a sleep-at-your-desk morning. Didn't the two of you go out last night? With the touchdown yesterday, he must have made like a quarter of a million dollars in incentive bonuses. I figured he'd want to take you out to celebrate."

"Well, we'd planned on going out, but something came up with the team at the last minute, and he had to cancel. They're playing in Green Bay next Sunday, so we'll need to find a night between now and when the team travels on Friday."

Lenny came out of his office and walked up to Sophie's desk. It was apparent he hadn't been getting a lot of sleep.

"Are you okay?" I asked.

"Yeah, I'm great," he said as he yawned and stretched his arms out behind him. "But this dating thing is starting to take it out of me. Elle and I went out Friday night, and she had me up until one thirty. Last night, I didn't get home until almost two. She went out with her girlfriends on Saturday night, and that's probably a good thing. I don't think I could've handled being with her three nights in a row."

"Are things still going okay between you two?" I asked.

"Yeah, so far, so good. But it's been years since I've had a girlfriend, and I'm still not used to it. Although, now that you've mentioned it, every time we've gone out, it's only for dinner, then over to her place. I've talked about us taking off together for a three-day weekend sometime, but I guess she's not ready for that yet. She says, 'All in good time,' whatever that means."

Lenny looked down at his Rolex and then up at me. "The client should be here in fifteen minutes. Have you finished reading the information they sent over last week? Everything's in the file."

"Um, just about," I said, holding up the folder so he could see I actually had it. "Let me review the last couple of pages before they get here."

Lenny looked at me like he didn't think I'd even started reading the file, which, of course, I hadn't.

"Get on that folder," he said. "You don't need to memorize it, but it'd be nice if you at least knew the background on the case." He then looked at me with a slightly puzzled expression. "Weren't you supposed to be sick? Like stuck in bed, not able to work, sick?"

"I was," I said. "I felt terrible and couldn't move from the couch until yesterday morning. But it only seemed to be a twenty-four-hour thing, and I'm pretty much over it now."

Lenny didn't say anything. He only gave me a look and walked back into his office.

I went into the conference room and flipped through the massive file until the client showed up. I then walked out to reception, and we made introductions.

Her name was Brenda Montoya, and she was the head of the Commercial Claims Adjustment Department for BisSure Inc., a local business insurance company. She was in her mid-fifties and was well-dressed. She had short dark hair and a no-nonsense attitude.

The four of us went into Lenny's office. Sophie came in last and left the door open so she could leave if the phone rang or a client came in. Lenny didn't offer anyone a pre-meeting drink.

"As we discussed last week," Brenda said. "Our department is looking into the case of a man named Rudy Rialto. He claims to have been injured three months ago while shopping at the Handy Hardware store on McKellips Road, a business we represent. Mr. Rialto claims to have lost seventy percent of the range of motion in his left leg and sixty percent in his left arm. He's claiming total disability, and his council requests a settlement of two point eight million dollars."

"What do the doctors say?" Lenny asked.

"His personal doctor says he's disabled to the limits I described. Our doctor says it's inconclusive. Unfortunately, it's one of those injuries there isn't a definitive test for. We have to go by what the injured party says. He was definitely injured, that's not in dispute, but it's the kind of injury that either heals quickly or never really gets better."

"I take it you need us to find out which it is?" Lenny asked.

"That's right," Brenda said. "A time-stamped video of him doing something that is clearly beyond what his doctor claims is possible would be best. Most insurance companies have someone on staff for this sort of thing, but unfortunately, we aren't large enough yet to hire someone full-time."

"It's not a problem," Lenny said. "We'll get right on it."

"Good," Brenda said. "All the information you need should be in the file. Call me if you need anything else."

We all stood and walked back to reception. We said our goodbyes as Lenny walked Brenda to the front door. After she left, he thought about the meeting for a moment, then turned to Sophie.

"Send over the standard business agreement to the contact at the insurance company," he said. "Give them a twenty percent discount off the full rate. Once they sign, invoice a twenty-five thousand dollar retainer. I doubt this assignment will take all of that, but see what they say. If it goes through, they'll have to use us for the next one as well. There's money to be made in insurance investigations, and we should be in on it."

Sophie said she'd get things going, and Lenny returned to his office. She looked like she was about to say something, but my phone started ringing.

I pulled it out of my back pocket and saw it was a Colorado area code. I walked into the conference room and answered.

"Miss Black," the man on the other end of the phone

said. "This is Mr. Barnes. We spoke yesterday concerning the security videos of your ex-husband."

"Mr. Barnes. I wasn't expecting to hear from you so soon."

"Yes, well, there's been an incident over here, and I need to speak with you about it."

"What happened?"

"It seems your ex-husband came into the hotel late last night and brutalized the employee we had covering the front desk. At least, we're assuming he was your ex-husband. We showed the clerk the security videos you mentioned from Friday night, and he says it's probably the same man. The image quality isn't the best. According to the clerk, his attacker was just a normal-looking guy, except that he had a large scar under his left eye."

"Yes, that's him."

"Well, your ex demanded all the information we had for your party, including your names, addresses, and methods of payment."

"My God. Is the desk clerk alright?"

"Unfortunately, no. He's been moved to the hospital, but the kid is still scared half to death. Your ex pulled him into a back room and roughly questioned him. Every time your ex didn't like an answer, he'd break one of the clerk's fingers. Your ex grabbed the clerk's hand and slowly bent one of his fingers back until it snapped. He ended up doing that three times."

"That must have been horrible."

"As you can imagine, the clerk gave him everything he wanted. I'm afraid your ex now has all the information we had on you and your party."

Damn.

"Are you doing alright, Mr. Barnes?"

"Frankly, I'm not even close to alright. This sort of thing has never happened at our hotel before. The detective from the sheriff's office just left. He's been here since right after it happened. I gave him your name and number, so I expect he'll be giving you a call within the next day or two. He'll want to know what you have on your ex-husband, including his name and last known address."

"Thank you for letting me know."

"Oh, and about the security videos. Due to circumstances, I'm using my discretion as hotel manager to release the videos to you. I trust you'll only use them to identify your ex-husband and have him dealt with."

"That's all I want them for," I assured the manager.

"You said you wanted the videos from the front entrance on Friday evening. Can you narrow down the time frame you were looking for?"

"Let's go from between eight and eleven. That should cover the time he was watching the entrance."

"Very well. I have your email address. I'll have someone from our IT department send the files right over."

"Thank you for the information, Mr. Barnes."

"Miss Black, I pray you'll do whatever is in your power to stop him. I hate to think someone like your ex-husband is free to roam our streets."

I disconnected and went back to reception. Sophie was looking at me with her head cocked to one side.

"What's going on?" she asked. "You've got a weird look on your face."

"That was the hotel in Vail. The shooter came in late last night and broke the desk clerk's fingers until he got everything the hotel had on Max."

"Jeez, this guy sounds like a total asshole. And you want to go out and find him?"

"It looks like it," I sighed.

"Well, be careful. I'd be really bummed if he started breaking your fingers too."

Lenny came back out of his office and walked to Sophie's desk.

"Gina owes me an alibi," he said. "Where is she on that?"

"She already came and went this morning," Sophie said. "We'll have the report on your desk by close of business today."

"Great," he said. "That's the first good news I've had this week. Hey, as long as you're both here, I have a question."

Sophie shot me a look that said she'd rather be anywhere but here talking with Lenny about dating.

"Should I stop using deodorant?" Lenny asked. "I've still got a good thing going with Elle, and I don't want to mess it up. I was reading over the weekend that a lot of women like their men to smell natural, like they just came back from hunting a wild boar or something. What do you both think?"

Sophie scrunched up her face at the thought of smelling Lenny in his natural state. I was afraid she was about to grab her trash can and spit up in it.

"Um," I said. "I'd probably ignore that article. But if you want a broad rule of thumb, if the woman shaves her armpits, you should probably wear deodorant."

Lenny stared into space, thought about it, and nodded his

head. "Yeah, okay, that's good advice. I once dated a girl in law school with hairy armpits, and she wasn't all that big on perfume."

While Lenny was talking, Sophie's desk phone rang. She answered, and her eyes grew big.

As Sophie listened to the caller, I could see her starting to panic. She asked the caller to hold, pushed a button on the phone, and then looked up at Lenny.

"What?" he asked, sounding annoyed.

"Um," Sophie said. "It's Tony DiCenzo, and it's for you."

Lenny's face went pale, and he looked like he was debating whether to take the call or not.

"Shit," he said quietly. "Okay, I'll take it in my office." He walked across reception, his shoulders hunched like a man heading to prison. Once in his office, he turned and slowly closed the door.

"Mr. DiCenzo?" Sophie asked. "Hold on, I'll transfer you to Mr. Shapiro." She pushed a button, then pulled her hands away from the phone like it had become something nasty.

"What did Tony want?" I asked. "Did he say?"

"No, and I wasn't about to ask. Look, I know you're friends with him and all, but he still scares the crap out of me. I've only met the man twice and neither time ended well. The first time, a building blew up, people were killed, and I had to take Alex Sternwood to the emergency room."

"Yeah," I admitted with a nod. "That was horrible."

"The second time, a wedding cake blew up, and people were almost killed there too. Both times, you ended up in the hospital."

Sophie shook her head and sighed. "Now that I've talked to Tough Tony again, I'm going to be waiting for something else to blow up. I only hope I'm not standing next to whatever it is."

Lenny opened his door about ten minutes later. Neither Sophie nor I had left the reception area.

From the look on his face, he hadn't enjoyed his conversation with Tough Tony. He motioned me into his office. After thinking about it for a moment, he motioned Sophie in as well.

Once inside, I opened both windows to create a soft, warm breeze. Sophie went to the wet bar and started dropping ice cubes into a glass.

She poured two fingers of Jim Beam while Lenny opened his drawer and pulled out his ashtray and pack of cigarettes. She set the glass on his desk, and we both took our seats.

Lenny sparked up his gold-plated Zippo and took a couple of long draws on his cigarette. After exhaling a few clouds of smoke, he picked up the glass and took a noisy sip of the bourbon.

"Alright," he said once he'd gotten settled. "I've just accepted an assignment from Tony DiCenzo. I didn't want to take it, especially after what happened the last time we tried to do something for him, but it's not like you can refuse to do a favor for the man when he asks."

We waited as Lenny took another deep draw on his cigarette and then took another long, noisy sip of the Beam. He stared into space for a moment before he was again ready to speak.

"Tough Tony's looking for help finding someone. He was a little vague on the details about who it was or what he wanted with him, but he wanted you to be the one to look into it," Lenny said, pointing at me. "I suggested that with Gina's background, she might be better at it, but I guess you impressed him with how quickly you found Alex Sternwood the last time."

Sophie made a noise, and I knew she was rolling her eyes. Lenny and I both ignored her.

Damn, I guess Tony talked Max into using my help.

"Tough Tony's set up a meeting with you and one of his guys to go over the details," Lenny continued. "His name's Maximilian. He's the same guy who was over here for the Sternwood case. I think he's some sort of business manager for the company. The meeting's this morning at eleven o'clock at Scottsdale Land and Resort Management. Their offices are on the second floor of the Tropical Paradise."

Lenny paused, took another puff of his cigarette, then crushed it out in the ashtray. "Now, I can't force you to take this assignment, especially since I don't know what all it'll involve, but I'd appreciate it if you'd accept it."

Lenny then smiled. I knew he was trying to look friendly, but it came across as more of a painful scowl.

"It's okay," I said quietly. "I'll take it."

"Really?" Lenny asked as he blew out a breath and visibly relaxed. "Um, very well. Sophie, write up the standard contract and send it over to the business contact at DiCenzo's office, same as last time. Go with a forty-thousand-dollar retainer and full hourly pricing. Maybe some good can come from this after all. I haven't been able to charge the full hourly rate since we had Stig Stevens in here, and that must have been three or four months ago."

~~~~

Sophie and I went back to reception. She still seemed a little nervous about the new assignment.

"So, what happened?" she asked. "I didn't think Max was going to let you work on this one."

"I guess Tony realized I was going to look for the shooter, with or without their blessing. At least this way, I won't need to explain to Lenny why I'm out of the office all week, chasing after some guy. It'll also give me a chance to tell Tony what happened last night at the hotel."

"If they want you for a meeting at eleven, you'll need to leave in a few minutes. When do you want to start on the Rudy Rialto assignment?"

"I'll have to work it in with looking for the shooter. But while Lenny was in there talking to Tony, I was thinking about it. The best way to get a video of Rudy doing something he shouldn't be able to do might be with a simple setup."

"Like what?" Sophie asked.

"If I show up at Rudy's house needing help with something, maybe he'd do something he shouldn't. I'll ask Lenny if you can come and shoot the video. We'll need to use the big office camera so we can get a time stamp."

"Well, I'll be glad to come and take the video, as long as we don't have to hide in a bedroom and listen to naked people having sex again. I can see why you hate it so much. That was like three weeks ago, and it still gives me the heebie-jeebies. Okay, it was sorta hot listening to it at first, but overall, it was just nasty."

I drove up Scottsdale Road towards the Tropical Paradise. The only thing that dampened my spirits was the traffic. In the summer, Scottsdale's a quiet town in the middle of the desert. In winter, it's an entirely different city.

Tens of thousands of winter visitors, or Snowbirds, descend on the city. They jam the restaurants, the hair salons, and, worst of all, the roads.

Many of them only feel comfortable driving between nine in the morning and four in the afternoon. That makes the middle of the day Snowbird traffic time.

Today was no exception. I was following a vintage Cadillac El Dorado with Wisconsin plates. Next to me was an RV from North Dakota.

I wouldn't have minded them being on the road and driving ten miles under the speed limit if it wasn't for the fact that they weaved back and forth in their lanes. It got to the point where I thought they would crash, either into me or someone else.

Chapter Five

I eventually made it to the resort and parked in the visitor's lot. It only took a moment to notice the extra security. I don't think a casual visitor would have seen the changes, but it really stuck out to me as unusual and a little creepy.

I walked up the hill to the main building, again noticing the extra security staff as I entered the massive lobby. They were keeping a low profile, but they were definitely there.

I walked past the waterfall and through the tropical foliage, then climbed the curved stairs to the offices on the mezzanine level. When I reached the Scottsdale Land and Resort Management offices, the big glass doors were closed. Two beefy guys in black polos stood to either side.

"Hold on," one of the guards said as I reached for the door.

"But, um, I have an appointment…" I started to say, but the other guard held up his hand to stop me.

"We know who you are, Miss Black, but we have orders not to let anyone in today without notifying the shift security supervisor first. Let me call it in. It'll just take a second."

The first guard used his radio to notify his superior that I was at the front door. He quickly received an answer, and his face relaxed.

"Miss Black, Mr. DiCenzo would like to see you in his office. Your escort will be here in a minute."

"It's okay," I said. "I know the way."

"Sorry, Miss Black," the guard said, genuine apology in his voice. "Everyone needs an escort today."

"Alright, I'll wait."

In two minutes, the bulk of Johnny Scarpazzi lumbered down the hall toward the front entrance. As soon as he appeared, the guards opened the doors and let me enter.

"Hey, Johnny," I said when we met in the hallway, giving him a hug. "How've you been? I hope you had a better weekend than we did."

"The weekend was pretty good, well, it was until Milo called about what occurred. Thank God neither you nor Max were injured. How come these crazy things keep happening to you?"

"I wish I knew. I always try my best to stay out of trouble."

Johnny snorted, but I couldn't tell if he was laughing at me or agreeing. I let it pass.

Something seemed off as we walked down the hallway toward Tony's office. Although the usual number of people were visible in the offices, the noise level was somewhat subdued. I guess the added security was also spooking everyone here a little bit as well.

We made it to the executive wing and walked down to Tony's office. Gabriella was at her desk, typing on a computer. Seeing her in her office outfit with dark slacks and a white cotton blouse was still a little strange, even though it was unbuttoned to the point where the top half of her boobs were showing.

Gabriella glanced up at Johnny, and there was an unspoken handoff. Johnny said he had a meeting and said goodbye.

"Hey," I said in a low voice as I walked up to Gabriella's desk. "Between the Black Castle and Vail, it's been an exciting couple of weeks. Are you any closer to finding the sniper?"

"No, we are being discrete in how we investigate, but there is no indication of anything unusual happening with other groups in Phoenix or throughout Arizona. If it wasn't for fact that someone tried to kill you and Max, it would seem like ordinary week."

"Tony's gone through my law office and hired me to help look for the shooter."

At that, Gabriella briefly flashed something that almost looked like a smile. "I know. Max doesn't want you to be so closely involved, but Tony say you will do it, with or without his approval, so he might as well make it official. He wants to talk with you about it."

"I thought I was coming over to see Max."

"Max will be in meeting with Johnny and director of sports operations for next hour. We're hosting pro golf tournament at the Blue Palms this week, and they are going over final security arrangements.

"Well, if I'm going to be working with everyone on this, let me know if there's anything I can do to help you out."

"So far, there's nothing to do. We're on lockdown here at offices, and we're restricting who has access to senior staff. Unfortunately, there's no indication if Max is only target or if there are others. For me, I would prefer to be stationed on roof with my rifle and scope. If your man with scar on his face comes back, I know how to take care of him."

"I should let you know about what happened at the hotel in Vail last night. The shooter came in, worked over the guy behind the desk, and forced him to give up the information the hotel had on Max. The shooter wanted names, addresses, credit cards used, everything."

"That is good information. It solves one problem."

"What problem?"

"Give information to Tony. He will explain."

She pushed the door buzzer, and I walked into Tony's office. As usual, he was sitting behind his desk with a stack of papers in front of him.

"Laura Black," he said as he took off his reading glasses and stood. "I'm glad you could make it. Have a seat on the couch. Before we get started, I've been wanting to try a little experiment. But I've been holding off until you could come over."

He stiffly walked to his wet bar and brought back a beautiful box. He opened it to show off a stunning bottle of scotch. The hefty bottle looked to be more of a glass sculpture than anything else.

"This is a bottle of Glenmorangie Pride 1974 single malt scotch. I've been told it's one of the best scotches in existence, and I'd like you to try it with me."

"Sure," I said. "Having a scotch that comes from a bottle that beautiful sounds like a good experiment."

I sat on the couch while Tony returned to the wet bar and prepared the drinks. When he brought them over, a single ice cube floated in each glass. Tony handed me the drink, and I held it in my hands for a few moments to warm the scotch and melt the ice.

"You're walking without the cane?" I asked.

"It was needed for a few weeks, but I don't want to rely on it. I can't walk very fast yet, but I can again walk."

"That's great. When it first happened, I feared the worst."

"Well," he said with a laugh. "I won't say I was unconcerned, but I knew I would find a way. Truth be told, the main reason I want to walk again is so I can get out to my golf courses. You get a different view of the fairways and greens when you're on foot as opposed to riding in a cart. I need to make sure nobody's been skimping on the maintenance of the courses while I was laid up."

Tony lifted his glass and proposed a toast. "To finding the asshole who shot at you and Max."

I lifted the glass and breathed in deeply. The aromas were subtle, complex, and delicious. I took a sip, and warm pleasure slid down my throat.

The sensation brought me back to the time I sat next to the pool with Muffy Sternwood, the day we'd first met. The fifty-year-old Balvenie she'd given me was the first truly great scotch I'd ever had.

The only way I'd been able to describe it was as *liquid sex*. It made me want to take a scotch-tasting class to learn more about the different flavors and sensations I had experienced.

As always, Tony watched closely to see my reaction to the drink. "Oh," I moaned as I took another sip. "This is so good."

"I agree," he said as he held up his glass to look at the remaining golden liquid. "This is a beautiful scotch, rich and complex. But, as I feared, I find that I'm judging it against the Balvenie Cask 191. What about you? You once mentioned that the Balvenie is what you also measured everything else against. You said it had ruined you for all other scotches. Did you experience that when you drank this?"

"Um, yeah, I sorta did. Honestly, I do it every time I have one of these wonderful scotches. It's nothing against this one. It's a great scotch, but I can't help it."

"No, I understand," Tony said with a nod. "I'm afraid the Balvenie has ruined me for all others as well. It's the notes of sherry from a scotch that's been in a barrel for fifty years that I find so extraordinary. I've never found anything to match it."

He let out a small sigh and looked thoughtful. "Unfortunately, it's not likely that I'll get another bottle of it. Only eighty-three were produced from that one remarkable cask. The one I found was likely the last that will be available on the open market for some time, at least at a price I'd be willing to pay. Once the bottle's gone, the memory of it will need to suffice."

"But, better to have loved and lost?" I asked.

Tony smiled and let out a short laugh. "Yes, something like that. Well, on to why you're here today. As you know, there was some excitement in Colorado during your recent trip. I assumed you'd be looking for the shooter. I also assumed Lenny wouldn't be too happy if you simply took off and did your own thing while he was trying to run his business. I thought that by making this a formal assignment for your job, you'd have an easier time helping us find out what's going on."

"Thanks, Tony. I appreciate you letting me help with this."

Tony gave me one of his dismissive hand waves. "It's not a problem. Max says you kept your head and were able to think clearly, even while you were actively being shot at.

From my experience, that's a rare ability, and I can always use that skill. Besides, you're part of my team. Truth be told, I would've been a little disappointed if you hadn't wanted to help."

"I think you're starting to know me. And yes, I've already started my investigation."

"As you may already know, we've had no luck in trying to identify the shooter or in learning if there're any targets other than Max. We've reached out to our contacts and talked with all of our intelligence sources. To this point, we've come up empty."

"So far, I know the face of the shooter," I said. "He has an unusual scar, but it doesn't ring a bell with anyone. We know the rifle that was used and where it was bought. We have a shell casing that I've turned in for analysis. I've also been talking with my contacts. So far, I don't have any indication who's behind this."

"Very well. What are your next steps?"

"I just found out some new information. Late last night, the shooter went back to our hotel in Vail and badly abused the guy who was working behind the front desk. Our guy broke three of the clerk's fingers to force him to give up all the information the hotel had on us. The only good that came out of the incident is that the hotel will send copies of the security videos. With any luck, we'll have a picture of the shooter."

Tony thought about it for a moment. "Do we know what information the clerk at the hotel was forced to reveal?"

"From what the manager said, the shooter was interested in our names, our addresses, and the credit cards used to pay for the rooms."

"Really? That is indeed interesting news. It tells us a lot.

And yes, I'd very much like to see the face of the shooter, if you're able to isolate a photo of him. What else?"

"If nothing else shakes out in a day or two, I plan to return to Vail. The shooter bought the rifle with cash, but there's a remote possibility he used his real name when he applied for the background check. No guarantees, of course. If he's a professional killer, he likely used a fake name, but I don't know where to go next."

"That seems reasonable. Are there any other avenues you wish to explore?"

"Um, maybe. Look, I'm not sure the best way to ask you this, so I'll be direct. Is everything still going okay with the plan for Max to take over the group? Is there anyone over here who seems, um, concerned, or maybe even upset about it?"

Tony looked at me for a moment, then started laughing.

"Laura Black, I think this is why we get along so well. You looked at the facts of the situation and came to the obvious conclusion. Yes, it's true. The most likely suspect would be someone from within my own organization."

"Um, well, I was considering it as a possibility."

"Don't worry about hurting my feelings. It was my first thought as well."

"Really?"

"Of course. It fits with the facts. But I'll tell you, ultimately, it doesn't make sense. Max taking over means all of my top guys move up. Everyone gets more responsibility."

"There isn't anyone other than Max who wants to run the group?"

"I wouldn't say Max actually pushed for the job. Truth be told, I think he'd be happier not to have it. But in all candor, Laura Black, the only man here who could gather enough followers to stage a takeover would be Johnny. And I know it's not him, because I offered him the position before I gave it to Max. I knew he wouldn't take it, but by rights, he was next in line."

"Really? I'm surprised."

"I think you know I originally brought Johnny out from New York to help me run things. He's a good leader, and the men respect him. Truth be told, Johnny likes the other side of the business, but he's never had an interest in the hotel and resort side of things. We found this out early on, and now Johnny mainly concentrates on our other activities. We both decided it would be in the interest of the group for someone comfortable with both sides to be the heir apparent. Matter of fact, that's about the time I decided to take on Max as my new number two."

"So, you don't think this attempt on Max's life came from anyone inside the group?"

"Honestly, I don't. The information you've just brought seems to confirm this. A man on the inside would already know all the information our shooter tortured someone to obtain. But let's both keep our eyes open. I've been wrong before. I should also let you know we've made some inquiries to learn if you might have been the actual target of the shooter instead of Max."

What? Seriously?

"Wow, I know I've pissed some people off over the last year or two, but I really don't think anyone would need to follow me all the way out to Colorado to shoot me. Besides, I ran into the guy on the street the first night we were in Vail. If he wanted to harm me, that would have been the perfect opportunity."

"Given what we currently know, I also think it unlikely.

But at this point, I want to leave nothing to chance."

I drove back down Scottsdale Road toward the office. Unfortunately, it was still prime time for Snowbird traffic. The drive that normally took fifteen minutes ended up taking over half an hour.

I can't wait for summer.

While sitting at a light, my phone pinged to let me know a new email had come in. I glanced at it and saw a link to the hotel security video.

Lenny and Sophie were there when I returned to the office, but Gina was still out. I went to reception to let Sophie know I was in and see if she'd already had lunch. When I got there, I saw she was already busy eating a slice of pizza.

"Hey," she said, her mouth still half-full. "There are still three or four slices left, and they're all yours." She pointed to a pizza box on the corner of her desk.

"Thanks," I said as I took a napkin and grabbed a couple of slices. "I'll be back at my cubicle. I got the raw security videos from the front of the hotel in Vail. I'm going to run through them and see if I can get a clear picture of the shooter."

I went to the back offices and booted up my laptop. With the link in the email, I was able to get a listing of the video files.

I downloaded the first file, which covered the time between eight and nine o'clock. I looked for the shooter, but the street seemed to be clear of everyone other than the expected tourists walking back and forth.

I fast-forwarded until I spotted the four of us returning to the hotel from the restaurant at eight thirty-seven. Five minutes later, the shooter emerged from the shadows.

He was across the street from the hotel, and once he appeared, he didn't move around much. Unfortunately, the only light in the scene was behind him, making him little more than a shadowy silhouette.

A few minutes before nine, I saw myself come out of the hotel and walk down the street. The man must have seen me, but he never moved from his spot.

In a way, this made me feel a little better. I would have been creeped out if he'd followed me through the village the entire time, but I hadn't noticed.

I downloaded the next hour of video to see if I could get a better view of the man. I fast-forwarded through almost the entire hour, but he barely moved.

At nine-forty-seven, I saw myself come around the corner and run into the man. We had our brief interaction, and I disappeared into the hotel.

The man looked up the street in the direction I'd just come from, then back to the hotel. Within a minute, he'd turned and merged back into the shadows. I fast-forwarded until the video ran out, but the guy was gone.

I reversed the video until I had a more or less full image of his face. I then copied the image as a picture and tried to brighten it to see if I could make out any details.

Unfortunately, the resolution of the image was poor. Between the darkness and the falling snow, it appeared I had little chance of getting a picture clear enough to identify the shooter.

Damn.

Gina came in while I was still working on the image. She

suggested we find a point in time when the man wasn't moving, copy three or four separate images of his face, and then overlay them on top of each other.

Doing this helped clear the picture, but the man still could have been half the male population. The scar on his cheek was barely visible and other than the overall shape of his face, there were no identifying details. Sighing with defeat, I printed a picture representing the best we could get.

Gina went up front to fill Sophie in on her current assignments. I used the opportunity to call Max.

"Hey," I said when he answered. "How are things on your end?"

"Hectic," he said with a chuckle. "Hosting a professional golf tournament is crazy at the best of times. Setting up for the network television coverage has been a nightmare all its own. Needing to divert half of our security staff to cover the Tropical Paradise isn't making things easier. This leaves our other properties with only a skeleton staff."

"Managing resorts seems to keep you busy."

"Busy isn't the word I'd use. Have you found out anything new?"

"Tony might have already told you, but late last night, the shooter went to our hotel in Vail and roughed up the guy working behind the front desk. He started breaking fingers until the desk clerk gave him all of the information the hotel had on you and where you were from."

"Yes, Tony mentioned that. He said you both had a productive meeting."

"We had a good talk. Plus, it was wonderful to see him walking without the cane. He's making great progress."

"I've learned to never underestimate Tony. Once he sets his mind to doing something, he'll find a way to do it. Is the desk clerk going to be alright?"

"From what I got, he was pretty shaken up, but broken fingers seem to be the extent of his injuries. That's bad enough."

"Still, it's important information. Attacking a hotel employee is a risky move. If the shooter was from Arizona, he would've already known that information."

"I was able to get the security tapes from the hotel in Vail. Gina and I worked on pulling a picture of the shooter's face, but it's still a little too dark and grainy to show any detail. I'll email over a copy to see if you can make out anything from it."

I said goodbye to Max and then started reading the background information on the Rudy Rialto insurance assignment. According to the file, he was fifty-eight years old and had been single since a divorce, twenty years before.

There was some information about Rudy's work history as a boat mechanic for a small local company. There were ten pages detailing his accident at the hardware store, which seemed to happen due to his carelessness.

He'd apparently been trying to get a heavy air compressor off an upper shelf and had climbed up on a lower shelf to get to it. When he pulled the compressor off the shelf, it fell on him and caused his injury.

There were then over thirty pages of various doctors' and physical therapists' reports. By the time I'd finished reading the file, my head was starting to spin.

Twice during the afternoon, my phone rang with a Colorado area code. I guessed this was the detective from the Eagle County Sheriff's office, so I didn't answer.

It wasn't that I was against helping law enforcement, but they would want to know my ex's name and his last known address. Since I didn't know either of these things, it would likely be a long and awkward conversation.

The second time, my phone buzzed to let me know I had a message. I listened to it, and it was indeed a detective from Colorado.

He gave me his name and a number to call. I didn't delete the message, but I also didn't call him back.

I went up front to see what Sophie and Gina were up to. Lenny had already taken off, and when I got to Sophie's desk, I saw she was packing up for the night.

"I'm starting to get hungry," I said. "It's too late to start anything with Rudy Rialto. Do either of you want to do dinner somewhere?"

"Well, I'm free tonight," Sophie said. "Snake's doing something with the team, and Pooh Bear's still, um, busy with work."

"Sounds good to me," Gina said. "But let's go somewhere without too many Snowbirds. How about sushi?"

"Oh, that sounds yummy," Sophie said. "It's been a while since I've had any hot saké."

We walked down the street to Geisha A Go Go, a fun sushi place that was starting to fill up but wasn't yet overly crowded. We found an open table and ordered some edamame.

We looked at the menus for a few minutes. Still, we ended up ordering the same sushi rolls we always get when we're here: a Hentai Heat, a Flying Kamikaze, a Bye-Bye Kitty, and a Super Junky Monkey.

The waitress delivered a bottle of hot saké, and I poured everyone a small cup of the rice wine. As we munched on the edamame and waited for the food to come out, we spent several minutes toasting each other's good health.

"I assume that picture we were working on today is for your new assignment from Tony DiCenzo," Gina said. "I hope you're being careful. Dating a mobster is bad enough, but you need to make sure you don't get sucked any further into their criminal organization."

I glanced at Sophie, but she had on her best, innocent face.

"I'm just helping them look for a guy," I said. "I guess they don't have a lot of people over there who are good at this sort of thing, and you know they won't go to the police, no matter what happens. Besides, Lenny's thrilled. He's getting to charge the full hourly rate."

"Still," Gina said. "There're a lot of people in law enforcement trying to build a case around his crime family. At some point, Tony's world is going to come crashing down around him. I don't want it to crash on you as well."

"Don't be such a Debbie Downer," Sophie said as she poured everyone another glass of saké. "The last time we had an assignment from Tony DiCenzo, we all got a bonus. Of course, it barely put a dent in my credit cards, but still."

I lifted up my glass. "Here's hoping for another bonus."

"I know I could use it," Gina said.

Sophie and Gina lifted their glasses and tossed back their wine in one swallow.

The sushi came out, and we spent twenty minutes munching away. We'd almost finished the dinner and had already paid the bill when the waitress appeared with three big saké bombers. "From the gentlemen," she said, indicating who'd sent the drinks.

We looked to where she pointed and saw there was a table of four cute Japanese guys, all in their late twenties or early thirties. From the way they were dressed, black suits, white shirts, and black ties, they must have been in town on business.

They all smiled and held up their drinks. Sophie waved, and the guy who looked the youngest waved back.

"That was so nice," Sophie said. "I'll go and thank them."

Gina and I started to work on our bombers while Sophie picked up her drink. She walked over to their table and talked with the guys for three or four minutes.

Before she left, she bent down and kissed the guy who'd waved at her. When she returned, her face had taken on the pink glow she got when she'd been drinking and was starting to lust after men.

"Those guys are in town to buy a hotel," Sophie said. "They've rented one of the karaoke rooms here and invited us to come and hang out with them."

The men had already gotten up from their table and started heading to the back rooms. Two of them waved for us to come with them.

"Well," Gina said, looking at her watch, "I can stay about an hour, but then I'll need to take off."

"What about you?" Sophie asked me. "Want to spend the evening doing karaoke with a bunch of cute Japanese guys? It could be fun."

"You both go ahead," I said. "Between the saké at dinner and this big bomber, I'm at my limit. I still need to get home."

"So, take an Uber," Gina said. "Our cars are parked at the office. They'll be fine for the night."

"You two go ahead. I need to function tomorrow."

"Party pooper," Sophie said as she laughed at me. With a wave, she and Gina picked up their drinks and followed the men into the back room.

I woke to the dueling sounds of the alarm and Marlowe purring in my ear. There wasn't anywhere I needed to be right away, so I hit the snooze button.

After the alarm had gone off several times, I started thinking about my two new assignments and that someone was trying to kill Max. That woke me up enough to get me out of bed.

My head was still a little fuzzy from doing the extra saké bomber the night before, but it cleared after the first cup of coffee. Marlowe followed me around as I got ready for the day, but I made sure not to feed him until right before I left.

I walked in through the rear door at about nine o'clock and found Gina at her cubicle desk. From the circles under her eyes, it was apparent she hadn't gotten a lot of sleep.

"How are you doing today?" I asked. "You look like you had a fun time."

"Yeah," she said with a laugh. "I really didn't mean to stay out so late. After we closed out the restaurant, we walked over to the guys' hotel and hung out for another hour or so. We ended up in at least ten pictures with all the guys."

"It sounds like they appreciated having you there."

"We're probably going to be well known in their social circles in Japan for a while. It was fun, even though each of them propositioned me at least once."

"Seriously?" I asked.

"At least they were polite about it," Gina laughed. "I didn't get home until almost one. Thank God for Uber. I don't know how many bottles of saké we went through last night, but it was a lot."

"Did you both at least have a nice time?"

"Oh, sure. They were good guys to hang around with, even though their English was a little hard to understand after they'd had a few bottles. Plus, I think they were struggling a bit trying to understand us. You know how fast Sophie talks when she drinks. But the karaoke room had a stripper pole in the middle of it, and after a while, she started working it. That sort of shut them up for a while, especially after she unbuttoned all but one of the buttons on her blouse."

"I can see Sophie doing a pole dance for a room full of drunken men," I said. "How was she?"

"She was actually pretty good. The guys certainly loved it. At one point, they started stuffing dollar bills in the waistband of her skirt. If the law office thing here doesn't work out, she should talk with Danica about getting a job at Jeannie's. She'd probably make more money there than she does being a paralegal here."

"I'll need to ask her about it. Well, assuming she still remembers doing it."

"Yeah, well, be nice to her today. I think her head still hurts a bit, and I had to give her some bad news this morning."

"What was it?"

Gina shook her head. "I'm sure she'll tell you all about it. Oh, one more thing. I got the results back on that shell casing."

"And?"

"And, as I suspected, I now owe the lab tech lunch."

"Sorry," I said. "I'll pay next time we go out to make up for it. What'd they find out?"

"It's a standard Winchester three-oh-eight match-grade cartridge. They didn't get any DNA, but they did find a partial fingerprint."

"That's great. Was there a match?"

"Unfortunately, no. That either means there wasn't enough of a print for a positive match, or the guy isn't in the database at all. They gave me the electronic file with the digital image of the print. I'm not sure if that helps us, but it might be handy if you get another print to compare it to."

"I guess a partial print is better than nothing. Thanks for having them do that. I owe you one, again. Unfortunately, it still doesn't tell us who the guy is."

"I'm assuming this has something to do with your assignment for Tough Tony. You already know how I feel about us working with them, but let me know how I can help. The sooner you're done with this, the better."

I walked up to reception, but one look told me Sophie was both hurting and in a foul mood. She wasn't wearing any makeup, her hair looked like it hadn't been brushed since the night before, and she was wearing her sunglasses.

"Hey," I said. "Um, what's going on?"

"What's going on?" she snarled at me. "I'll tell you. This is what's going on."

She opened a newspaper on her desk and flipped it to the back-society page. "Look at this," she growled.

Sophie reached out to grab a big doughnut-store coffee on her desk while I slid the paper closer and read the article.

Cardinals Players Relax After Big Win

After their win against San Francisco, several Cardinals players were seen celebrating Sunday night in the VIP room at Nexxus. Pictured is running back Josh Taylor and his wife Keisha, wide receiver Thomas Mann with his wife Belinda, and quarterback Snake McCoy along with Cardinals cheerleader Hayley Reynolds.

The picture showed the three smiling couples gathered together at a table with several half-full glasses of champagne in front of them. The woman sitting next to Snake had big curly blonde hair and a dress that was low-cut to the point where her oversized fake boobs were all but falling out.

"This is why Snake couldn't go out with me after the game," Sophie growled. "He said it was a team thing, but I guess it was more of a cheerleader thing."

She slid open her desk drawer and pulled out a big bottle of Advil. She shook out four tablets, tossed them back, and washed them down with the coffee.

"He was probably with her last night as well. Now that he's starting to make some serious money, he probably thinks he can do better than me."

"Well, that sucks," I said. "Has he told you anything about going out with a cheerleader?"

"Nope, this newspaper article is the first I've heard about it. Gina's the one who spotted it. She showed it to me when she came in today."

"What are you going to do? Are you going to confront him with the evidence? Are you still going to see him?

Besides, I thought players weren't allowed to date the cheerleaders."

"That frickin jerk? He's dead to me. He knows the rules."

"Um, about the rules. I know when you start going out with a guy, you tell them you may not be exclusive with them. Do they have the option of not being exclusive with you?"

"Why would they want to go out with anyone but me? I'm available pretty much seven days a week. I'm only dating two guys right now, so they each get me a minimum of three or four times a week. I only go out with the Cougars when neither of them is available. They both know that."

"Well, I'm sorry you had to find out from the newspaper."

"Oh, that's just Gina. She doesn't approve of me dating multiple guys at once. She wasn't smiling or anything when she gave me the paper. Actually, it seemed to upset her. But on the inside, I think it made her happy to prove me wrong."

Sophie looked up at me for a moment. "I know why I feel crappy, but why are you looking so moody today?"

"Oh, it's the assignment for Tony. It isn't going anywhere. The only real clue I had was the shell casing, which came up with jack squat. I'm no closer to finding out who this guy is than before. All I have is a physical description that could match at least a thousand guys and a partial print that doesn't match anything in the police database."

"Nothing else?"

"No. My next step is to go back to the gun shop in Vail and then canvas the hotels. He must have stayed somewhere around there."

"Assuming he used his real name."

"I know, like I said, it's a long shot, but I'm out of actual clues. Hey, you know the secret software better than I do. Is there some way I can use it to pull up guys who match his general physical description? He has a prominent scar on his face. Maybe I could narrow down who he is with that."

"I don't think so. At least, I've never seen a way to do it. But I'm still on trial and error with most of that stuff."

"You'd think it'd have some sort of capability to do things like that."

"Hey," she grumbled, "it's not like it came with instructions, and I don't think they have tech support. If I tried to call the DEA to ask about it, I'd probably get arrested just because I had a copy of the database. It's not like I have a receipt for it."

"Well, what about the fingerprint? According to Gina, not getting a hit on a print is either because it isn't complete enough to get a match or the print isn't in the database."

"Well, sure, there's a way to submit fingerprints to the secret software, but I think it has to be in a specific FBI-fingerprint format."

"I have the digital file from Gina's friend in forensics. I'd think they'd have put it in the right format."

"Okay, email me a copy. I'll run it through the software and see if it works."

"Any idea how long it takes to get a fingerprint back?"

"No clue. But a regular search usually takes about a day, so I wouldn't think it would take much longer than that."

My phone started ringing with *The Love Boat* theme. I walked into the conference room and answered.

"Good morning," I said, thrilled that Max had called.

"Good morning, yourself. I'm sorry I haven't been as good at calling as I should be. Between the shooter and the golf tournament, it's been a hectic week. How are you doing today? Keep in mind, until we find out what's happening with the shooter, I'll need you to stay alert."

"I'm fine, and I haven't seen anything the least bit suspicious."

"Alright, but let me know if you sense that something's wrong. My offer to let you stay at one of the resorts is still on the table."

"Thanks," I said, "but things here are going well. Besides, I'd miss Marlowe. What's going on with the hunt for the shooter?"

"I wish I had some positive news on that, but every avenue we've looked at has come up empty. We seem to be at peace with our neighbors. No one new is trying to come into Arizona. And I believe Tony mentioned that we even looked internally."

"You haven't found anything?"

"Everywhere we've investigated has been a dead end. It's like the shooting never happened. If I hadn't been there, heard the bullets, and seen the tree trunks splintering across the snow, I'd probably start to doubt that it happened at all."

"It's the same on my side," I confessed with a sigh. "So far, the shell casing we found has led nowhere. There was a partial print, but it wasn't in the police database. I told Tony that if I can't come up with a fresh lead here, I'm going back to Vail and starting over again with the gun shop and the hotels. I don't have a lot of hope for either of those, but I'm not sure where to go next."

"Well, before you return to Vail, I'd like to see you. Actually, it was one of the reasons I called. I should have a couple of free hours tomorrow night. Would you like to come over and have dinner together? Around six? We'd probably have until the nine o'clock meeting. That would give us some time to discuss strategy."

"Three hours? You know, that's time for more than just dinner and strategy."

"I know," he said. I could tell he was smiling as he talked. "Think you'd be up for some cuddle time?"

Oh yum.

"I can't wait."

Chapter Six

I walked back into reception. Sophie was sitting upright at her desk, but she wasn't moving. With the sunglasses, it was hard to tell, but I think she was asleep, or possibly dead.

"Sophie?" I asked.

She woke with a start. "What?" she asked as she looked around to make sure Lenny wasn't there.

"Sorry to wake you. Since I'm still stuck on finding out who shot at Max and me, I'll start to work on the Rudy Rialto assignment. I have his address from the file. I'll go over to see if I can find anything obvious, then figure out how I want to play it and call you in. You can position yourself somewhere nearby and shoot the video with the time-stamp camera. If we're lucky, we'll have this wrapped up later this afternoon."

Sophie was still looking in my direction, but she'd stopped moving again. As I looked to see if she was still awake, I heard her snore softly.

"Sophie?" I asked.

"What?" she asked as she again woke with a start.

"I'm going over to Rudy's house. I'll give you a call once I figure out what to do."

"Um, okay, that sounds great. Sorry, I fell asleep. I spent

the first half-hour today deciding if I was going to throw up or not, and then Gina gave me the news about Snake. Now, all I want to do is curl up somewhere and pass out for a few hours."

"Will Lenny be here this morning?" I asked. "I didn't see his car out back."

"He was here when I came in. He dropped off some motions for me to type up, and then he took off. He'll be out all morning at a hearing."

"So, lock the door, flip over the 'Open' sign, and take a nap. You'll feel better after you wake up."

"Yup, that's the plan. But I was going to wait until after Gina takes off. Otherwise, she'll give me another lecture on being responsible and all that garbage."

I walked to my cubicle in the back. I told Gina about Rudy and my idea to get a video of him doing something that would invalidate his insurance claim.

"I'd go with the damsel-in-distress routine," Gina said. "When I was on the force, and we needed a suspect to do something out of character, that always seemed to be the best way to do it."

She then got an annoyed look on her face. "Of course, since I was the youngest female in the department, I usually got the job of putting on the short skirt with the low-cut top and strutting my ass in front of the guy until he reacted. It was one of the parts I liked least about being a detective."

Gina then started packing to go out for the day. Her primary assignment was gathering evidence for an upcoming civil suit.

As soon as she left, I buzzed Sophie's desk and let her know the coast was clear. From the mumbled response, it sounded like Sophie had already started her nap, whether

Gina was there or not.

I sat in my cubicle and went through the Rudy Rialto notes again. Not finding anything new, I opened the web page for the company he had worked for, *The Mesa Dry Dock*.

From what I could tell, it seemed like a legitimate, well-run company. They even had a picture of Rudy as he worked on some sort of big boat.

I then scanned through Rudy's social media pages. From what I could tell, he didn't seem to have an active social life.

Most of the pictures he posted were of his grandkids and his bird, a sulfur-crested cockatoo named Billie. There were pictures of Billie sitting on Rudy's shoulder, pictures of Billie eating various things, and videos of Billie flying across the room from one perch to another.

In addition to learning about Billie, I was able to get a better sense of Rudy. He was a big man with a round pink face, a scruffy-looking beard, and long, messy hair he sometimes tied back in a ponytail. Although he appeared in a dozen pictures with his grandkids and his cockatoo, he never smiled once.

While scanning the internet for information on Rudy, my phone started ringing. It was the Colorado number belonging to the Eagle County sheriff's office.

Again, I let it roll into voicemail. I wasn't sure how long I could keep this up before they'd call the Maricopa County sheriff to track me down for an official conversation.

It's always one more thing.

When my phone buzzed to let me know I had a message, I listened to see if there was anything new. It was the same detective as the day before, wanting me to call him. The only new piece of information was that he gave me a case number to refer to when calling him back.

I was starting to get hungry and went up front to see if Sophie was still asleep. When I got to reception, the window shades were down, the lights were off, and Sophie had her head on the desk.

I've never figured out how she can sleep like that. But she's somehow able to take a quick power nap, then wake up ready to go.

My first stop was lunch. I went through the drive-through line at In-N-Out and got a cheeseburger, animal style, fries, and a Diet Coke.

Eating as I drove, I headed out to Val Vista Lakes, a high-end community south of the Superstition Freeway in Gilbert. According to the file, Rudy owned a house and had been living there for the last fifteen years.

What makes the community unique is that most homes sit directly on the shore of one of three vast man-made lakes. I've noticed the area is especially lovely during sunrise and sunset when the red and orange colors of the sky bounce off the water and give everything a wonderful warm glow.

I drove down Rudy's street and quickly found his home. Like most houses in this part of Val Vista Lakes, it was a well-maintained white stucco with a pink tile roof.

There was a small patch of grass, an orange tree, and a queen palm in the front yard. From what I could tell, all of the houses here had the typical tropical oasis pool and landscaping in the backyards.

As I drove past the house, the door to Rudy's garage was up, and I could see him inside, sitting on a stool, working on some piece of equipment. A tallboy beer sat on the workbench next to him.

On the far side of his workbench were a couple of

oversized tool cabinets. The rest of the garage was taken up by a small car, probably a convertible, covered by a green tarp.

An almost new black Chevrolet pickup truck sat in the driveway, which I assumed was Rudy's. With the entire garage space used for storage and a workshop, there wasn't any room for him to park in there.

I drove to the end of the cul-de-sac and slid into one of three public parking spaces. I knew Rudy had worked as a mechanic in a boat repair shop. Seeing the garage full of tools started to give me an idea. I pulled out my phone and called Sophie.

"Hey," I said when she answered. "How are you feeling?"

"A lot better than this morning. I should know better than to go out drinking and dancing the night before I have to be at work. But after you left, I slept at my desk until almost noon, and it helped."

"I'm parked down the street from Rudy's house. He has a garage full of tools and used to be a mechanic. I was thinking if I had a car problem in front of his house, I could ask him for help. Then you could shoot the video of him while he's working on my car. If the problem was way in the back of the engine compartment, he'd have to stretch and bend to fix it. It should be an easy way to get our video."

"Um, that sounds pretty obvious. You really think he's going to fall for it?"

"Sure, why not? I was talking to Gina about this, and she said the police use the woman-in-distress ploy all the time. She said it was one of the best ways to make a guy do something out of character."

"Well, okay," she said skeptically. "What do you want

me to do?"

"I'm going to head back to my place and change into something a little more provocative. Meet me at the parking area at the end of the cul-de-sac on Rudy's street in about two hours."

I drove back to my apartment, searched through my closet, and pulled out a low-cut cranberry knit top. I had to search through the back of my drawer until I found my black push-up bra.

I grabbed a short white skirt and a pair of four-inch wedge sandals. I then quickly put on the outfit.

Looking at myself in the mirror, I decided I needed to go bolder. I gunked up my eyes with a load of eyeliner, shadow, and mascara.

Satisfied I looked slutty enough, I drove out to my mechanic. His name was Butch Carbone, and I'd been using him since my Honda's warranty ran out, several years ago.

"Hey, I remember this car," Butch said in his deep gravelly voice when I pulled into the shop. "You had it towed in last week from the middle of the desert. I didn't expect to see you back here so soon."

He walked to my car and used a small red rag to absentmindedly rub the oil off his hands. "You know, somebody putting an explosive in your car was a pretty sick practical joke, even if the damage was only to your belts and hoses. Something like that could easily have started a fire. What can I do for you today?"

"How can I sabotage my car so it will sort of run but still not work very well?"

"You want me to sabotage your car?" he asked as his eyes drifted down and focused on my cleavage.

"Well, I want you to show me how to do it. And whatever it is, it needs to be way in the back of the engine compartment."

"Are you trying to get back at whoever put that bomb on your engine?"

"Um, sort of."

"Man, remind me not to mess with you. You and your friends play too rough for me."

"Well?"

"Alright," he said as he reached in and popped open the hood release. "Let's take a look."

We walked to the front of the car, but it took him a couple of tries to get the hood up. The week before, it had gotten bent from the explosion and seemed to have been knocked out of alignment.

I scooted around to stand next to him while he peered down at the engine. I noticed he spent almost as much time looking down my shirt as he did looking at my car. At least the outfit seemed to be having the desired effect.

"That's the damaged area from last week," he said as he pointed to the blackened front of the motor. "Fortunately, we got away with only replacing your hoses and belts and then re-timing the engine. It could easily have been a lot worse."

I gave him my best *thank you, but hurry* look.

"Okay, I can tell you're in a rush. See that hose attached to the engine?" he asked as he pointed to a thick black tube attached to the far side of the motor. "It's held on with that hose clamp. If you loosen the clamp and disconnect the hose, your car will still run, but it'll sound terrible, and it'll most likely backfire like crazy."

"Perfect," I said. "Um, it won't damage the engine, will it?"

He pulled his head out from under the hood and stood back to take in my car. The look on his face seemed to say: *What's the difference?*

Instead, he tactfully said: "Well, it won't be great on your engine, but if you only go a few miles with it like that, you should be okay. To fix it, simply use a socket wrench or a screwdriver to reattach the hose from where you disconnected it. It'll fix the problem right away. Just make sure the car isn't running when you do it."

I thanked him and gave him a twenty for his advice, making a mental note to write out a receipt so I could get reimbursed from Lenny. I then drove back to Val Vista Lakes and Rudy's house.

When I got there, I saw that Sophie had parked in one of the three public spaces down the street from Rudy's. The top on her Volkswagen was down, so I parked, hopped out of my car, and stood next to her.

She was wearing an oversized pair of red plastic sunglasses, had her seat tilted back, and seemed to be taking in the sun. As I got closer, I could see she was asleep again.

"Hey, Sophie," I said.

She slowly woke up and then stretched a couple of times. "Oh, hey, Laura," she said. "I think I fell asleep."

"Well, you sound better than you did this morning. Were you able to get anything done after you got up from your nap?"

"Oh, sure. I'm all done with Lenny's motions. He got in about an hour ago and signed them all. The courier service picked everything up right before I left. I also returned all the phone messages people left while I was asleep."

"You were busy."

"Yeah, I even filed another stack of folders, ones I need to keep track of. That now only leaves the unimportant files lying around. All I have to do tomorrow is work on a deposition and send out some invoices. After that, I'll be pretty much done for the day."

"Anything come back on the fingerprint?"

"Not yet, but it's only been a few hours. Have you figured out how you're going to do this?"

"It should be pretty simple. I stopped by my mechanic, and he showed me how to sabotage my car. I'll drive it to Rudy's house and see if he'll help me fix it. You sit here with the camera. When he comes out, you start the video."

"Okay," she said as she took the camera from its case. "You flush him out. I'll get the evidence."

After a few tries, I was able to get the hood of my car open and identified the correct hose. I then went to my trunk and disconnected the faded red bungee cord that kept it shut.

I found my toolbox underneath a blanket and opened it. Among the six or seven miscellaneous tools that were rattling around in the box was a screwdriver that looked like it should work.

I went to the engine and looked at the hose. It was held in place with a silver band that had a sort of screw mechanism.

After a bit of trial and error, I found that the screwdriver could loosen the band until it was just flopping around. I then pulled on the hose, but getting it off wasn't as easy as I'd been led to believe. It took three or four good yanks to finally pull it off.

"Okay," I told Sophie. "I'm going to drive to Rudy's. I'll

position the car so you'll get a good view."

I put the hood down but didn't completely latch it into place, then tossed the screwdriver into the trunk and reattached the bungee cord. I turned the key in the ignition and hoped for the best.

It took the car several seconds to start. When it did, it sounded terrible. It was knocking and shaking, and smoke was coming out of the tailpipe. Despite the best assurances from my mechanic, this had to be rough on the engine.

I drove to the end of the street, swung the car around, and returned to Rudy's house. As I neared his driveway, a loud backfire shot out from under my car.

I parked where he'd get the best view of me, and then I left the engine running and pumped the gas a few times. This was enough to cause it to backfire twice more.

Well, at least he'll know I'm here.

I turned off the motor and got out of the car. I lifted the hood and looked down at the engine. I made sure to position myself, so I'd be clearly visible to Rudy.

Sure enough, the plantation shutter in the living room opened after about thirty seconds, a large shape looming behind it. I moved slightly to make sure he noticed what I was trying to do under the hood, and then I walked up the sidewalk to his door.

I knocked, and he answered right away. I noticed he was leaning on a cane with one hand and holding a beer in the other.

"Car problem?" he asked, even as his eyes focused on my chest. For such a big man, his voice was surprisingly high-pitched.

"Yes," I said in my best helpless voice. "There's a hose that comes loose sometimes, and then nothing works. I watched my ex-boyfriend fix it a couple of times. If I could borrow a screwdriver, I might be able to fix it myself. I'd hate to call a tow truck for something simple like a loose hose."

"Sure," he said, still focused on my cleavage. "I have tools in the garage. Come on in."

I stepped into the house and was hit by a loud squawk. I saw Billie the cockatoo sitting on a perch, eyeing me with curiosity and obvious suspicion.

There were several different perches in the house. One was in the kitchen, and one was in the living room. I saw a third on the upstairs balcony, and I imagined that there was probably another one in Rudy's bedroom.

"That's a sulfur-crested cockatoo, isn't it?" I asked. "My neighbor had one when I was a kid. He's beautiful."

"That's Billie, and she's a she. I got her almost thirty years ago."

"Wow, that's amazing. I'm guessing cockatoos have really long lifespans?"

"Yes, they do," he said as he walked over to the bird. I noticed he wasn't limping and that he'd forgotten he needed a cane. "Billie can easily live for sixty or seventy years. She's already outlasted my two marriages and will likely outlast me."

"Cracker?" Billie squawked out.

"Oh my God," I squealed out. "She's adorable. Can I feed her a cracker?"

"Go ahead," he said as he easily used his supposedly bad arm to hand me a box of bird biscuits. I took a cracker and held it up to Billie. She delicately took it and started munching on it.

"Let's get you a screwdriver," he said as he smoothly walked to the door leading to the garage, all trace of a limp now gone.

Once inside the garage, he hit the button to raise the door. There was a walker next to where he was standing, and he quickly bent over to use it.

He certainly didn't need it. But he must use a cane or walker in public to show anyone watching him that he was indeed injured. I had to admire his cleverness, but I was still determined to get the video.

He slowly shuffled to the toolbox and used his "good" arm to pull out a couple of screwdrivers. I briskly led the way back to my car, hoping he'd race to keep up, but he only slowly shuffled behind me.

We stood next to the open hood, and I pointed to the hose. "That's the one. When it comes loose, it makes my whole car shake."

"Okay," he said. "Let me take a look."

He quickly assessed the situation and saw the issue. He started to reach in with his bad arm, and I felt a brief thrill of excitement.

Instead, he seemed to remember he was in public and twisted his body around to use his good arm to shove the hose back into place. He then used the screwdriver in his good hand to tighten the metal band back into place.

"That'll fix your problem," he said. "But I don't understand how the hose could come off like that. It's almost like someone purposely pulled it off…"

As his voice trailed off, I could see him thinking.

All at once, his head shot up, and he started looking around. He quickly focused down the street on Sophie's Volkswagen and at Sophie, who was clearly holding up a video camera.

"You goddamn bitches," he growled at me. "Well, you can tell that cheap-ass insurance company they'll never see me doing something I'm not supposed to do. I was injured at that crappy hardware store, it was their fault, and I'm going to get what's owed to me."

He then turned and slowly shuffled back towards his garage. His motions were now exaggerated to the point that it would have been funny if it wasn't for the fact it was completely screwing up my assignment.

I put down the hood and started the car. This time, it turned over quickly and ran well. I drove down to Sophie and stuck my head out of the window.

"Did you get all that?" I asked.

"Yeah, but what happened? I thought we'd get some usable material, but then he stiffened up and went all lame on us again."

"He figured out what we were doing. I guess he's been waiting for something like this from the insurance company."

"What are you going to do next?" Sophie asked.

"I don't know. I'll come up with something. It's getting late. Do you have any dinner plans?"

"No, Pooh Bear's still on lockdown, and after last night, I'm afraid to ask if the Cougars are going out. I don't think I should have any more alcohol for at least a day or two. Actually, I think I'm going to go home, do some ramen, then go back to sleep."

I drove back to my apartment and parked in the back lot. I scanned the area but didn't see anything out of place.

The only other person in the parking lot was Mr. Latimer, who lived on the fourth floor. He was walking out to his car, a large Pontiac sedan that looked like it had been lemon yellow back when he'd bought it, sometime in the early nineteen eighties.

I took the elevator up to my apartment and then walked down the hall to my apartment. I didn't hear the TV on at Grandma's, so she must have been out for the evening.

When I got into my place, I set the deadbolt and washed off my eye makeup. Feeling much better, I went into the kitchen to see what was there. Marlowe had been asleep on the couch but quickly appeared at my feet as soon as I opened the refrigerator.

I scanned the interior for some actual food but could only find a frozen pizza. I turned on the oven to warm it up and pulled out a caffeine-free Diet Pepsi.

I then sat on the couch and flipped through the notes I had for my current assignments. It didn't take long.

I still had jack-squat for Tony's assignment, other than knowing the shooter's face. I decided if nothing shook loose tomorrow, I'd head up to Vail on Thursday morning.

I wasn't looking forward to it, mostly because I already knew it wouldn't give me a lot of helpful information. My best lead was the gun shop, and even that seemed like a long shot.

Thinking about it, I'd need to come up with a convincing story to give the shop owner. It needed to be good enough to have him look up the name the shooter had used on his firearms background application.

But even if I did get a name, the odds were low that it would be the actual name of the sniper. Most likely, it would be an alias of some sort. If so, I'd still need to spend a week tracking the name down, only to have it come up empty.

The Rudy Rialto assignment wasn't doing any better. I

thought it would be easy enough to catch him doing something inappropriate. Still, from his reaction today, he'd been expecting the insurance company to try to flush him out. It looked like I was going to need to be a lot more creative with the next attempt.

On a positive note, I knew for a fact Rudy was scamming the insurance company. I probably would've felt bad if he really had been injured and the insurance company was simply too cheap to pay what they owed. But after seeing him casually walk around his house without a cane or a walker, I wanted to nail the guy.

I ate most of the pizza, with Marlowe watching me the entire time. I'd been hoping to hear from Max again, but after talking to him once today, I really wasn't expecting it.

I sent a few texts to let him know I was okay and was calling it a night. By ten fifteen, I crawled into bed and quickly fell asleep.

I had a restless night and woke up an hour before the alarm went off. I tried to go back to sleep but was still feeling edgy.

Somebody who seemed to be a trained assassin was hunting Max. In the three days since the shooting, I hadn't been able to do a lot to identify the sniper or find a way to stop him.

I crawled out of bed and made a pot of coffee, but that didn't do a lot to help my mood. I was supposed to have a romantic dinner with Max later in the day, and I didn't want to tell him I'd come up completely empty.

After fiddling around for half an hour, I decided to get

ready and see if Sophie had anything new for me.

I drove into work and parked in the back. It was after nine, but only Sophie's yellow Volkswagen was parked under the carport.

"Hey," I said as I walked up to reception. "Where's everyone?"

"Gina's doing interviews, and Lenny's at a hearing. I'm still doing the billing and typing up a new stack of motions that Lenny dumped on my desk before he took off."

"You're looking better. You must have gotten some sleep."

"Well, I feel better than yesterday. Between reading about Snake and the boozing the night before, I felt like crap."

"The thing with Snake and the cheerleader really sucked," I said. "What are you going to do about him?"

"Not a thing. I texted the jerk to let him know I'd seen the picture in the paper. I told him it was pretty obvious he'd made a choice and wished him well. If I never hear from him again, all the better."

"So, that's pretty much it for Snake? How do you feel about it?"

"I slept like a baby last night. It'll make things easier in a lot of ways. I won't have to worry about juggling both of them anymore. The only downside is I won't have anyone to go out with when Milo's busy, which has been happening more and more lately."

"There's always the Cougars," I said.

"Thank God for that. After a crappy day at work, there's nothing like having a bunch of hot guys buy you drinks. Oh, I almost forgot. I got the report back on your fingerprint last night. It turns out they had a lot on this guy. But, um…"

"Um, what?"

"I don't think you're going to like it."

"What am I not going to like?"

"The guy who belongs to the fingerprint. His name's Nikolay Malakov."

"Nope, that doesn't ring a bell."

"No reason it should. It turns out he was an international assassin who was active until like fifteen years ago. According to the secret software, he was a major in some sort of government military organization in Eastern Europe."

"Really? Who did he work for? Our side or there's?"

"The software was a little fuzzy on which government he actually worked for. It mostly gave a lot of acronyms that meant nothing to me. I tried to Google a couple of them, but they also came up blank.

"Wow, seriously? Okay, that's something. Does it say where he is now or what he's doing?"

"Um, that's the part I don't think you'll like."

"Well?"

"It says he was killed. Over a dozen years ago."

"That can't be right. The guy was shooting at us like three days ago. He pretty much seemed alive at the time."

"Okay, I get that, but that's what the report said. He was killed in a forest near the town of Stepantsminda, wherever that is, by someone called Agent Kingfisher and Lieutenant Krovopüskov. After that, it's case closed."

"Well, crap. That doesn't help me any. The guy's walking around shooting at us. I don't think he's dead. Does it have any information on Agent Kingfisher or Lieutenant

Krovopüskov? I'd like to talk to them."

"Nope. I tried to do a search for both of them, but that part of the database seems to be off-limits."

"Seriously? It figures. That doesn't do a lot to help us."

"Hey, don't complain to me. Call up Washington and bitch to them about their crappy secret software. The kind I don't think we're even supposed to know exists."

"You're right. I'm sorry. But for a second, I thought we might actually get somewhere with the investigation. Instead, it turns out we're back at square one."

"But at least you now have a name to go along with your fuzzy picture."

"Yes, but he's dead. I'm not sure how much good it does to know the name of a dead assassin, even if he's still walking around and shooting at us."

"Maybe Max would know who he is? Even if the guy is dead, it may still ring a bell for him."

"Maybe. I'm supposed to have dinner with him tonight, but I should probably tell him this news right away. If he knows anything, it'll give me something to track down this afternoon."

"You mean other than Rudy Rialto? Don't forget about him."

"I won't, although compared to someone trying to shoot Max, it honestly doesn't seem as important."

I punched up Max's number and walked into the conference room as it rang.

"Good morning," he said when he answered. "It's good to see you're up and going."

As always, hearing Max's deep and steady voice made

me feel safe and loved. "I've been up for hours," I said. "Are we still good for tonight?"

"So far, so good. I have between six and nine o'clock blocked off. I'll meet you in the Kokopelli Suite. Think you can find it?"

"That sounds perfect, and I'm sure I'll be able to find you. I called because I want to discuss with you where I am on the assignment and to let you know about the casing. The forensics results came back last night."

"That sounds good. Do you have time to stop by and do it in person? Gabriella will also want to hear what you've learned so far, and she might have questions."

"Sure, I'd be happy to come over. Most of my information, including the casing analysis, are leads that seem to go nowhere. Still, maybe you and Gabriella can figure out something."

"We'll be glad to take a shot at it. Besides, I haven't seen you since Saturday night. I'm starting to miss you."

Hearing this made my heart beat faster and gave me tingles all over. "I've missed you too."

"Alright, I'll meet you up in my office. Say about forty-five minutes from now?"

I thought about how I looked. When I'd left the house, I'd swiped on some mascara but hadn't done a thing with my hair. "Um, can you meet in an hour?"

"No problem," he said with a small laugh. "Need to fix your hair first?"

I could feel my cheeks getting warm. "Yes, shut up."

Chapter Seven

I drove to the Tropical Paradise and parked in the visitor's lot. Again, security personnel were visible around the grounds and in the parking lots.

I walked into the lobby and then made my way upstairs to the entrance to the offices. This time, the security guards opened the doors and let me in without an escort.

Max had told me to meet him in his office. I realized that of all the times I'd been here, I'd never actually seen where he worked.

I assumed it would be near Tony's office, but really, it could be anywhere. I walked through the hallways until I came to the executive suite. Gabriella was at her desk and stood as I approached.

"Max says you have report on shell casing?"

"Yes, but there isn't a lot to tell."

"Well, we still have found nothing, so anything you have will be helpful."

Gabriella led the way to an office halfway down the hall. There wasn't a nameplate on the door, but I assumed it was Max's. I followed her in.

Max's office was much like how I'd imagined it would be. Simple and uncluttered. There was a seating area with a black leather couch and two comfortable leather chairs. I took the couch while Max and Gabriella took the chairs.

"What do you have for us?" Max asked.

"Like I said on the phone, not a lot. We got a partial fingerprint from the shell casing, but I don't think it's going to help us. It took some work to track it down, but according to the fingerprint, the guy who was shooting at us was named Nikolay Malakov. He was a military officer working in southeastern Europe and the Middle East."

When I said the name, both Max and Gabriella looked up in surprise. They glanced at each other and had one of their silent conversations.

"Unfortunately," I continued, "according to our source, the guy's been dead for a dozen years. Since he can't be both dead and still shooting at us, my source must somehow be wrong."

"But your source does confirm that he's dead?" Max asked.

"From what we were able to dig up, he was supposedly killed by someone called Agent Kingfisher, along with a military officer named Lieutenant Krovopüskov, near the town of Stepantsminda. I looked it up, and it's in the country of Georgia. It sits between Turkey to the south and Russia to the north."

The look on Max's face was one I'd never seen before. He looked like he was pissed.

"I'm not sure how you got that information," he said slowly. "But you must never repeat either the Kingfisher or Krovopüskov names again. Those are things that need to stay hidden. Even after all this time, if that information fell into the wrong hands, it could lead to trouble.

"And you are sure name was Major Nikolay Malakov?"

Gabriella asked. "It is not possible. What your informant told you about his death is correct. He died many years ago."

I looked over at Max for an explanation.

"Most of the countries between southeastern Europe and the Middle East have been unstable ever since World War II," he said. "I was part of the covert military forces sent into one of those countries to help them maintain their democracy."

"Okay, that makes sense," I said. "I vaguely remember hearing about all of that on the news."

"About a dozen years ago, we started getting intel on a guy who was going around killing top-level assets, both from our side and theirs. At first, we only knew him as Nikolay, but as time went on, we found out more about him. Major Nikolay Malakov was one of the top assassins for the insurgents in the country of Georgia."

"I read something about the fighting there. But why were there insurgents in Georgia?"

"Georgia used to be part of Soviet Union," Gabriella said. "There has been bad blood between the two countries ever since Georgia broke away from Russia in 1991. When Russia started to re-form old Soviet Union, Georgia was obvious target."

"Nikolay was leading a ten-person squad of snipers when he suddenly went rogue," Max said. "We have no idea what set him off, but he killed several of their top officers, then started killing people from our side, seemingly at random."

"I could see why that upset everyone."

"I was the asset assigned to take care of the Nikolay Malakov problem. During that time, I was given the codename of Kingfisher."

"What happened?"

"It took me almost a month to track him down. Even after I made visual contact, it took me another week until I was in a position to take him out. I actually had him in my sights when I was shot."

"You were shot?" I asked.

"You know that scar on my shoulder? That's the one. It turns out the other side had also sent someone to take out Nikolay, and they didn't want me interfering."

"So, what happened? Did the guy from the other side get Nikolay?"

"Not then. There was some bad luck, and the Major was able to get away."

"What'd you do then?"

"Well, I knew I couldn't get my target with another guy also hunting him, so I decided to find the other guy instead. I thought maybe we could come to some sort of understanding."

"That couldn't have been easy."

"No, sneaking up on a trained field operative is harder than it sounds. It took several days for me to make visual contact. I then followed the other agent, who was following Nikolay. But at last, I made my introduction."

"Did you, um, take him out?"

"No, it wasn't necessary. They weren't a threat to me, and I only wanted the mission to succeed."

"But he shot you!"

"The bullet only grazed me. One sniper's way of telling another one to back off. They could have easily planted the bullet in the middle of my forehead."

"So, what happened?"

"Well, after some initial arguing, we decided to go in together as a two-person team."

"Did you get Nikolay?"

"I thought we had," Gabriella spoke up. "But if your information is correct, perhaps we did not."

"Wait a minute," I said. "You were the other operative? You're Lieutenant Krovopüskov? You shot Max?"

"It was only scratch," she said with a smile. "He is such baby. Max was interfering with me, so I removed him. Unfortunately, he was very persistent and decided to follow me. If I had known that, maybe I would've shot something more vital."

"Gabriella wanted to be the one who made the kill, so she took me out rather than risk not being able to finish her mission," Max said.

"But I assume you finally got him?" I asked Gabriella.

"The distance was long, but shot was clean, and I did confirm the strike," she said quietly.

The look on Gabriella's face was horrible, as if someone had told her there was no Santa Claus. "You say the man you saw in Vail had large scar under left eye?" she asked slowly. "I would not have believed it possible for Nikolay to have survived, but if what you say is accurate, maybe he did."

"I'm not sure if he's been tracking us or if our meeting in Vail was a chance encounter," Max said. "But we're going to have to assume he's been actively hunting us for some time."

He paused and thought for a moment. "Well, if there's a bright side to this, he's only after me and possibly Gabriella. That means the rest of the organization won't be in direct danger."

"Assuming we're talking about the same guy, what do

you know about him?" I asked. "My source didn't have a lot of information beyond his name and occupation. If he's as deadly as you say, what can we do to protect ourselves?"

"At the time, I remember we learned a lot about him," Max said. "He was born in Belarus and educated in Germany. He speaks several languages fluently and has been trained to blend into his surroundings, which can either be outside in nature or in a city. If he's stalking you, he could be ten feet away from you in a crowded bar, and you'd never know he was there. He's proficient in hand-to-hand fighting and in the use of weapons, including knives, explosives, and all manner of firearms. He's one of the world's most deadly killers, and now he's after Gabriella and me."

"You want to know about Major Malakov?" Gabriella asked, sounding upset. "He is very bad man. He often abuses women and takes pleasure in torturing men. He kills people for sport. The army was able to use his skills for many years, but the Major did not like being subject to army discipline and control. He eventually rebelled at all authority and started killing anyone who tried to stop him."

"So, how can we fight someone like that?" I asked.

"We need to go on the offensive," Max said. "Between Gabriella and me, along with some of the people from the organization, we're going to start hunting him."

Gabriella seemed to have gotten over the shock of hearing that Nikolay Malakov was still alive. Her eyes were now wide open, and her face was lightly flushed. I've come to know this as the look of excitement she gets when she knows she might get to hurt or kill a man.

"Did you still want to do dinner tonight?" I asked. "I'll understand if you need to work on this instead."

Max thought about it for a moment. "No, let's keep our date. With everything going on, I might not be able to see you again for several days. In fact, after tonight, you should probably stay completely away from us until we get this business with Nikolay cleared up."

"That might be a while."

"True, but I don't want to worry about you getting caught up in the crossfire."

"Fine, but text and call whenever you can. I'll want to know you're okay."

"Fair enough," he said. "Gabby, would you walk her out? I need to let Tony know who we're up against."

I gave Max a hug and a kiss, then followed Gabriella as we made our way back to the hotel lobby.

"It looks like you're eager to get another shot at this Major Malakov guy," I said as we walked through the hallways.

"Oh yes, I liked killing him the first time. He was good assassin, but he is very bad man. I will very much enjoy getting to kill him again."

Something in the eagerness of her response made me stop. I looked around to make sure no one was in earshot. "Maybe it's just me," I quietly said. "But do I take it you don't mind killing men like him?"

"I don't mind hurting or killing any bad man," she said. "In fact, I take very much pleasure in doing it."

"Um, I think I've noticed that. Did something happen, or have you always liked doing that?"

"No, not always. When I was young girl, I was happy. But by the time I was twelve or thirteen, some men in my village began to make me do things to them. If I didn't do what they say, they put me in basement room, and they take turns hurting me. I joined army to leave my village, but some men in army made me do the same things to them. So, I joined special army unit and trained how to kill men. I became very good at it. Now, I kill anyone who hurts me, or my friends."

"You seem to get along pretty well with Max and everyone in the organization."

"Max is one of the few men I know who treat me with kindness and respect. I like him, and I work for him. Max introduce me to Tony and Johnny. I like them too. I like our organization, and I protect it. Besides, in my job, I sometimes get to hurt and kill bad men. It is nice bonus."

I looked at the clock and saw it was almost noon. I was getting hungry, but I didn't want to eat alone.

I'd thought of having lunch with Max, but those plans had gone up in smoke. I called Sophie to see if she'd gotten anything to eat yet.

"No, and I'm starving. Where should we go?"

"There's a new burger place up here, next to the resorts on Scottsdale Road, called Joey's. From what I've heard, it's supposed to be as good as The Chuckbox."

"That sounds great. I haven't had anything all day. When can you get there?"

"I'm still at the Tropical Paradise. It looks like it'll be quicker for me to walk than to get in my car and look for parking there."

"Okay, I'll leave now and should get there in about fifteen minutes."

"Good luck with that. It'll be more like half an hour with

the Snowbird traffic."

It was an easy ten-minute walk from the resort lobby to Joey's Burgers. I arrived and studied the menu until Sophie's car pulled into the parking lot.

The restaurant itself was nice, although it was done up in a rather non-descript Southwestern cowboy theme. I got the feeling it would look better in a year or two after they had time to decorate the place more fully.

We waited in line while we took in the aroma of sizzling burgers grilling over charcoal. It made me so hungry that I ordered a double bacon cheeseburger, along with fries and a Diet Pepsi. Sophie was behind me and ordered the same, except with a chocolate shake.

We went to the condiment table, loaded up the burgers, then grabbed a table in the back corner and dug in. The food was delicious.

Like all good charcoal burger places, it reminded me of my dad cooking burgers in our backyard as a kid. Even the fries were good. They were fresh-cut from real potatoes, rather than being frozen and shaken out of a bag.

I'd pretty much finished up the burger and was picking at my fries. Sophie had been doing most of the talking and was still working on the last of her burger.

Halfway through taking a sip of her shake, she saw something over my shoulder, and her eyes grew big. After a second, they narrowed down, like she was pissed about something.

"What is it?" I asked.

"Milo," she growled.

"What about Milo?"

"He's here, and he's with another woman. He said he

couldn't do anything with me because he had to work all day."

"I thought you were the one who liked having an open relationship with the guys you go out with. Does it really surprise you if they go out sometimes as well?"

"But why would he want another woman? I'm with him whenever he has time off. You'd think I'd be enough for him."

"Well then, you'd better tell Pooh Bear. I don't think he got that part. Besides, think about it. We're next door to the Tropical Paradise. He's probably out on his lunch hour. Does it look like an actual date, or are they only eating burgers together?"

"Well, he's not holding her hand or anything, but they look pretty chummy. I think maybe I should go and ask him about it."

"I'm not sure if that's such a good idea..." I started to say. But it was too late. Sophie stood and marched across the room.

I turned to see Milo at a far table with a woman. I didn't know her by name, but she looked familiar.

I'd seen her a few times, working at the resort next door. She was about our age, had long dark hair, and wore a black Tropical Paradise security polo.

"What the hell are you doing out with her?" Sophie demanded. She was standing in front of Milo, hands on hips. Her tone and volume were a bit much for a family restaurant, so the room went silent as everyone turned to watch.

"We're on our lunch break, so Angelique and I decided to come over here and grab a burger," Milo said, trying his best to sound reasonable.

"You know I don't like you going out with other

women," Sophie fumed, her voice rising. "Especially with a nasty skanky bimbo like Angelique here."

"Wait a minute," Milo reacted, his voice now rising. "You go out with other guys all the time, and when you aren't actually on a date with someone else, you're out with your friends at the clubs trying to pick up as many men as you can. I don't know how you can come over here, when we're just having lunch, and accuse me of doing something inappropriate."

Upon being called a skanky bimbo, Angelique slowly stood up and glared down at Sophie. Like all of the security personnel at the Tropical Paradise, she was strong, athletic, and no doubt had at least one black belt. She towered over Sophie by several inches and was scowling down at her.

Since they were all the way across the restaurant, it was sort of hard to tell, but I think Angelique was growling at her. It was as if she actually wanted Sophie to start something, so she could get some exercise by beating her skinny ass across the restaurant.

Sophie took in a breath to continue insulting the woman, but after looking her up and down, she seemed to think better of it. Instead, she looked at Milo.

"Jerk, don't talk to me anymore." She then turned and came back to our table to grab her purse.

"Looks like I'm the one having the shitty day today," she said, then quickly left the restaurant.

Milo looked over at me with a confused *What the hell just happened?* look. I only shook my head and shrugged my shoulders. I quickly cleared off the table, tossed everything in the trash, then took off after Sophie.

When I reached the parking lot, Sophie's yellow Volkswagen was already pulling out into the street. From the way the gravel flew out from her tires, I knew she wasn't going to be in the mood to talk anytime soon.

I walked back to my car and then drove to the office. Sophie's car wasn't there, but Gina's was. I walked in and found her up in reception.

"Hey, Gina," I said. "Do you know where Sophie is?"

Gina gave a snort of annoyance. "She called to say she wasn't feeling good and probably wouldn't make it back from lunch. She asked if I could cover the reception desk, which is a strange request since she normally doesn't mind closing the entire office when she wants to take a nap. Lenny's out for the day, and I have an interview scheduled soon. So, now *I'm* going to be the one who closes the office when I leave."

"Oh, go ahead and do the interview," I said. "I know what happened. Sophie saw Milo out with another woman. I don't think it was a date, but on top of the Snake thing yesterday, I think it was a bit much for her. My assignments are still going nowhere, and I can cover for the afternoon, well, at least until about four thirty."

"Thanks," Gina said. "That'll really help me out. According to Sophie, the only thing going on today is someone's coming in to pick up a file."

She then seemed to think about Sophie and her situation.

"Honestly," Gina said, "I don't understand how Sophie thinks she can juggle all these men and still maintain a long-term relationship with any of them. This sort of thing will keep happening until she finds one guy and sticks with him, at least for a little while."

I sat at Sophie's desk all afternoon, answering the phone and stuffing invoices into envelopes. The client came in around three o'clock and picked up the documents Sophie had left sitting on her desk, but that was the only bit of excitement for the afternoon.

I tried to think where either of my assignments should go next, but I was at a complete standstill on both of them. I needed to come up with a way to get a video of Rudy doing something physical. I also needed to find a way to help Max and Gabriella track down the killer, without either of them noticing I was doing it.

Gina came back a little after four. We chatted for a bit, but by four-thirty, we decided we could close things up for the day.

I drove home and changed into some black capris and a silky sapphire blue top. It was low-cut enough to give Max the right idea but not so obvious that it looked like I was desperate.

I thought about heels, but every time I wear a pair, I end up trying to run after someone. I've pretty much given up on those, except for a few special situations.

~~~~

As I drove to the Tropical Paradise, I wondered how Sophie was doing, so I gave her a call. I'd never seen her act out like that before, and I was worried about her.

"Hey," I said when she answered. "How are you doing?"

"I feel like crap. I probably shouldn't have blown up at Milo like that. But after finding out about Snake yesterday, I was feeling like the walls were crashing down, and everything sort of happened on its own."

"Did you call him yet? I imagine he'll want an apology."

"No, but I'll probably do that tonight or sometime tomorrow. We're supposed to go out on Friday, assuming he can get it off, and he still wants to."

"I hope you can patch things up. Now that you've dumped Snake, Milo will probably be happy to know he's the only one."

I drove up Scottsdale Road and pulled into the main entrance of the Tropical Paradise. As I parked and got out of my car, the increased security presence was even more apparent. I wasn't sure if this made me feel safer or more paranoid.

I walked up to the lobby and found a resort map. The Kokopelli Suite was on the top floor of the main building, looking out over a cluster of pools. I navigated the curved hallways until I found the right elevator.

Once I made it to the top floor, I walked down the hall until I found a sign that pointed to where the suite was located. I was a little surprised that Gabriella wasn't standing in the hallway, watching to see who was approaching. This struck me as somewhat odd and made me curious if I was in the right place. Maybe there were two Kokopelli Suites, and I was at the wrong one.

When I turned the corner to go into the suite, I found Milo in the vestibule leading to the room, lying face down on the floor. He wasn't moving, and I couldn't tell if he was breathing.

Oh crap.

I dropped to my knees and rolled him over. I didn't see any blood, but I still couldn't tell if he was alive or not. Looking closer, I saw his chest rise faintly, then fall. In my numb terror, I merely registered the fact that he wasn't dead.

The door to the suite stood open, and I briefly wavered between seeing if Milo needed assistance and wanting to check on Max. Knowing whatever I did was probably wrong, I stood up and ran inside.

My purse was looped over my head and was lying against my side. I shoved my hand into it, feeling around for my pistol.

A lamp had been knocked over on a table, and one of the chairs had been overturned. Max was sprawled haphazardly across the couch, his eyes closed.

Again, I didn't see any blood, but he also didn't appear to be breathing. For some reason, a large hotel laundry cart was sitting in the middle of the room.

Crap, crap, crap.

There was a desk against the wall with a phone on it. My first thought was to call resort security.

I was also worried that the person who did this might still be nearby. Now that I'd learned all about the assassin today, I had no desire to confront him.

After I contacted security, I was going to check on Max, then back myself against the wall and stay put until someone showed up. I had a gun and would be able to protect myself. My fingers had started to close around the butt of my pistol when there was a soft popping sound and something sharp jabbed into my back.

I reached around to grab whatever was stabbing me and turned to see who my attacker was. As I did, Major Nikolay Malakov stepped into the room.

He was wearing a Tropical Paradise housekeeping uniform. The large scar that had been under his left eye had somehow disappeared.

He looked around the room until he was confident I'd come in alone. He held a semi-automatic pistol in one hand and a tranquilizer gun in the other. In my dazed state, I registered that the side of his face was red, like something had recently hit it.

"Do not pull out the dart," he calmly said. "If you do, I will shoot the next one in your face. That will be extremely painful."

Ignoring his words, I tried to pull out my gun with one hand while the other hand went up to the dart in my back. Unfortunately, whatever drug had been in the syringe was already well into my system. My vision began to swim, and my legs had gone wobbly.

I gave up trying to get the gun and took a step toward him instead. I tried to raise my hand. My goal was to hit him squarely in the face, one last parting shot before I went out, but instead, darkness closed in on me.

As I slowly came back to consciousness, I found myself being roughly dragged across a bumpy surface in a very bright place. My head was pounding, and I felt nauseous.

As my eyes slowly came into focus, I became aware I was outside in the desert, and it was daytime. Major Nikolay Malakov was half-carrying and half-dragging me across the hard-packed dirt in the general direction of an enormous saguaro cactus.

He was still wearing the housekeeping uniform from the

night before, and his scar was still missing. From the coolness of the air and the position of the sun, it must have been six-thirty or seven o'clock in the morning.

Damn, I've been out all night.

I looked down and saw my hands cuffed together in front of me. One look told me that these were an expensive police model, and I wouldn't be able to simply slip out of them.

As we got closer to the giant saguaro, I noticed something lying on the ground, maybe ten feet away from it. As my eyes continued to clear, the shape on the ground became Max.

He was unconscious, and his hands were also in cuffs. These appeared to be attached to a metal stake that had been driven into the desert floor.

I tried to struggle and run away, but the effects of the drugs still lingered in my system. I desperately looked around, but there wasn't any sign of civilization from horizon to horizon. I had no idea where we were other than somewhere deep in the Sonoran Desert.

Crap, this isn't good.

Ten feet from where Max was lying, another metal rod had been driven into the ground. There was a ring on a swivel at the top of the rod, like it'd been designed to keep a dog on a leash in a backyard.

As we got to this pole, Nikolay pulled another pair of handcuffs from his pocket and effortlessly used them to attach the chain between my hands to the metal ring. He turned and walked back to a red Wrangler Unlimited, parked thirty feet away, while I collapsed in the dirt.

My head was still spinning, and I was on the verge of throwing up. I put my head down to try to stop the whirling and quietly passed out.

When I regained consciousness, the air was warmer, and the sun was higher in the sky. The Major was sitting on a beach chair next to the Jeep.

The chair had a rainbow-colored umbrella attached to it, and he was relaxing in its shade. The tranquilizer dart gun sat in his lap, probably for use in case one of us started to get out of hand.

He'd changed into white slacks, a white Panama hat, and a bright blue Aloha shirt. He wore a pair of oversized black sunglasses, and he smiled when he saw I was awake.

The side of his face that had been red the night before was now faintly purple with a bruise, and the scar had reappeared under his eye. I realized he must have used some sort of special-effects makeup to hide it.

It now made sense that no one at the hotel had tried to stop him. They would've been told to look for a man with a large scar.

Half of my face stung painfully, and I knew it was bright red with sunburn. If it wasn't for the fact that I was staked out in the open desert and I'd been lying in direct sun all morning, I would've found the situation to be almost comical.

I mentally assessed my situation. Yes, I had a bad sunburn, but I could live with that. My throat was dry, but not painfully so, at least not yet. My head still hurt, but the nausea had thankfully subsided.

All my clothing seemed to have been shifted around, and I hated to think what that implied. My purse was still looped over my head and was lying against my side. Unfortunately, pressing against it showed that my Baby Glock was missing.

I slowly rolled to my side and carefully felt around in my back pocket. With a rush of relief, I realized he hadn't taken my phone.

I knew I'd need to ignore the fact that I still had it. Otherwise, he'd take it away from me. Nikolay must have been watching me because he seemed to read my thoughts.

"It's okay," he said, almost like an understanding father. "You may keep your phone, your purse too. They'll do you no good. I carefully checked as I drove you both out to this remote spot. There's been no signal for several kilometers. You will not be able to call for rescue. I did, however, remove your pistol. Otherwise, I fear you might have been tempted to shoot me."

Well, duh.

For the next hour, I sat on the ground and positioned myself so the sunburnt side of my face was more or less in the shade. The day was warm for November, but fortunately, it was not overly hot.

My mouth was beginning to feel gummy and sticky. I could still swallow, but it was becoming more problematic. Max was still unconscious, but he seemed to be breathing without difficulty.

As I sat, I could feel several bruises on my body. I must've been roughly handled between being smuggled out of the hotel in a laundry cart and then stuffed into the back of a Jeep. The bumpy drive out to this remote spot probably didn't help.

When a shadow briefly passed over my face, I looked up

to see a vulture high in the sky. It flew in wide circles with its long wings outstretched, catching the desert thermal updrafts. It didn't seem to be in any sort of hurry, but it could likely sense the tight spot we were in.

I tried to start a conversation with my kidnapper. I asked him who he was and why he was doing this to us, but Nikolay didn't say anything the entire time. All he did was pull out a pack of cigarettes, smoke several of them, and play a noisy video game on a tablet.

Chapter Eight

It took another half-hour for Max to wake up. As he did, he blinked his eyes and shook his head in an effort to try to make sense of things. From the look on his face, I knew his head was pounding, and he was just as nauseous as I had been.

"Ah, Agent Kingfisher," Nikolay said as he lit another cigarette, a broad smile on his face. "Good to have you rejoin our little party. I was beginning to think that after taking two full darts, you might've received a fatal dose of the drug. I will admit, I would've been upset if you'd died before your suffering had even properly begun."

As Nikolay talked, I couldn't detect an accent. I did note how he carefully enunciated each word, like maybe he'd been trained as a broadcaster or an actor at some point in his career.

"Who are you?" Max asked. His voice was strained with the effort of talking through the nausea and drug haze. "What do you want?"

"Please do not play games. You've had my description for a week, and I left you a clue to my identity under the bed in the condominium in Vail. By now, you will have discovered who I am. Therefore, you know why I must kill both you and Lieutenant Krovopüskov."

He paused and took a long draw on his cigarette. "A

dozen years ago, you led the American team that tried to kill me. The Lieutenant used to work for me, but then the bitch switched sides and joined your little assassination squad. I should add that she'd been a pain in my ass for several years before you showed up. So, taking her out would have been a pleasure in either case."

Nikolay got up from his chair and took a few steps toward us, the dart gun still in his hand. He flicked away the cigarette, removed a small camera from his pocket, and used it to take several pictures of both Max and me.

"Souvenirs," he said as he held up the camera. "I'm afraid I can't use my phone because the photos would then become a permanent record. But have no fear, even though you'll soon be dead, your images will live on in a very exclusive private collection I've amassed over the years."

"You're sick," Max said. "You do know that, don't you?"

The Major let out a small laugh as he put the camera back in his pocket. "It may not surprise you to learn that you're not the first person to mention that."

He paused and looked out over the vast open desert. He shook his head and walked closer to us.

"Although, Agent Kingfisher, I must say, I'm rather disappointed. I've always heard the deserts of Arizona are very hot. But perhaps this is the wrong time of year for that. It was my hope you'd die from the extreme heat and that your suffering would be intense. I would have enjoyed watching your torment as you slowly baked to death under the desert sun."

He again looked out to scan the horizon. "Instead, it looks like you'll simply die of thirst, like a stray dog who's been abandoned by its owner. But in a way, this may be a crueler death. In the heat, you'd both have been dead by the end of the first day. This way, left to slowly succumb to the elements, it will no doubt take you three or four days to finally die. Perhaps, in the end, this will be a more agonizing death than simply passing out with heat stroke. I will leave that for you to decide."

"How did you find us?" Max asked. His voice sounded a little stronger, but I also saw the sharp wince of pain he made. From the way he held his arm against his side, I guessed he might have some injured ribs.

"Finding you was the most amazing luck," Nikolay said. "After you and Lieutenant Krovopüskov tried to assassinate me, I went through a dozen surgeries and several years of physical therapy to feel like my old self again, but I won't bore you with those details."

He pulled out his pack and lit up another cigarette.

"When at last I was physically able to begin the hunt for my shooters, I easily traced both you and the Lieutenant to America, but then the trail went cold."

He took a long draw on his cigarette, then let out the smoke in a stream. "You did an excellent job of covering your tracks, and I congratulate you for that. I came into this country and gained employment with various criminal groups. It seems that being a professionally trained killer is a useful job skill to have in America."

As he was speaking, Nikolay walked back to the SUV and opened a cooler he had sitting on the passenger seat. He took out a liter bottle of Arizona iced tea and shook off the water that was clinging to it. He then walked back over to us as he removed the top and took a couple of long swallows.

Watching him tease us with the iced tea reminded me of a similar occurrence that had happened only a week before, when a vicious killer named Jonathan LaRose had done something remarkably similar. Thinking about how I'd suffered, locked in a cell without having anything to eat or drink, made me dread what was going to happen to us here in the desert.

"About two years ago," Nikolay continued, "I started hearing rumors of a female assassin working as a bodyguard for the head of a crime syndicate somewhere in the southwestern United States. From her age and physical description, I thought it could be the Lieutenant. I've spent the last year and a half in Los Angeles, working my way through the various gangs, looking for her."

He shook his head and chuckled to himself, as if this amused him. He spent a moment watching us as he took a couple of long, slow drags on his cigarette.

"I had no success in locating the Lieutenant in LA, of course, since she was apparently in Scottsdale the entire time. But I was able to make an amazing amount of money. Southern California is a perfect place for an assassin to work. It's very much like the Wild West of your movies. After I kill both you and the Lieutenant, I may go back there and continue until I have enough to retire. I've discovered the beaches of Malibu and quite like it there. As they say, America is the land of opportunity."

The Major paused to take another drink of the tea. He was purposefully sloppy about it, so we could watch as some of it dribbled down his chin. This time, he let out a long *aaahhh* after he swallowed.

"You may not know this," he said, "but I'm not the only person who's been searching for the both of you. There's even been somewhat of an informal bounty on the Lieutenant since she left Georgia. This is not surprising, considering what she did for a living. Your old friend Viktor has openly stated that he'd give a million dollars to anyone who could tell him where she is."

At hearing the name Viktor, Max seemed to stiffen. "So, how did you find us?" he asked again, this time with a touch of anger in his voice.

"As I said, it was the merest stroke of luck. With my new fortune, I decided to take a small break and go skiing. I booked myself a room at a very nice hotel in Vail and had been spending the last two weeks there, skiing and simply enjoying life. Then, last Friday, as I was on my way to dinner, who do I see? You and the Lieutenant were walking down the street and then into an Italian café. I simply waited until you left the restaurant and followed you to your hotel."

Nikolay took one last swallow, draining all but the last inch from the bottle. His smile was mischievous as he carefully set the bottle down on the dirt of the desert floor.

It was well out of our reach but close enough that we both could see the liquid in the bottle. Swallowing had started to become difficult, and the sight of the iced tea forced me to think about how thirsty I was.

"At first," he continued, "I'd thought about shooting you both when you came out of your hotel in the morning. Not very satisfying, I grant you that, but effective. Unfortunately, when your girlfriend here ran into me that night, I knew you may have been alerted to my presence. I even thought you may have sent her out to confirm my identity. So, I made a new plan."

"Really?" Max asked hoarsely. "Tell me all about it."

"It was obvious that you and the Lieutenant would be skiing for the weekend, so I decided to fall back on my sniper training and take you both out from a distance. I thought it would add a proper sense of symmetry to your deaths. I bought a very nice rifle and set up in a location where I could see a part of the slope that I knew you'd both be skiing. I will admit, it was a wonderful feeling waiting for the two of you to appear in my rifle scope. Rather nostalgic, actually."

"You must've been disappointed when it was too windy for a clean shot," Max said.

"Yes, between the wind and the unfamiliar rifle, I was not able to kill you that day. I never even saw the Lieutenant. But it didn't matter. The hunt was on. After you left, I merely went back to your hotel and tortured a member of the staff until they gave me the information I needed. You both checked in under false names, of course, but your rooms had been paid for by the Scottsdale Land and Resort Management company. From there, it was a simple matter of tracking you both down."

Nikolay walked back to the Jeep and began to clean up his makeshift camp. He put the beach chair and cooler in the back of the vehicle. After a few minutes, he'd finished packing and walked back over to us.

"I would gladly stay and watch as you weaken and die, but I must go. I need to find the Lieutenant. She and I have unfinished business, and she's no doubt looking for you. I was somewhat disappointed not to get both of you at once last night, but such things are to be expected."

He paused and looked into the sky, where the vulture was still circling. "Now, where your death will be a long and drawn-out affair here in the desert, I promise you, her death will be shorter but far more painful. I'm not sure which of you pulled the trigger on me. I've always imagined it was you, Agent Kingfisher, but it doesn't matter. If we're being honest here, I've always wanted your death to be slow and lingering. Still, I've always imagined her death to be one of screaming agony. I'm going to use a razor blade on her face. I would have preferred to perform her torture in front of you, but as long as you know she'll die shrieking in pain, it will suffice."

"You're simply going to leave us staked out here to die of dehydration?" Max asked.

"Yes, that's pretty much it," the Major said with a smile. "Of course, after I leave, there's nothing to prevent you from pulling out your metal poles and wandering around the desert until you die. In fact, I rather expect you'll do just that. It's all part of the human will to live. But it doesn't matter. You're over thirty kilometers from the nearest road that will have a vehicle traveling on it. Neither of you has had anything to eat or drink for over eighteen hours, and you'll soon start to weaken as your bodies begin to shut down. You've perhaps already started to feel the first effects?"

Nikolay walked over to Max and bent over him. He talked very quietly, like a father giving advice to a son. "Agent Kingfisher, it's my hope that you'll take the remaining hours of your life to review the error of trying to kill me. Perhaps, even now, at the very end, it's not too late for you to gain wisdom from this experience."

He straightened up, took a few steps back, and gave us both a salute. "Very well, I bid you *adieu*."

Nikolay climbed into the Jeep, started it up, and then took off. As I watched the dust cloud recede on the horizon, I noticed he was driving on a faint dirt road.

With both Nikolay and the Jeep gone, it suddenly became very quiet. There was a faint breeze that came and went, but nothing that made any sound. I looked around one more time, but I still didn't see anything that would give a clue as to where we were.

We were stranded in the open desert, a long way from anywhere, with no hope of rescue. I also noticed that a second vulture had joined the first and was making lazy circles in the sky, high above our heads.

Damn.

"Well," Max said, looking over at me with a tired smile. "You did say you wanted us to spend more quality time together."

"That's true," I replied. "But being handcuffed and staked down in the middle of the Sonoran Desert wasn't exactly what I'd had in mind for a romantic getaway."

"When I took you to Vail, it was only supposed to be for a fun vacation weekend. I'm sorry it's led to this."

"Vail wasn't so bad," I said. "At least I learned how to ski. That was fun. Plus, we got to sip champagne in a hot tub in the snow. I loved that part."

"It wasn't too cold? You looked like you were half-frozen, standing on the roof in only your bikini. You were shivering so hard I could hear your teeth chatter."

"Yeah, it was cold. I've never had ice in my hair like that before. But we were together, and it was so romantic."

I sat in the dirt and thought about the weekend in Vail and how wonderful the first part of our vacation had been. Hearing Max speak brought me back to the present and our crappy situation.

"Milo was on security outside the room last night," Max said. "Do you know what happened to him?"

"He was down when I got there. But he seemed to be breathing, and I didn't see any blood. I assume he got hit by the same dart gun that got both of us. I was surprised Gabriella wasn't there."

"She was originally scheduled to be on duty, but I sent her to the clinic last night to get the final evaluation of her gunshot wound. She told me she was fully capable, but I wanted the doctors to put their stamp of approval on it. It's only been a little over a week since she was shot. With the Major on the loose, I wanted to make sure it wouldn't split open again the first time she got into a fight with someone."

"With Milo down and us missing, everyone will be on the alert that Nikolay is here," I said. "It will be tough for him to go after her."

"One thing about Gabriella, she's always on the alert. I'd imagine Nikolay's next move will be to somehow attempt to draw her into a trap, maybe using Tony or us as bait."

"I'm not sure how we could be bait when we're in the middle of nowhere. But even if he tried something, she'd know it was a trap, wouldn't she?"

"Yes, but that still wouldn't stop her from coming after us if she thought she could perform a rescue. Nikolay's the one who trained her, and he knows that as well. We'll need to get out of here and somehow warn her."

"He let me keep my phone. He said there wasn't a signal out here, and I believe him. My bigger worry is that it's been on all night, and the battery is probably close to being dead."

I twisted around and was eventually able to pull the phone out of my back pocket. As expected, the *No Service* indicator showed, and the battery was down to six percent. I shut off the phone to save what little power I had.

"There's no signal here," I said. "We'll need to walk to where we can find one. Nikolay said he lost the signal several kilometers back. That sounds difficult but manageable. I'm assuming he came in the same way he went out. So, in theory, we'll have to follow his tracks for a few miles, and we should be able to call out, assuming he wasn't lying and that my battery holds out."

"The first step is to pull out these metal pegs," Max said. "I don't know how deep they are in the dirt, but maybe we can wiggle them out."

I tried to twist and pull on the metal rod, but it was solidly in the desert floor. Max didn't seem to be having any better luck with his.

We then both started kicking at the pegs. Neither of us wore the best shoes for doing this. I had on my black flats, and Max had on a pair of brown loafers. I saw him wince in pain when he started kicking at the stake.

"Are you alright?" I asked.

"I might have a cracked rib or two," Max said with a touch of annoyance. "I think Nikolay used the opportunity while I was unconscious to give me a couple of kicks. I probably should be thankful he didn't injure me more severely."

"Will you be able to do this?"

"I'm not sure, but we really don't have a choice. We need to escape. Even if Tony sends out every person on staff, it's unlikely anyone will come across us. Sitting here, waiting for a rescue, seems to be a certain death sentence."

We both continued kicking at the metal poles, although I think I was able to kick more effectively than Max. After a few minutes, the top of my peg had moved about half an inch.

I scooted around on the dirt so I faced the other way. I then started kicking at the metal stake again.

Max saw what I was doing and said it looked more effective than only attacking the pole from one side. He then slid himself around and did the same thing.

We slid around on our asses for the next half-hour, kicking at our metal poles. We found that we had better luck if we scooped out the loose dirt as the rods moved back and forth.

Every few minutes, we'd stop kicking to try to pull them out. Not having any luck, we'd both go back to kicking.

"Why do you think Nikolay is doing all of this?" I asked as I kicked at my metal stake. "Wouldn't it have been easier for him to shoot all three of us in the hotel room last night? Why go through all this extra effort?"

"From what Gabriella has told me, a quick kill's not his preferred style. He'll make killing us a game of blood sport. You heard what he said. He's been planning this for years. He wants my death to be slow and painful, and he's especially hostile toward Gabriella. He wants her to die while she's sitting right in front of him. I'm starting to think he wasn't trying all that hard to kill us on the mountain the other day. I think shooting at us was only his way of saying the game was on."

We sat in the dirt of the desert and kept kicking. Max had only been using his right foot for the last twenty minutes. He'd occasionally kick a few more times with his left, but that was the side of his rib injury, and it seemed to hurt him too much to continue.

With all the sliding around on my ass, I was glad I was wearing capris and not a skirt. Unfortunately, I could feel holes starting to wear in them.

After another fifteen minutes of kicking, I was painfully sore and tired, but the top of my pole could now wiggle back and forth about two inches. By mutual agreement, we both stopped kicking and got on our knees and pulled.

I watched as Max strained to pull up his stake, although I could see it was hurting him to do so. Unfortunately, his pole was still stuck. As I pulled on mine, the metal rod slid up an inch but then got stuck again.

"I've got mine to come up a little," I said. I knew I should have been excited at the thought of being free, but I was already mentally exhausted.

We sat back down in the dirt and went back to kicking our poles. After another ten minutes, I got to my knees and pulled again with a loud grunt. This time, the metal rod slowly slid upwards.

As I pulled, I was a little shocked at the length of the pole. With a feeling of relief, the rod finally came free. It ended up being a little over three feet long. No wonder we'd had such a hard time getting them out.

I slowly got to my feet and spent a few seconds stretching. I then picked up a rock, roughly the size of a brick, and used it to pound against the side of Max's pole.

After doing this for two or three minutes, we both pulled on the metal rod. With a crunching grinding noise, it slowly came up. From the look of relief on Max's face, he was also thrilled that he was no longer staked down to the ground.

I helped Max to his feet, and we both spent several minutes stretching out the kinks. I walked over and picked up the bottle of iced tea Nikolay had left.

There was a large palo verde tree about twenty yards from us, and we both went over to stand under it. Even though the day wasn't extremely hot, it was nice to be out of the direct sun.

We each took a sip of the meager amount of tea. It was warm, but the liquid in my mouth gave me a feeling of relief and renewed energy.

"How are your ribs?" I asked.

"Painful, but I think they're only cracked. If they'd been fully broken, all of that exertion would have caused more internal damage than I felt. Are you ready for a hike? We need to find a signal for your phone."

"Which direction should we go? I know the Major went north on what sort of looks like a road. But he's in a Jeep, and we're walking."

"Where do you think we are?" Max asked. "This part of the desert doesn't look familiar."

"I'm guessing either west or southwest of Phoenix, but there's no way of knowing. The direction he went is as good as any."

We both started down the road, going in the same direction Nikolay had gone when he'd left. It felt a little weird still having our hands cuffed together with the metal poles dangling from them, but after a few minutes, I stopped noticing it.

After walking for two or three miles, the scenery hadn't changed a lot. The desert was mostly flat, with some rocky hills in the distance.

The road was still visible and seemed to be gradually climbing, but there wasn't any sign of civilization. I'd been hoping Nikolay had been lying about being so far from the nearest road with vehicles on it, but it was starting to look like he'd been telling the truth.

As we walked, the road began to parallel a dry riverbed,

known in Arizona as an arroyo. From the angle of the sun, it must have been about one thirty or two o'clock in the afternoon. The temporary relief from the mouthful of liquid had quickly faded, and I was again finding it hard to swallow.

"Still think this is the best way to go?" I asked.

"We're on a road of sorts, and we're following the arroyo downstream," Max said. "If there's any civilization to be found, it'll be in this direction."

"Is that from your army training?"

"No, the Boy Scouts." He then smiled wearily at me.

"Somehow, I've never pictured you as a scout."

"I guess there's still a lot you don't know about me."

"Yeah, I think I'm finding that out."

We walked another two miles or so, and it must have been around three o'clock. My headache had gotten worse, and I was finding it hard to talk without croaking like a frog.

The shoes I wore weren't meant for this kind of hike across the desert, and I could feel some hot spots forming. Max had developed a limp from trying to favor the side without the cracked ribs.

"I think we're being set up," Max said.

"What? How do you mean?"

"Think about it. Nikolay let you keep your phone. He made it possible for us to escape. Now, we're walking down the only road for miles in any direction, which is also our most likely way back to civilization. Why would he let us do that?"

"I don't know. Maybe he wanted us to have some false hope. After all, there isn't a signal out here, and we're a long way from anywhere."

"Maybe, but it all seems too convenient. Want to try your phone again?"

I powered it on and waited to see what would happen. "Hey," I said, excitement rising in my voice. "I've got a signal."

"Can you call out?" Max asked.

"Let me try to get Gabriella." But even as I looked at the phone, the one bar of signal winked out, and the *No Service* warning was displayed again. "Damn it. I had a signal, but now it's gone."

"How's your battery?" Max asked.

"Almost dead. I'm down to four percent. I'll shut it down again."

"Right," Max said. "But even if we're only getting an intermittent signal, I'd say we're still headed in the right direction."

Although he was trying to sound upbeat, I could tell the situation weighed on him as much as it was on me.

We plodded on for another mile or so as the road gradually climbed to the top of a slight rise. There was a rocky hill half a mile away on the west side of the road and a flat desert on the east side. As we walked, I could tell that the warm spots on my feet were slowly turning into blisters.

"This would be the most likely place for a signal," Max said. He sounded weak, and his voice was getting hard to understand. "From here, the road slopes down for a couple of miles. If you don't have a signal here, perhaps we should try to climb that hill over there?"

I glanced at the hill and had no desire to go for a hike up its rocky sides. I pulled out my phone and powered it up. With a sense of excitement, I saw it had one bar.

"I have a signal. It's weak, but it seems to be holding." I pulled up Gabriella's number and hit the Send button.

"Gabriella," I said when she answered. "We're out in the desert somewhere."

"We know where you are," she said in a matter-of-fact voice. "We will be there in approximately five minutes. Do not move from your position. Stay on east side of road, but stay close to road. Find cover if you can."

"Okay," I croaked out, confused by how she could know where we were and how she could be here so quickly.

"We'll stay here. But you'll need to be careful. Max is worried about an ambush…"

As I started to say the words, my phone beeped that it had lost the connection.

Damn it.

"Can you get her back?" Max asked. "We need to warn her."

"Let me try." But even as I hit the Send button to call her back, the phone powered itself down.

Damn it.

"The battery's dead," I said. "But Gabriella says she knows where we are. For some reason, she told us to find cover on the east side of the road."

"The sun's in the west, so east is this side," Max said, pointing. "The ground on this side is flat, so there's nowhere to hide. The best we can do is to try to find some shade."

We got off the road and walked twenty yards to a palo

verde tree, which offered some amount of protection from the sun.

After three or four minutes, we heard the faint rumbling of a vehicle, but it didn't sound like one of Tony's SUVs. As the sound got louder, a dust cloud billowed in the distance.

Looking down the road, some sort of sizeable tan-colored vehicle was racing toward us. It must have been doing thirty-five or forty miles an hour, which was insane on the narrow and winding dirt road.

Two minutes later, a military personnel carrier slid to a stop on the road directly across from where we were standing. The vehicle had come in so fast that the entire area was immediately blanketed in a thick cloud of dust.

The back driver's side door opened, and Gabriella stuck her head out. "Hurry! Keep low."

Even as she said this, we heard the loud *thump* of something heavy hitting the truck's passenger side window, like someone had thrown a large rock at it. Fortunately, it was on the side facing away from us. A second later, we heard the crack of a rifle shot.

Crap, not again.

"It's Nikolay," Max called out. "He's on the hill. It's a trap. Hurry, but stay low."

Three seconds went by, and another shot hit the passenger side window. It sounded like someone had thrown a brick at it.

As we ran to the vehicle, shot after shot rang out. Most of the bullets hit the personnel carrier with the sound of a hammer hitting a steel bathtub. Still, none of them seemed to be doing any serious damage.

The vehicle's armor and the thick bulletproof glass seemed to provide a good level of protection. Fortunately, from the angle of the rocky hill where Nikolay had been waiting for us, we were protected by the bulk of the truck.

I jumped into the vehicle with Max close behind. Milo was driving and urged us to get in faster. The windows on the passenger's side were a spiderweb of pitted and cracked glass, but so far, nothing had penetrated.

Milo gunned the big engine and performed a tight turn that sent the vehicle back in the direction it had come from. After a mile or so of going full out, he slowed to a more reasonable speed.

From the beads of sweat on Milo's forehead, he'd been a little nervous about the rescue. Gabriella didn't seem the least bit troubled by the situation.

Sitting on the floor was a small cooler. She calmly opened it, pulled out two water bottles, and handed one to each of us.

"Drink slow," she said to Max. "Otherwise, you throw up. We have to give vehicle back to army, so we must keep it clean and in good condition."

As I looked at the cracked and partially shattered windows, I realized Gabriella had made a joke. I think it was the first one I'd ever heard from her.

I took a small sip of the water and felt a rush of relief as I could swallow again. I tried to take Gabriella's advice and drink slowly, but my animal instincts took over, and I downed half the bottle in three large gulps.

My stomach tightened, and for a moment, I thought I really was going to throw it back up. But after a few seconds, my stomach relaxed, and I felt strength rush back into my limbs.

Gabriella then handed me a box of moist towelettes. I used one to wipe my face and another to clean my hands. I knew I still looked terrible, but I felt a lot better than I had.

"Thanks," I said. "That helps a surprising amount."

"Is no problem," she said. "I've been there, many times."

"There's probably only one road Nikolay can drive down from that hill," Max said. "Is this the only vehicle we have out here? If we have more, the others can swing around from behind, and we can trap him."

"Tony try to get three of these so we could get Nikolay," Gabriella said. "But his army contact could only let him have one on short notice. Tony say to get you first, and we take care of Nikolay later."

"How'd you find us so quickly?" I asked.

"I put tracking app on your phone when we were on airplane coming back from Vail," Gabriella said, still in her matter-of-fact voice. "I knew Max would not let me do it, so I not ask."

"You put a tracker on my phone?" I grumbled, feeling dismayed at the violation of my privacy.

"With the tracker," Gabriella continued, "we were able to follow your movements last night from the Tropical Paradise to the desert. We lost your signal about three o'clock this morning at approximately this spot here in the desert."

"You should have put the tracker on Max," I protested, still feeling a little upset. "He's the one Nikolay's after, not me."

Gabriella shrugged, ignoring my comments. "Nikolay knew you would call in for rescue as soon as you reached point where your phone worked again, and he knew that spot would be right here. Fortunately, I know how Nikolay thinks. He train me. He likes to kidnap someone then ambush the rescuers."

"You explained this to Tony?" Max asked.

"Yes, we realized it would be trap, so Tony borrow armored vehicle. When we got signal a few minutes ago, it was right where we lost it last night. We knew there was prominent rock formation less than thousand meters from your position. If I was Nikolay, I would set up there. I told Milo to park between you and where Nikolay must be."

"Where'd you get the vehicle?" Max asked.

"Tony call in favor from contact in Army. She let us have it for up to three days."

"I don't know a lot about army trucks," I said. "Is this a Humvee?"

"No," Milo called back to us. "It's a JLTV. It stands for Joint Light Tactical Vehicle. They're newer and offer more protection than a regular Humvee."

"From the sound of the slugs hitting the vehicle," Max said, "Nikolay's traded in his three-oh-eight for a fifty caliber."

"Yes," Gabriella said. "I would've done same thing. That is why we needed to get vehicle rated for fifty-caliber cartridges. Fortunately, Nikolay assumed we would attempt rescue in civilian vehicles, and he wouldn't need armor-piercing rounds. If he'd been shooting black-tipped ammunition at us, we might not have been so lucky. We must assume he will not make that mistake again."

"How're you doing?" Max asked up to Milo. "I heard you took a dart full of the same stuff we got."

"I'm doing okay," Milo said. "I woke up with a bitch of a headache and felt like I was going to toss my cookies for about an hour, but you probably know about that."

"All too well," Max said. "I ended up taking two darts. I was still able to get in a couple of swings after the first one, but the second one put me down. Plus, I got a couple of kicks in the ribs for my trouble."

"I'm sorry I let you down, Boss," Milo said. "He must have come up behind me, and it was only two or three seconds between the time the dart hit and the time I went out. Maybe none of this would've happened if I'd been paying more attention."

"Don't beat yourself up over it," Max said. "There was nothing you could've done. He was dressed in a resort uniform, and he looked completely legitimate. When I saw him enter the room, I hesitated for a second before realizing who he must be. You would've had no reason to suspect him until he shot you."

Max then shifted in the seat, wincing with pain. "Although, before we go back to the Paradise, I'm going to need to stop by the clinic and get taped up."

"They've already been alerted," Milo said. "They'll be waiting when we get there."

Max looked down at the metal pole dangling from his cuffed wrists. "I don't suppose either of you brought a handcuff key or maybe a pair of bolt cutters?"

We drove north over the faint dirt road. The first few hard bumps caused Max to wince in pain. Gabriella opened a white first-aid box and pulled out a small syringe and an alcohol pad.

"I think it is your turn to have this," she said. "Let me do it."

Max turned, and she swabbed his arm and then smoothly gave him the injection. Within about twenty seconds, he visibly relaxed, and his eyes seemed to grow more alert.

"Thanks," he said, his voice already sounding stronger. "That's much better. I'm glad you remembered it."

"What is that stuff?" I asked. "You gave it to Gabriella last week when we came off the river."

"I don't know the proper name," Max said. "We always called it jungle juice. It was developed for the Army about twenty years ago. It kills the pain yet leaves you ready to fight. We, um, obtained a small supply for situations like this.

Chapter Nine

Milo continued to drive us north along the dirt path. The road seemed to disappear for long stretches, forcing him to go through the arroyo.

I could see why Nikolay had used a Jeep to get us out into the desert. A standard SUV would have gotten stuck a dozen times over. Happily, Milo had fresh tire tracks to follow, so I knew we wouldn't get lost.

Fortunately, Gabriella had thought to bring a box of snacks. Once my stomach had more or less returned to normal after drinking the water, I grabbed a package of peanuts and experimentally tossed back a few.

When nothing terrible happened, I quickly finished the package. This was followed by a box of goldfish crackers, a Snickers bar, and some Famous Amos cookies.

As we got closer to civilization, I was able to plug in my phone and see where we were. It turned out we'd been stranded in a vast area of open desert, about forty-five miles west of Phoenix and about twenty miles south of Interstate 10.

Looking at the map, I had to admit Nikolay had found one of the state's most remote areas to abandon us in. Even with the mild November temperatures, I doubted we would have made it out alive if we hadn't been rescued.

Once I got a steady signal, my phone pinged me that I had two voice messages from the Eagle County sheriff's office and three from Sophie.

Ignoring the detective from Colorado, I gave Sophie a call. She answered right away.

"Hey, girlfriend," she said. "Where have you been all day? Lenny's been driving me nuts looking for updates on the Tony DiCenzo and Rudy Rialto assignments."

"Sophie, I'm sorry I was out of touch. But I've been having a really shitty day."

"Yes!" Sophie said as she started laughing and clapping her hands. "Laura's having a shitty day!"

What the hell?

"Sophie? Why are you laughing at me? I could have been killed this time. I mean, seriously."

"Sorry, I'm not laughing at you," Sophie said, even as she started laughing again.

This went on for fifteen or twenty seconds before I heard the phone change hands, and Gina came on the line.

"Hi, Laura. Sorry for Sophie. We made a bet about half an hour ago. She bet you were having another shitty day, and I bet you were just really involved with the assignments and couldn't call in. Based on her reaction, I think I now owe her lunch."

I don't know why I bother.

"Well," I said, still feeling a little annoyed at both of them. "Just so you both know, I'm doing okay, and I'll be in tomorrow. Would you hand the phone back over to Sophie?"

Gina did so, and I glanced around the noisy personnel carrier. Max and Gabriella were deep in a conversation, and Milo concentrated on driving. I lowered my voice so no one else could hear. "Did you ever call Milo and straighten things out?"

"No, I've been trying, but I think he turned his phone off. It keeps rolling to voicemail when I call."

"It hasn't been off. He's with me, and we're in the middle of the desert. He hasn't had a decent signal for the past few hours."

"Oh, really?" Sophie asked, brightening. "Okay, that's good. Do you know when he'll be free? I should call and try to straighten things out."

"We'll be back in Scottsdale in about two hours, give or take. I'll give you a text to let you know when he's free."

After bouncing on the dirt road for almost an hour, we made it to the interstate. Three of Tony's black SUVs were waiting for us.

We all got out of the vehicle and stretched. Even with the painkillers in his system, Max looked worn down by the experience.

The sun was going down, and it was a beautiful desert sunset, but I didn't take the time to admire it. It had already been a long day, and I only wanted to get back home.

Two security men hopped into the Army truck and drove onto the interstate toward California. The four of us got into the middle SUV, and we all took off. After bouncing around in the back of the personnel carrier, sitting on the comfortable leather seat seemed like laying back on a living room couch.

As we drove back towards Scottsdale, Max and Gabriella had a long conversation about what'd happened. She reported they were still piecing together how Nikolay managed to get in and out of the Tropical Paradise without being seen by anyone.

They had mapped out his movements from the locations

of four other staff members also hit with tranquilizer darts. Fortunately, all four seemed to have recovered with no ill effects.

"No one has any memory of seeing man with scar," Gabriella said. "Since it is notable feature, I assume he did something to change his appearance."

"When I first woke up this morning," I said, "the Major was dragging me across the desert. I noticed his scar had disappeared. Then, later, it was back. At the time, I chalked it up to being half-conscious, but I remember he also didn't have it when he was at the Tropical Paradise. I think he must have used some stage makeup to hide it."

At the mention of Nikolay covering his scar, Gabriella nodded her head as if a piece of a puzzle had fallen into place. The only other things I could add were how I'd found Milo in the hallway, that I determined he was still breathing, and how I'd gone into the suite to investigate. Still, I'd only gotten a tranquilizer dart in the back for my efforts.

The lights of the western edge of Phoenix came into view in about thirty minutes. From there, Scottsdale was still another hour away.

Conversation in the SUV slowed as Milo drove us to the clinic on Frank Lloyd Wright Boulevard. Unfortunately, I was starting to know the place all too well.

I've never understood Tony's relationship with the clinic. They seemed to be able to offer his organization complete medical services and even clear out entire wings at a moment's notice. I've never gotten a bill from any of my stays there, and other than my first name and medical history, I've never told them a thing about me.

As soon as we arrived, Max and Gabriella were quickly ushered back into the emergency room while I was checked out by a nurse. After taking my vitals, she directed me to an examination room. I waved Milo back with me.

A doctor stopped by and again checked me over. She cleaned and treated some of my larger scrapes, especially around my wrists. She also said I was looking a little dehydrated.

She left but soon came back with some sports drinks. I then told her about the knockout drug.

She said they already knew what it was, having treated others earlier in the day, and that it was relatively harmless. After that, Milo and I went back to the waiting room.

I was concerned about Max and was restless. I felt like pacing around, but since I'd worn at least one large hole in the seat of my capris from sliding around on the desert floor, walking around in the waiting room probably wouldn't be a good idea.

As we sat, I relaxed for the first time since the night before. Talking with Milo, it was clear he still wasn't doing well. But I thought it was more than the drugs he'd taken or worry over Max.

"How are you doing?" I asked. "I know the stuff in the tranquilizer darts gives you a hell of a headache. Thanks for coming out and rescuing us."

"Don't worry about it," he said, his head down, a tone of sadness in his voice. "The headache went away after about an hour, and I'm only doing my job."

He then looked up at me. "What's going on with Sophie? She snaps at me all the time. Sometimes, I think that's just her way of talking. But I've never heard her act like that. She's a lot of things, but she's never been rude in public before. And then she tells me to never talk to her again."

"It's not you. She's been going through some things the past couple of days, but I think she'll come around. I wouldn't be surprised if she called you sometime soon to apologize."

"I hope so. Some of the guys I work with think it's a bad idea to go out with someone like her, someone who can't even commit to dating one guy at a time. But there's something about Sophie. I've never found anyone quite like her."

There was an awkward pause, then a doctor came into the waiting area and said we could both go back. When we found Max, he was sitting on a gurney in a room with Gabriella.

"What's the verdict?" I asked.

"Four cracked ribs," Max said. "Unfortunately, I know from experience there isn't much they can do about it other than tape everything up and wait a few weeks for them to heal."

Max laughed and shook his head. "For some reason, they didn't even want to tape them up. The doctor said the guidelines for treating cracked ribs have changed, but I asked him to tape them up anyway."

While we were milling around the room, waiting for the last of the test results to come back, I texted Sophie and let her know Milo was free at the moment. A few seconds later, when Milo's phone buzzed, he walked down the hall to answer it.

Max walked over to talk with me. "Nikolay's still out there," he said. "He's going to continue to come after Gabriella and me. I'd still feel better if you stayed at one of the properties, the Blue Palms, perhaps. I would say you should stay over at my place, but since I'm one of his primary targets, it probably wouldn't be a good idea."

"Thanks for the offer, but I'd rather stay at my apartment. Nikolay seems to know how to get around hotel security. I honestly don't think I'd be any safer in a resort than over at my place."

"Maybe, but I'd feel better if you stayed somewhere with at least some level of security."

"I'll be fine. But I promise, if things start to heat up, I'll take you up on your offer. You can get me a room somewhere fabulous and let me order room service for a few days. But for now, I need to go home and feed Marlowe."

Max gave me a look that seemed to say: *You were just kidnapped and threatened with death. How exactly can things start to heat up from there?* But fortunately, he knew me well enough not to say anything.

After talking with Sophie for about five minutes, Milo returned to the room. He looked to be in a much better mood. I guessed that Sophie had not only apologized but had probably asked him over to her place after work.

Twenty minutes later, Max was released, and we were back in the SUV, heading towards the Tropical Paradise. Max said he wanted to meet with Tony first thing, plus I needed to get my car, which was still sitting in guest parking.

By the time I got home, I was dead tired. It had been a very long and crappy day.

When I stepped off the elevator, I automatically looked around for the Major. Of course, from what I'd learned, he was very good at not being seen.

I knew Marlowe would be over at Grandma Peckham's, and I wanted to see him, so I went up to her door and listened to see if she was still awake. When I heard an episode of *Law and Order: SVU* blasting out of the TV, I knocked.

I heard the shuffling of feet and saw the peephole briefly go dark. I then listened to the security chain being unlatched and the deadbolt being unlocked.

"Why, Laura," Grandma said as the door swung open. "Land's sakes, I wasn't expecting to see you tonight. Come on in."

"Hi, Grandma," I said. "I came for Marlowe. I've had a long day and didn't want to sleep alone tonight."

"I understand, dear. He's been keeping me company all day."

I looked over to see Marlowe fast asleep on his afghan. He hadn't even bothered to wake up as I'd come in.

"I'm about to make myself a nightcap," Grandma said. "Would you like one too?"

"How's the arthritis? Are you on the pills today?"

"When I woke up this morning, I was so stiff I could hardly get dressed. I've already taken three of the damned things today, and I'd hate to do any more. But I figure a Jerk or two on top of the pills will keep me comfortable for the night."

"Well, I'd hate for you to drink alone. And honestly, a Jamaican Jerk sounds pretty good right now."

Grandma went into the kitchen and made the drinks while I turned the sound on the TV down to a more manageable level.

"How are the wedding plans coming along?" I asked Grandma as she handed me the highball.

"Well, I've made a list, and I'm slowly working my way through it. It's not as bad as it could be since most of the details were already planned out. Today, I sent out emails to everyone. I usually think things like wedding invitations should be mailed out as something formal and hand-written. Still, I have to say email is a lot quicker. I sent out over thirty invitations this morning, and most of the people have already responded. I've sent you yours, but I don't have Sophie's, Gina's, or your cousin's emails. Would you be able to give me their addresses or at least ask them about coming?"

"I've already told Danielle, and she said she'd come. I also imagine Gina and Sophie can make it. I'll send you their addresses so you can send the invitations and get their RSVPs."

Grandma spent a moment looking me over. "My goodness, you look like you have a bad sunburn on the side of your face. That looks painful."

"Yeah," I said. My face had become more painful as the day had gone on. Taking the hike through the desert definitely hadn't helped it.

"I once had that happen when I passed out at a party some of my friends were having on the beach one afternoon," Grandma said. "No one thought to roll me over or even throw a shirt on me. When I woke up, half my face stung like the dickens."

"Speaking of that," I said as I stood and turned. "Would you look at the back of my capris and see how bad they are? I had to slide around in the dirt a lot today, and I know I put at least one big hole in them."

Grandma looked for a moment and shook her head. "I'm afraid they're ruined. It's a good thing you weren't wearing a thong today. As it is, your blue panties match your shirt, and it almost looks like you planned the outfit that way. Fashions change so quickly. I don't even try to keep track any more. I'm glad it's not still popular for girls to have the top inch of their butt cracks showing anymore. That trend always seemed a bit overboard."

Grandma and I spent the next twenty minutes talking and having a second Jerk each. She was going to meet with friends from her lady's club the next day, and she wanted to tell me all about it.

By the time we'd finished the drinks, Grandma had started to get sleepy as the alcohol mixed with her painkillers. It was just as well. My head was beginning to spin from the events of the day, and I also needed to get to bed.

I picked up Marlowe, who seemed to have suddenly become boneless, and carried him to my apartment. After setting him on the bed, I pulled off my clothes and checked out the damage to my capris.

As Grandma had said, there were several holes in the seat, and there was no way I could save them. Feeling a little melancholy, I carefully folded them and gently placed them in the trash can. They'd been a good pair of pants, and I hated to see them go.

Marlowe had already stretched out and fallen asleep on his spot next to where my feet go. I pulled on a T-shirt, set the alarm for seven the next morning, and fell asleep almost immediately.

When I awoke the following day, I was so stiff I could hardly move. The bruises from being handled roughly and the effects of our long walk across the desert were all crying out for attention.

I took a look at myself in the mirror and saw I was a patchwork of scrapes and bruises. A couple of them were in some strange places. I tried to think back over the events of the day before but had no idea how they'd gotten there.

The one thing I hadn't counted on were the scrapes and bruises on my wrists, caused by yanking on the pole while wearing the handcuffs. Both of my wrists were bright purple, and there were several deep scratches along both forearms.

I also felt a little fuzzy and out of sorts. I didn't think it was from the Jerks at Grandma's last night. Even though the doctor had pronounced the drug to be mostly harmless, whatever the Major had shot into us seemed to have some lingering effects.

I took four Advils, washing them down with a cup of coffee. I decided to keep the outfit simple and didn't bother to do a lot with the hair.

My walk across the desert had also resulted in a couple of sore patches on my feet, so I picked out some comfy sneakers. Marlowe was in an affectionate mood, and he demanded to be petted right up until the time I fed him.

When I got to the office, I was happy to see Sophie's yellow Volkswagen sitting in its space. I went in through the back door and walked past Lenny, who was pulling a Monster energy drink out of the breakroom refrigerator.

"I still don't know about this dating thing," he said as he popped the top and took a swallow. "Elle had me up until after midnight, again. I've been doing two or three cans of this stuff a day just to stay awake. It's only Friday, and I'm already beat. I don't know how I'm going to survive the weekend."

He stopped and stared at me. "What the hell happened to you? You're walking like you got beat up or something. Do you realize half your face is bright red?"

"I know," I said. "It's a sunburn."

"Did you do that working on your cases, or was this from something wacky you decided to do on your own?"

"It was for the Tony DiCenzo assignment."

"Oh, okay then. Make sure to log it. Although, next time, you should probably wear some sunscreen or at least rotate your head occasionally. That looks really weird."

"Thanks," I said. "I'll keep it in mind." Although I knew the sarcasm would likely be lost on Lenny.

"How's the investigation for DiCenzo going? He hasn't called me for an update yet, but I want to be ready for him when he does."

"Um, I had a meeting with Tony on Tuesday and had another meeting with Maximilian yesterday."

"And? Anything to report? How close are you to finding that guy they're looking for?"

"Well, we now have a name to go along with his description. We know he's somewhere in the Scottsdale area. And we know some of the places he's likely to be over the next few days. How much do you want to know?"

"That's good enough. I don't need to know the details. As long as you can legitimately get me a butt-load of billable hours, I'll be happy."

Lenny took another swig of his Monster. "And don't forget about the log. Go overboard on your descriptions of what you did for DiCenzo during the investigation. I don't mind charging Tough Tony an arm and a leg over this, but I don't want him sending any of his boys over here because he feels I somehow cheated him."

"Sure, no problem," I grumbled, feeling a little annoyed as I walked up to the front, as much to visit with Sophie as to get away from Lenny.

When I got to her desk, Sophie looked tired but didn't have the bloodshot eyes from being hungover.

"Hey," Sophie said. "Thanks for letting me know about Milo last night. After I yelled at him the other day, I figured he turned off his phone or maybe even blocked me."

"I take it everything worked out between you two?"

"Pretty much. He came over about eleven last night and stayed until he had to go back to work this morning. It's a good thing he had a clean shirt at my place."

Sophie then got a strange look on her face. "At least, I think it was his shirt," she slowly said. "It seemed to fit him okay and everything, but, um, now that I think about it, it might have been Snake's. They're both about the same size."

She shrugged as if to say there wasn't anything she could do about it now.

"Did you talk with Milo about the multiple boyfriends?"

"Yeah," Sophie said, sounding a little annoyed. "I made a deal with him. He won't go out with anyone but me, and I won't have any other boyfriends but him."

"What about taking home the guys you meet in the clubs when you're out with the Cougars?"

"Um, we really didn't get around to addressing that."

"Don't you think he's going to make an assumption?"

"Well, maybe, but I'm already making a pretty big concession here. I haven't had only one boyfriend since my divorce. You'd think he'd be willing to meet me halfway on this."

"Hey, I'm not Gina." I said, holding up my hands. "You can do whatever you'd like. But I'm your friend. I understood what happened with Snake. You found out he was going out with a cheerleader, you got mad, and you dumped him. I get that. But Milo's different."

Sophie looked at me. "Different? Like how?"

"You weren't pissed when you saw him with that woman the other day. You were jealous. It upset you to think of Milo being with someone else. That must mean something. Maybe you should consider being completely exclusive with him? You can still go out with the Cougars and flirt with the guys, just don't take any of them home."

Sophie paused, and I could see her mind working. "Oh, I've been thinking about that," she said. "I don't know. Maybe I'll give it a try."

"Let me know what happens?"

"You'll be the first to know," she said. "Now, what about you? What happened yesterday? You said it was a shitty day, but that seems to happen to you once or twice a week anymore."

"Shut up. It does not."

Sophie looked at me.

"Fine," I said. "Whatever. Do you want to know what happened or not?"

"Yeah. Milo was pretty tight-lipped about it. From the way he acted, he must have messed up somehow. I suppose it all has something to do with the new bruises you have on your wrists. You haven't had marks like that since Raul hung you up in that torture chamber over at the Black Death headquarters."

"Yeah, well, I think I told you, two nights ago, I was going to head over to the Tropical Paradise to have dinner with Max."

"You said it was going to be in one of the high-end suites, and you would have him all to yourself for like three hours. I take it that didn't work out like you planned."

"Not even a little bit. Remember that international assassin we were talking about, Major Nikolay Malakov, the one who died a dozen years ago?"

"Yeah, what about him?"

"It turns out he wasn't as dead as we were led to believe. He disguised himself and snuck into the Tropical Paradise. He then shot Max, Milo, and me with some fast-acting tranquilizer darts. When I woke up yesterday morning, I was staked out next to Max in the middle of the desert."

"Seriously? Like in the dirt? With the ants and scorpions and stuff? That sucks."

"Yup. He had us out there most of the day. The weird part is how much the guy seems to enjoy hurting and killing people. He sat in a lawn chair for hours just so he could watch as we slowly baked to death. He was really disappointed when he found out how mild the desert temperatures are in November. He even took pictures of us, staked out in the dirt, for some kind of sicko photo album he has of everyone he's killed."

"Wow. That's pretty messed up."

"He eventually took off to hunt Gabriella and left us alone to die out there."

"Well? What happened?"

"We managed to get loose, although I ruined a good pair of capris in the process. We then walked through the desert until we were able to call Gabriella and Milo. They came to rescue us in an Army personnel carrier. It turns out the Major had set up the rescue as an ambush, and he started shooting at us. Fortunately, the vehicle they came in was bulletproof, so we were able to get back to Scottsdale last night. Everybody's okay, but Max ended up with some cracked ribs."

"What about Milo? Why'd he feel so crappy about what happened?"

"He was doing guard duty covering Max and got hit with the first dart. He blames himself for not stopping the Major. But honestly, the guy's really sneaky. I don't think there was anything Milo could've done about it. The guy might even be a match for Gabriella."

"I bet it's going to be pretty stirred up at the Tropical Paradise. They'd already stepped up security, but from what you said, the guy blew right through it."

"You're probably right. I wouldn't want to be working in security over there today."

Sophie's smile was devious.

"What?" I asked.

"I wish I could be there when Tony yells at the security staff. I'd like to watch that bimbo, Angelique. It'd be great if she started to cry. You know, with her chin quivering and her shoulders bouncing up and down and everything. That'd be pretty funny. Maybe she even did something that made the whole thing her fault. Then Tony could fire her in front of the whole security team. She'd hurry out of the meeting with tears running down her face while everyone looked at her like she was a dumb-ass loser. I'd really love to see a video of that."

"You know," I said. "You take jealousy to a whole new level."

"Maybe. What are you going to do about your psycho killer?"

"The Major isn't after me, only Max and Gabriella. I

think it'll give me some leeway to go after him. He certainly won't expect it. Max wants to hide me away at one of his hotels until everything blows over. But honestly, that could take weeks. I couldn't do my job, and I don't want to be stuck somewhere like that."

Sophie's eyes opened wide. "Wait a minute," she said. "Maybe you need to think about this. Max offered to put you up at a fancy resort for a couple of weeks? All expenses paid? You wouldn't have anything to do but lounge by the pool and sip rum drinks, the kind with little umbrellas in them. You could go to any of the restaurants or have room service brought up whenever you felt like it. You could invite me over, and I could hang out by the pool with you. And you turned that down? Are you nuts? Offers like that don't come around very often."

"I couldn't stay hidden in a resort while a killer's stalking Max."

"So, what are you going to do? If you go after this Nikolay guy, Max will say you're placing yourself in needless danger."

"He doesn't need to know. It's not like I'm going to be obvious about it."

"How are you going to go after a trained international assassin without Max knowing about it?"

"I don't know. I might need you, and maybe Gina, to help me."

"Are you sure you don't want to rethink this? Sitting by the pool at a resort drinking piña coladas seems a lot safer."

"Shut up and help me out here. What do we know about him?"

"Um, he's a killer. And from what you've told me, he's also kind of a jerk."

"Yes, but according to Gabriella, there's often a pattern to his kills. He likes to kidnap someone, then ambush whoever comes after them. All I need to do is make myself available to be kidnapped, then Gabriella and Max can take him out when they come to rescue me."

"Hold on," Sophie said. "That's the worst plan you've ever come up with."

"Do you have a better one?"

"No, but making yourself a target for a sadistic killer doesn't seem like such a great idea."

"Max will probably say the same thing, but I bet he hasn't come up with anything better."

As we talked, Lenny came out of the back offices and walked up to Sophie's desk.

"I'm glad you're both here," he said. "Look up my nose."

"Um, did you just ask us to look up your nose?" I asked. I was having some trouble processing the request. Sophie started to gag, and I was afraid she'd thrown up a little bit in her mouth again.

"Yeah," he said. "Take a look up my nose. How bad's the hair in there? I was looking at it in the mirror in the bathroom just now, and it looks kinda shaggy. Do you think I should trim it, or do ladies like the natural look?"

"Um, sure," I said. "I'd keep it trimmed. I imagine most women don't want to feel your nose hairs brushing against their face when you kiss them."

"Thanks," he said as he turned to go back to his office. "I'm glad I have everyone here to give me advice on the dating thing. Maybe you can't tell, but I still feel like I really don't know what I'm doing."

When the door to Lenny's office closed, I returned to my

cubicle and called Max. When he answered, he sounded like he was outside, walking somewhere.

"Hey," I said. "I know you're busy, but…" I then heard what sounded like a large crowd of people cheering. "Where are you?"

"I'm at the Blue Palms. There've been a couple of minor incidents at the golf tournament already, and we're going over some of the new security arrangements."

"Nothing to do with the Major, I hope. Besides, it's only Friday. I didn't think that really got going until the weekend?"

"No, nothing to do with the Major. And it actually started Monday with the practice rounds and Wednesday with the Pro-Am charity tournament. You'd be surprised how many A-list celebrities come to those. They get some free PR and a decent round of golf in front of several thousand cheering fans. Didn't you say you worked with Stig Stevens? He was here, and his team came close to winning."

"So, you're saying the actual pro tournament started yesterday? I don't typically follow golf or anything. Still, I can only remember seeing the tournaments on TV on Saturday and Sunday."

"Those are the final two rounds. The tournaments always start on Thursday, and the field is cut to seventy players after everyone finishes on Friday. The networks then cover the final two rounds."

"I'd like to get together and discuss the Major Malakov thing. I have some ideas. Would you have any time this afternoon?"

"Gabriella and I are scheduled to meet with Tony later today to discuss the situation. His office, one o'clock. I don't think he'd object if you were there as well."

"I'll be there. How are you feeling today?"

"Honestly, I feel like I got run over by a truck. Between the cracked ribs and the after-effects of whatever drug the Major shot into us, I'm feeling a little rough today. How are you doing?"

"I didn't get as much of the drug, so I'm only a little fuzzy, but I've got my share of bruises and blisters. It'll take me a couple of days to feel like myself again."

I had a few hours before the meeting with Tony, so I drove back to Val Vista Lakes to see if I could learn anything at Rudy's. I stopped at a store along the way to get a six-pack of beer.

That way, if he caught me sneaking around his house, I'd hold up the beer and tell him it was an apology. I'll admit, it was a pretty lame excuse, but it was all I could think of on short notice.

When I arrived at his house, the pickup wasn't in the driveway. Thanking my lucky stars, I parked in a spot at the end of the cul-de-sac and walked back to his house.

Still holding the six-pack like it could protect me from flying bullets, I rang the doorbell. I heard Billie squawking and flapping but no footsteps or movement of any other kind.

When nothing happened the third time I rang the bell, I walked around to the side of the house, hoping I could look in a window. Ideally, I could place a tiny spy camera in one of the windows and catch him as he freely walked around in the living room. Unfortunately, the interior shutters in all of the rooms were closed.

I tried the gate to the backyard, but it was locked. If I

wanted to see into the rear of the house, I'd either need to hop the wall or take a boat and come in off the lake.

I knew climbing over the wall should only be used as a last resort. I'd learned from many bad experiences that nice neighborhoods like this were filled with nosy people. If I hopped the wall, I'd no doubt have to explain myself to the police.

On the other hand, coming in off the lake seemed like the safer bet. I'd be less visible, and people generally aren't as suspicious about strangers in backyards as they are of people looking into windows in the front.

I returned to the street and looked over the wall into Rudy's backyard. From here, all I could see was a large tree.

It wasn't the typical desert palo verde or mesquite tree. This one was more solid, like a ficus. There were thick branches visible on the lower part of the tree, and they still seemed pretty substantial towards the top.

It was the kind of tree that if something valuable was stuck in it, Rudy might be tempted to climb up the branches in order to recover it. Thinking about this gave me an inkling of an idea.

I walked back to my car and then drove to the Val Vista Lakes clubhouse, which was the name of the big community recreation center. It was on the shore of the main lake.

It had swimming pools, tennis courts, and many other activities, including paddle boat rental. As I looked at the colorful little boats tied up in a row and floating in the water, I started to firm up my plans for getting evidence of Rudy doing something he shouldn't be able to do.

"I have an idea about getting the video for the insurance scam," I said over the phone as I drove down the Superstition Freeway.

"I hope it's a better idea than last time," Sophie said. "That one didn't work out so well."

"Rudy has a big tree in his backyard. If I could put something valuable on one of the branches, something he'd be desperate to get to, maybe I could get a video of him climbing up to get it."

"What could you put in the tree that he'd want? And how would he even know it was there? His house has a pretty high wall around the backyard. How would you get the thing in the tree anyway? And when's the last time you actually tried to climb a tree?"

"I don't know all the details yet. Let me work on it."

"Okay, you do that. Are you coming back here? I'll be heading to lunch soon."

"No, I'm heading for a meeting with Max and Tony. I'm going to pitch my idea for catching the Major."

"Good luck with that. Somehow I don't think Max is going to be too keen on using you as the bait in the assassin trap."

Chapter Ten

Driving up Scottsdale Road, I wracked my brain, trying to think of something I could put in Rudy's tree. It not only had to be something he'd want, but it also had to seem like it had legitimately become tangled up in the branches. If I wanted him to break character enough to climb up and get it, he couldn't be suspicious about the item or how it'd gotten there.

I pulled into the Tropical Paradise, found a relatively close parking space in the visitor's lot, and hiked up to the main building. Once inside the massive lobby, I slowly climbed the curved stairs to the offices on the second floor. As I approached the glass doors, the security guards opened them without a word.

I made my way to the executive offices and walked down to Gabriella's desk. She was typing at her computer and looked up as I approached.

"Hey," I said. "I haven't gotten a chance to thank you for what you did yesterday. Everything happened so fast, but I can't tell you how relieved I was when I saw you and Milo in that Army vehicle."

"Is no problem. But it was unfortunate we had to perform rescue at all. If I had been where I was supposed to be, on guard duty Wednesday night, rather than sitting at doctor's office, perhaps none of this would've happened."

"After learning about the Major, I've discovered how devious and clever he is. If you'd been on guard duty, there probably would've been a shootout. As it is, we thwarted his plans, and everyone lives on to fight another day."

Gabriella gave me a look that said she wouldn't have been caught off guard and a shootout would have been okay with her, but then she shrugged her shoulders.

"Maybe, but past is past, and we'll never know." She then seemed to remember something and looked up at me. "According to what Max say, Major Malakov thought Max was the one who shot him. Did you also hear that?"

"That's what the Major said. He said he wasn't sure, but he thought it was probably Max."

Anger flared in Gabriella's eyes. "That is not good. The Major suffered, but he did not know I was the cause. I will need to teach him I was the one who caused his pain. I think I will shoot him under his right eye this time. Then he will have matching scars, and he will know who made him suffer."

Remind me never to piss her off.

"Is Tony ready for us yet?" I asked.

"Max is already in with Tony, and we are to go in as well. I was only waiting for you to arrive."

Gabriella got up and used a keycard to buzz us into the office. Max and Tony were already seated at the small conference table on the far side of the room.

Tony slowly stood, and I walked over and gave him a quick hug. I then sat next to Max while Gabriella sat next to Tony.

I wanted to throw my arms around Max, but between his cracked ribs and everyone watching, I didn't think it would be a good idea. Instead, I had to settle for putting my hand on his leg.

"So, I see that all three of us are walking stiffly today," Tony said with a slight chuckle. "We're indeed a fine lot. Max was downloading me on the new security arrangements that he and Gabriella have come up with. It's pretty fuckin' embarrassing how our target could simply stroll in here and kidnap both you and my top guy."

"Max probably already told you," I said. "But the Major used stage makeup to cover his scar. When I saw him wearing the housekeeping disguise, he was clean-shaven, and the scar had disappeared. And honestly, without that to identify him, he pretty much looks like anyone else."

"No need to sugarcoat it," Tony said. "It's my fault. I was told how dangerous this guy was, and I didn't take enough precautions. I think we're secure now, but this Major is a slippery son of a bitch. I'm not going to assume anywhere is completely safe."

"We're as secure as possible under the circumstances," Max said. "Our next task is to draw him out. I believe if we don't go on the offensive, he'll simply fall back on his sniper training and take us out one at a time."

"And there's no way to defend against a determined sniper?" Tony asked.

"No," Gabriella said flatly. "We know he has fifty-caliber rifle, so he is lethal within a kilometer. Unless we voluntarily imprison ourselves in building and never leave, there's no way to defend ourselves against him. He has both the time and money to do as he pleases. He could hunt us for week or two, go to California for month to do job, then return to Scottsdale at his leisure."

"Alright," Tony said. "We'll need to draw him out. So, how are we going to do that?"

"Gabriella and I have been discussing this," Max said. "I'll present myself as a target. Not an obvious target, mind you, but enough of a target that even with some security to overcome, I think he'll come out of hiding to get to me. Gabriella will be stationed nearby, along with some of our armed guys. The goal will be to turn him over to the authorities. He's still on their capture or kill list, but we need to get rid of him, one way or another."

"I understand your feelings about completing your mission on the guy," Tony said. "But I wouldn't be overly concerned with taking him alive. The only weakness I see in the plan is this Major guy is as likely to shoot you on sight as he is to come out into the open. I understand that you're using yourself as bait in hopes he'll keep you alive as a way to also bring down Gabriella, but I wouldn't want to bet my life on it."

"Um," I said. "From what I understand, the Major's favorite way to flush out his targets is to kidnap someone close, then pick off the rescuers one by one. Why not make me the easy target to kidnap? As long as you're both secretly watching over me, I should be relatively safe."

"No," Max said. "I'm not going to let you purposefully be the target. We'll find another way."

"It could work," Gabriella said. "The Major already knows you are Max's girlfriend, so he knows Max would be guaranteed to come after you."

"Um, maybe I should ask," I said. "The people the Major kidnaps. What happens to them?"

"Sometimes they are killed," Gabriella said. "But not too often. The Major typically does not kill the hostages. Most of the deaths occur when they are accidentally shot by rescuers. We would need to make sure that does not happen."

"No," Max said as he looked at me. "I'm not comfortable

with this. Maybe it would work, but there are a dozen ways it could go wrong. I don't want you placing yourself in harm's way. There's always another answer."

"Fine," I said. "Come up with something better, and I'll go home. It's not like I want to be the bait in a trap. But if you can't find another solution, then I think I should do it."

"Now, you realize what you're volunteering to do?" Tony asked. "I understand why you're doing it, and it shows great courage. I honestly expected nothing less from you. There's no guarantee on something like this. Plus, this might take some time. We'll be performing a play for a guy who may not even be watching. I can see this maybe going on for weeks."

"I know," I said. "But I really don't see another way. And honestly, I don't want to sit around while people I care about are slowly picked off, one by one."

"I don't like having you anywhere near this psycho, you know that," Max said. "But if we're going to do this, we'll figure out what to do while keeping you as safe as possible. We can try for tomorrow, in the evening. I'll give you a call when we've set everything up."

I drove over to a hobby shop on Scottsdale Road to look for inspiration. I was hoping to find something I could put in Rudy's tree that could plausibly get there on its own, like maybe a radio-controlled airplane. I often see people out on the desert flying them, and they look pretty valuable.

I walked over to a display cabinet and saw half a dozen airplanes of one type or another. Although any of them would've likely interested Rudy, all of them were very smooth. It was almost like they were purposefully designed not to get stuck in a tree.

Just as I was turning away from the airplanes, I noticed a display of flying drones. This was more like it.

The drones looked very technical and expensive. Most of them had high-definition cameras and all sorts of sophisticated electronics in them. The sight of the cameras triggered a bunch of ideas and scenarios in my head.

A nerdy-looking clerk came up and asked if I had any questions. After talking to him for about twenty minutes, I made my purchase.

Sophie was at her desk when I got to the office. I walked up and set the drone on it.

"What are you doing with that, and why is it on my desk?"

"I've figured out the Rudy thing," I said. "I went to the hobby store and picked this up. I told you about the big tree in his backyard. I've seen it from a couple of angles, and it seems perfect. I'll stick the drone high enough in the branches so that he'll need to climb a ladder and then reach up to get it."

"Okay," she said. "I can see that."

"Everybody loves drones. I bet he won't even think twice about doing it. We'll position ourselves somewhere nearby and should be able to get a good video."

"How are you going to get the drone into the tree? All the houses there have walls that seem pretty high. It doesn't seem like the kind of place where you can pull a ladder out of your car and climb over. Somebody on the neighborhood watch would probably call it in."

"It should be simple," I said. "His house sits on a lake. I'll get a boat and paddle to his backyard. I'll put the drone in the tree, then get in the boat and float back."

"You know," Sophie said. "It's a drone, and there's a camera on it. Does the camera work? Maybe you could fly it into Rudy's tree?"

"The camera works, and there's a recording feature on it that feeds the video directly to an app on my phone. It doesn't have a time stamp, but we can probably use it as a backup to the main video."

"So, what do you think about flying it into the tree?

"I thought about it, but I don't think I have the skill. I've watched people playing with these things, and it looks like it takes months of practice to get the drone to go where you want it to. Honestly, I think it'll be easier to stand underneath the tree and toss it into the branches until it gets stuck."

"Okay, I get that part. But then, how's he going to know there's a drone in his tree? He'll get pretty pissed if you knock on his door and ask him to get it down for you."

Sophie's eyes suddenly got big. "Wait a minute," she said, holding up both hands. "I hope you don't want me to be the one who knocks on his door. That's way too much involvement for me. Besides, he'd probably recognize me from the other day."

"No," I said. "You won't be directly involved. In fact, that's the beauty of this plan. Neither of us has to tell Rudy about the drone. Watch this."

I pulled out my phone, opened an app, and pressed a button. The room suddenly filled with a harsh beeping sound from the drone.

It beeped once every eight or ten seconds and was loud enough to be painful. After the drone beeped four or five times, I again used the app on my phone to shut it down.

"Jeez, what was that?" Sophie asked, shaking her head to clear it.

"It's the location-beacon feature on the drone. It's to help you find it if it gets lost. I imagine Rudy will be able to hear that, even if he has his TV on."

"I think everyone in the neighborhood will be able to hear it. Are you really sure this is such a good idea?"

"Well, unless you have a better one?"

"No, but I can easily see this plan ending up like the last one."

"Where's everyone?" I asked.

"Lenny's gone already, and Gina's still out on her assignments. I think she has a date with Jet later on."

"Are you doing anything tonight? Tony agreed with my ideas, and starting tomorrow, I'm going to be the bait in the trap."

"Really? How'd Max take it?"

"I could tell he wasn't thrilled about it, but he also couldn't think of anything better. The alternative is for them to try to protect themselves against a sniper who can attack anytime and anywhere."

"Yeah, that would suck. I was planning on going out with the Cougars tonight. Milo's still doing security. I guess between the golf tournament and the crazy Major, everyone's pulling double shifts. You should come along. It'd take your mind off being a target for an insane assassin."

"I don't think staying out all night will help, but I was thinking about dinner. You interested?"

"Yeah, I'd like that. What'd you have in mind?"

"I'm thinking something spicy," I said. "Are you up for Los Dos Molinos?"

"Oh, I love that place. It tastes so good, then it burns for two days after. That sounds perfect. I'll drive."

After dinner, Sophie dropped me off at the office, and I drove back to my apartment. I didn't see the Major or anyone else lurking about, so I took the elevator.

I grabbed a caffeine-free Diet Pepsi from the fridge, then Marlowe and I sat on the couch and started watching *Friday Night Smackdown*. We were about half an hour into it when the theme to *The Love Boat* rang out from my phone.

"Laura," Max said in his deep and steady voice. "Sorry, it's taken me so long to call. What are you doing tonight? Something fun, I hope."

"Nope, Marlowe and I are sitting on the couch. We're watching big, sweaty men beat each other up."

"That sounds interesting. How are you feeling?"

"I'm not as bad as I was this morning. I popped another four Advil about two hours ago, and that took the edge off. I'm thinking I still might need a therapeutic beer or two. How are your ribs doing?"

"Still tender. It's been a few years since I've broken anything. I'd forgotten how painful it is to breathe with a couple of cracked ribs. And seriously, don't do anything to make me laugh. That's downright painful. But I know from experience that after a day or two, they'll mostly calm down. Then they'll just be sore for a couple of weeks."

"Didn't they prescribe painkillers at the clinic?"

"Yes, but I don't like taking them. They make me fuzzy-headed and a little queasy."

"I don't see how you do it. Whenever I break a bone, the

painkillers are a necessity."

"Actually," Max said, "not counting the ribs, my wrists got the worst of it. The handcuffs cut in when we were trying to pull out those metal rods. I didn't think it was doing that much damage, but today, I'm nothing but cuts and bruises."

"Same here. Fortunately, with the cooler weather, I can get away with long sleeves for the next couple of days. Remind me never to do that again."

"Does that mean you've changed your mind about the Major? You know you're under no obligation to help with this."

"No, I haven't changed my mind. What have you come up with?"

"We believe the Major must be monitoring activities here at the Paradise. It's the only way he could've slipped through security the other night. We'll place you somewhere visible, one of the lounges, maybe. Then give the Major some easy kidnapping opportunities. We'll set them up so it won't be obvious what we're doing, but we'll still be able to control the situation."

"So, you want me to hang out in the resort's restaurants and bars for the night and give the Major the opportunity to kidnap me whenever I go to the bathroom?"

"Something like that. What do you think?"

"I would say it sounds a little iffy, but honestly, I was thinking along the same lines. You know, if we end up doing this for two or three weeks, you're going to have a much larger girlfriend."

"That's okay, I know some special exercises designed to help you lose weight."

Oh, yum!

"You're so naughty," I said, smiling. "Of course, doing something like that may hurt your ribs."

"Alright," he said, ignoring me. "Dress for a night out and come over here around six thirty tomorrow. There's a three-piece combo playing at the Bistro from seven until midnight. We'll start you out there. I'll be waiting at a table and we can be seen having dinner together. If I'm being monitored, he'll see you as well. I'll have a security detail visible, but you won't. When I leave, you'll appear to be alone. Hopefully, it'll be a temptation he can't resist."

"With all the extra security you have there, how will he even be able to watch your movements?"

"Based on what we know, there's nothing that'll keep the Major out of the resort. He's too good, and we're still a large and open public space. Most of the new security measures involve surrounding our top guys with an observable staff. That's why we need to strike first. Otherwise, Gabriella and I will be sitting ducks."

I continued to watch wrestling but was still feeling restless. The idea of placing myself as the bait in a trap for a sadistic killer like the Major was starting to creep me out.

I went to the fridge, pulled out a Corona, and watched two episodes of *The Big Bang Theory*. By the time the second show was over, I'd had three more beers and wasn't hurting at all.

As I climbed into bed, Marlowe hopped onto the comforter and curled up in a ball. I turned off the light, rolled over, and eventually fell asleep.

I opened my eyes and knew something was different. I

was in the office reception area, but everything had grown to gigantic proportions. I seemed to be sitting on top of Sophie's desk, but it was now roughly the size of a football field.

It was nighttime, and everything was dark outside except for the faint glow of the lights up and down the street. The only illumination in the office came from Sophie's computer monitor. From where I was, it looked to be the size of a screen in a drive-in movie theater.

I looked at the monitor, and it seemed to comfort me. It wasn't what was displayed on it, which seemed to be the Southern California Surf Report.

It was more the light itself that was soothing. It was somehow compelling, calling out to me.

I found that I desperately wanted to get closer to the light of Sophie's monitor. Without thinking about it, I jumped and was suddenly flying. I looked over my shoulder and saw I had a pair of wings.

Once over the initial shock, I found I had the ability to fly wherever I wanted to go, just by thinking about it. I could move up or down. I could go fast or slow.

If I concentrated, I could even hover in the same position. Giddy with excitement over my new abilities, I flew around the reception area until I started to get tired.

I was flying next to a wall and decided to land on it. For some reason, I knew I could do so without falling off.

As I rested on the gigantic vertical surface, I walked around and explored what was there. I walked down to an old legal document in a frame that I'd seen a hundred times before, but really never paid attention to.

I hopped onto the glass to see what it was. It seemed to be an old deed from the 1890s for a piece of land along the Salt River. It made me wonder what the other framed documents on the wall were.

I then flew over to the bookshelf behind Sophie's desk. I landed on top of a set of legal books on an upper shelf.

I'd always known these law books were only for show, but seeing the thick dust that had accumulated on them only confirmed my suspicions. I guessed they hadn't been opened since they were originally put there, back when the law office first opened, sometime in the 1980s.

I was beginning to feel vaguely uncomfortable. I quickly realized it was because I'd moved away from the light of Sophie's monitor. With a jump, I flew across the room and landed on the middle of the screen.

Walking across the immense lighted surface, I felt happy, but I was also overwhelmed by the brightness. It seemed to completely surround me so that I couldn't sense anything else in the room. I thought about flying away, but all I wanted to do was to get closer to the light.

I suddenly felt myself being grabbed and pulled off the screen. I struggled to get away, but someone had me by the wings.

As I moved away from the light, my senses seemed to return. I saw that my wings were being held firmly between two huge fingers. I struggled to escape, but it was no use. I was trapped.

I looked out to see who was holding me. The giant face of Major Nikolay Malakov smiled down upon me with an evil smirk, then leaned toward me. I was able to see every detail of his scarred and battered face, down to the individual pores of his skin.

"Well," he said, his hot breath washing over me. "It looks like I have you. You thought that by turning yourself into a fly, you could hide from me? You should know by now that nowhere is safe if I decide to hunt you down. You can hide in the office, in your apartment, or even in a fancy golf resort. I'll find you and collect you as easily as pulling a fly off a computer monitor."

I then felt an incredible force as the calloused tips of his fingers started to press together. They were surrounding my body, and I couldn't struggle or even move.

The pressure kept building, and I couldn't breathe. I fought to take in a single breath, but it was no use. I gradually became lightheaded and knew the Major was going to finish me off...

I sat up in the bed, panting for breath. I looked around my bedroom and was confused when Nikolay wasn't still crushing me between his fingers.

Marlowe looked up at me as if to ask why I was disturbing him. I looked over at the clock and realized it wasn't even midnight yet.

Damn, that dream sucked.

I picked up my phone and called Max. When he answered, he sounded awake and alert.

"Why are you still up?" I asked. "I figured you'd be asleep by now."

"As you can imagine, there's a lot going on over here. Why are you up? Is everything alright over there?"

"Um, is your offer to put me up somewhere still good? I think I'll take you up on it."

"Are you okay? Did something happen that made you change your mind?"

"Um, no, I'm fine. But I've been thinking about it and I'd probably feel safer in one of your hotel rooms rather than in my apartment."

"Do you want to come over now? I'll send Gabriella to drive you to the Blue Palms. I've been keeping a room open for you."

"No, I'd have to take a shower and pack first. Besides, I need to tell Grandma that I'm going to be gone for a few days and ask her to take care of Marlowe."

"I could come over and stay with you tonight," Max said. "Then tomorrow morning we'll get you packed and over to the resort."

"Um, yeah. If you wouldn't mind, I'd like that."

"I was in the process of finishing up for the night," he said. "I'll be there in about forty-five minutes."

Max knocked on my door, exactly on time. I'd been sitting on the couch with the TV on, trying not to fall back to sleep.

I checked the peephole, then opened the door. Max stepped into the apartment and gave me a long warm hug. I tried to not hug him back too tightly.

"That's nice," he said. "I didn't think I was going to see you until later tonight."

"I'm glad you came over. I had some stupid dream and I really didn't want to be alone."

"Well, whatever the excuse, I'm glad to see you." He walked to the kitchen table, grabbed one of the chairs, and walked back to the front door. "If it's okay, I'm going to need to borrow one of these for the night."

"Sure," I said, already knowing why he wanted the chair. "I imagine Gabriella would appreciate having something to sit on."

"Yes, but it's not Gabriella tonight. She's a superwoman, but even she needs to sleep sometimes. I've pulled someone new into my security detail. Her name's Angelique. She's been with us for a couple of years, mostly working resort security."

Oh crap. The woman from the burger place. The one Sophie called a nasty skanky bimbo.

"She's not Gabriella," Max continued. "But she's no slouch by any means. She has an extensive military background, including time in the military police. I'll need to introduce you sometime soon. You'll probably be seeing more of her, especially if you start spending the night with me on a more regular basis."

Oh, meeting her should be interesting.

"Um," I said. "She probably already knows this, but there are bathrooms on the ground floor in the atrium."

I wasn't so much worried about Angelique's needs. It was more that I wanted to put off meeting her for as long as possible. Having her knock on the door to use the bathroom in the middle of the night didn't seem like the best way to get reacquainted with her.

"She knows about the facilities," Max said. "We did a perimeter check when we first got here. You sound tired, are you ready for bed?"

"It's almost one in the morning," I said. "I'm beat."

"Don't you have any food here?" Max asked. He was already dressed and seemed to be wide awake. I'd heard him get up and take a shower but really hadn't paid a lot of attention. I was still mostly asleep, even though it was now fully daylight outside.

"I have coffee," I said, trying to be helpful.

"No, I mean actual food. I was thinking about making you breakfast, but I searched the kitchen and you don't have any."

"Um, there's some strawberry Pop-Tarts in the cupboard, although the toaster's broken. You have to hold the handle down the entire time or else it just pops back up. There's a pepperoni pizza in the freezer and there's probably still a box of chocolate chip granola bars somewhere in the living room."

"Come on then," he said. "Take a shower and get dressed. We need to get some actual breakfast. Then we'll get you settled in at the Blue Palms."

Knowing Max was waiting, I quickly got ready for the day. When I went out to the living room, he was on the couch with Marlowe curled up on his lap.

Max had his phone to his ear and it seemed like he was having some kind of meeting about the golf tournament. When I walked over to where they were sitting, he held up his finger to gently shush me.

I went back to the bedroom, grabbed my suitcase, and opened it up. It was still halfway packed from the trip to Vail.

I pulled out the hat, the gloves, and the balaclava. I then tossed in three casual outfits, a couple of nice-looking dresses for enticing the killer, several pairs of shoes, and a bag of makeup.

I also walked around the room and grabbed a couple of miscellaneous things, including a semi-naughty negligée and a bikini. I'd be staying in a fancy resort and hopefully Max would be visiting me in my room from time to time.

I zipped up the suitcase and rolled it into the living room. Max seemed to be finishing up his conversation.

"Are you ready?" Max asked as he disconnected.

"Let's go," I said, dreading the look I was about to get from Angelique.

We stepped into the hallway and I braced myself. But instead of the bimbo skank woman, Gabriella was calmly sitting in the chair in a small alcove next to the elevator. She held a newspaper and appeared to be reading it.

"Darn," I said, trying not to sound too relieved. "I thought I was going to meet Angelique today."

"Her shift ended at seven," Max said. "Don't worry. I'm sure you two will get another chance soon."

Gabriella stood and walked the chair down to Max. He took it and looked back at her. She seemed to understand the look.

"Three people left their apartments and used elevator to go down. No one has come up. Old lady in pink jogging suit came out at seven thirty, then came back fifteen minutes ago. She wanted to have conversation, but she seems harmless."

"That's Grandma Peckham," I said. "She's nice. Oh, I need to tell her I'll be gone."

I knocked on Grandma's door and she answered after about thirty seconds, still wearing the pink jogging suit.

"Hi, Grandma," I said.

"Why Laura," she said. "Come on in." Grandma then saw Max coming out of my apartment and Gabriella standing down the hall.

"You can invite your friends in too, if you'd like. I knew

you had a gentleman caller last night and I got to meet this young lady earlier today. She was sitting on one of your kitchen chairs, so I assumed she was with you."

"This is Max and Gabriella," I said. "And we really can't stay."

"Nonsense," Grandma said. "I enjoy meeting your friends and I'm sure you have time for a Diet Pepsi." She looked up at Max who'd finished locking my apartment door. "Do you prefer soda or tea?"

"Tea would be great," Max said as he stepped into Grandma's apartment."

Feeling a little frustrated, I followed them into Grandma's living room."

"Isn't Gabriella coming in?" Grandma asked.

"No," Max said. "I think she'd prefer to stay out and walk around."

We went in and Grandma told us to have a seat while she got everything ready.

As she busied herself in the kitchen, we went over to the desk and looked at the pictures of her family. Every few months, Grandma seems to add another photo and must have twenty of them by now.

Grandma came into the room carrying a tray with two cups of tea and a Diet Pepsi. Max picked up a small medallion that sat behind a picture of her granddaughter Meghan and Xiu Mei.

I'd seen it before, but it didn't mean anything to me. He looked at it for a moment, then over at Grandma. "You were with the Bureau of Intelligence and Research?" he asked.

"Oh, for a few years, back when I was younger. One of my professors at Cambridge thought I'd have the knack for it and he made some introductions. It's where I met my husband. I'm surprised you know about the bureau. They keep a low profile and most people have never heard of it. Can I take it you worked somewhere similar?"

"Yes," Max said with a smile. "Somewhere similar."

Grandma nodded as if that was the answer she'd expected to get.

"In case Laura hasn't mentioned it yet," Grandma said. "I'm getting married next month, on New Year's Eve. I hope you can make it."

"That sounds like a perfect night to get married," Max said. "Laura hasn't mentioned it yet, but I look forward to it."

There was a squeaking noise from Grandma's bedroom and a few seconds later, Marlowe sauntered in. He took a few sniffs, but after he determined there wasn't going to be anything to eat, he hopped up on his chair and curled up.

"That reminds me," I said. "I'm going to be gone again for a few days. Would you mind keeping an eye on Marlowe?"

"Oh, I'd be glad to. Whenever you go somewhere, he moves in over here anyway. Of course, when only one of us feeds him, he gets fussy after a day or two. I've never seen a cat that likes to eat as much as Marlowe. I'm surprised he doesn't weigh twice as much as he does."

"This is wonderful tea," Max said after he'd had a couple of sips. "Would this happen to be a Taiwanese high-mountain oolong?"

"Yes, it is. You seem to know your teas. I used to travel to Taiwan for work and I do miss the tea. It wasn't until you could start buying it over the internet that I've been able to get any at all. Most of the teas sold as Taiwanese mountain oolongs are only cheap knockoffs from Vietnam, but there's a dealer in Taipei who can get the real deal. Now, it's about the only tea I drink."

"I haven't had it for years," Max said. "It's a nice treat. Thank you."

"I'm glad I've finally gotten a chance to meet you," Grandma said. "I knew Laura had been seeing someone new, but she was being a little mysterious about it. Now, if I have it right, you work with Tony DiCenzo and you help him run all those golf resorts here in town?"

What? I never told Grandma that.

"Why, yes, I do," Max said. He then gave me a look that I didn't need for him to translate.

"Oh, Laura didn't say anything directly, but you know her. She leaks information. Plus, I've lived in Scottsdale for a long time and I've kept my eyes open as to who is who. From what I can tell, you both get along pretty well. Not like her and that detective. Land's sakes, you should have heard them argue. Every week it was something new."

Max looked at Grandma and then at me.

"These apartments have thin walls," Grandma said. "You can't keep a secret here."

"Good to know," Max said as he smiled at me.

Chapter Eleven

We walked down to the parking lot, and Max put my bag in the back of a black SUV. Gabriella climbed into the big vehicle and got ready for us to take off. Max and I got into my car, and he started looking around the interior with a sense of amusement.

"Hey," I said. "Don't laugh at my car. You know all too well why I'm still driving it. Besides, it's paid for, and it still runs pretty well. Unless someone puts another bomb on the motor, it probably has a good fifty thousand miles left in it."

"I wasn't looking at your car," he said with a smile. "I was looking at the piles of fast food wrappers you have in the back. I see Filiberto's, In-N-Out Burger, McDonald's, and is that Jack in the Box?"

"I like the Jumbo Jack," I said. "And yes, I'll clean it out sometime soon. I've been sorta busy lately."

With Gabriella following close behind, I drove us to Old Town and parked in front of the Morning Squeeze, my favorite breakfast place.

Max and I were seated in one of the lemon and turquoise booths against the back wall while Gabriella took a seat near the main entrance. When the waitress came, we both ordered coffee.

Max had a sensible breakfast of eggs, toast, and bacon. I

had the eggs benedict, a weakness of mine whenever I was here.

"After breakfast, we'll get you settled into your room," Max said as he sipped his coffee. "I suppose it's too much to expect that you'll stay there today and not leave the resort?"

"I'm still working on an assignment for Lenny. We're trying to get a video of a man who claims he's injured but is clearly not. Unfortunately, he's been expecting the insurance company to do something exactly like this, and it's making my job harder. At first, I felt a little bad about tricking him, but the guy's kind of a jerk, and he is scamming the insurance company."

"Alright. We're still setting up something for the Major. I won't ask if I can assign someone to watch over you while you're gone since I already know the answer. But make sure to let Gabriella know whenever you leave and when you get back."

"Alright, but I have a question. You asked Grandma about working at a bureau somewhere. What's that about?"

"It's the intelligence division for the Department of State. They provide intelligence and analysis for U.S. diplomats around the world."

"I didn't know there was such a thing," I admitted.

"That's the way they like it. They're a small group, but they're highly skilled."

"I'm sorry Grandma knew so much about you. I didn't think I'd told her anything."

"I'm not worried about Grandma Peckham. I think she knows a lot more about what's going on in Scottsdale than she lets on, but I don't think she'll spread any of it around. Actually, I'm glad you have someone like that to keep an eye on you."

After breakfast, we drove up Scottsdale Road to the resorts and pulled into the Blue Palms. The place was buzzing with activity.

The parking lot had semi-trailers with ESPN, Fox Sports, and Golf Channel logos plastered across them. Portable generators, lights, and thick black electrical cables were everywhere.

"This is amazing," I said. "Is it always like this for a tournament?"

"Not usually. But for the major tour events, the networks come in and cover them pretty extensively. We end up hosting a pro tour event at one of the resorts three or four times a year."

"It's certainly exciting."

"I normally wouldn't put you somewhere this busy; it'll make security more of a headache. But we already know how the Major blew through security at the Tropical Paradise. Having you over here should help throw him off the scent. We'll still keep our efforts at capturing the Major over at the Paradise. I'd rather he tried to kidnap you over there while you're under close surveillance than over here."

We pulled up to a white three-story building that was covered in vines and wide balconies. Max grabbed my bag from the SUV, and the three of us walked up a broad flight of curving stairs with vine-covered railings to a landing on the third floor.

Gabriella pulled a keycard from her pocket and tapped it on the reader for a set of double doors. There was a mechanical noise, she opened the door and then went inside to make sure all was well.

At her all-clear signal, Max and I followed her in.

The suite had a large living room with a balcony, a

kitchen, a dining area, a bedroom, and a huge bathroom. More than anything, I was impressed by how fresh and clean the room smelled.

"Wow," I said as I looked around. "This is a beautiful room, and it's bigger than my apartment."

"I'm glad you like it," Max said. "The resort manager has texted me twice, wanting to offer it for the tournament."

"Well, I do appreciate it. Thank you for giving me somewhere nice to stay."

"When are you taking off? Are you at least going to be staying here for the morning?"

"No, I'll stay long enough to unpack, but then I need to get on my other assignment. I'll let Gabriella know when I'm on my way back."

"Whenever you're here, we'll have someone stationed outside of your door. Make sure you let them know if you're going to be leaving."

After Max left, I used the coffee maker in the kitchen to have something to drink while I unpacked the suitcase. After everything was more or less put away, I opened the big sliding glass door and went out to the balcony.

There was a small table along with two comfortable white chairs. I sat in one of these, sipped the coffee, and looked out over the resort.

Even though I've lived in Scottsdale all my life, there's something uniquely relaxing about being at a hotel like this. The place was beautiful and conveyed a feeling of tranquility.

From where I sat, I could look out over one of the larger pools and a pool bar. Maybe they were only doing this for the tournament, but next to the bar, somebody was already playing a steel drum. I could hear him clearly but at a low and relaxing level.

Between my room and the pool was a small field of grass surrounded by date palms and queen palms. Even though the grass already looked like it was manicured to perfection, there was a man on a riding mower going over it again. I could smell the freshly mown grass, and it was wonderful.

I knew that behind the scenes, everything was buzzing with activity, but even with a crazy assassin hunting Max and the golf tournament going on all around me, sitting on the balcony seemed to drain all of my tensions and cares. Maybe Sophie was right, I thought. Perhaps a week or two staying at a resort would do me a world of good.

I grabbed the keycard Gabriella had left for me and went outside, hoping the person guarding the door wouldn't be Angelique. I was fairly confident that after I explained the whole story about Sophie and Milo, she'd understand and not hate me, but that was a conversation I wanted to put off for as long as possible.

Fortunately, when I opened the door, Angelique wasn't there. Instead, it was a big security guard with a blond crewcut in a Blue Palms polo.

He eyed me as I came out of the room. I'd seen him around before but didn't know his name.

"Hey," I said as I held out my hand. "I'm Laura."

"Carson," he said as his monster hand wrapped around mine. He was a solidly built, good-looking man, a couple of years older than me. "Ma'am, is everything alright?"

"It's all good. I'm going to be out for a few hours. Would you let Gabriella know?"

"Roger that," he said. "I'll escort you to your vehicle."

I was going to say that it wasn't necessary, but one look at the man told me it would do no good. We took off down the curving white stairs while he radioed in that I was leaving.

I drove down Scottsdale Road in the direction of Old Town. Before I headed out to Rudy's house, I needed to stop by the office and pick up the drone.

Thirty minutes after leaving the office, I made it to Val Vista Lakes and drove down Rudy's street. I was happy to see that his truck wasn't in the driveway. I could've planted the drone while he was at home, but it would have been a little risky.

I next drove to the Val Vista Lakes clubhouse and rented a two-person paddleboat. It would have been nice to have something faster, but gasoline-powered boats weren't allowed on the lakes. Besides, I didn't think I would look as suspicious if I pedaled up to his backyard in a little yellow boat.

I put on the required life jacket, set the drone on one seat, and climbed into the other. It'd been years since I'd been in one of these tiny boats.

They worked by pumping your legs on a set of bicycle-style pedals, which connect to a paddle wheel underneath the boat. The faster you pedal, the faster the boat goes. There was a little handle next to my seat, and by pointing it where I wanted to go, I was able to steer.

I then started pedaling the plastic boat toward Rudy's house. The paddle wheel was in the water underneath where I was sitting, and it made a pleasant rhythmic splashing noise as I pumped my legs.

As I slowly crossed the wide lake, I kind of felt like a

ninja. I was on a mission to sneak unseen into the enemy's fortress, plant something vital, and then sneak out again.

Although the distance on the map wasn't very far, the boat was barely going at walking speed. I wanted to get to Rudy's before he came back, so I tried to hurry.

Even with my legs pedaling as fast as they could, it took almost twenty minutes to go the quarter mile to where he lived. When I got there, my legs were already starting to ache. I didn't want to think about having to pedal all the way back.

I slid the boat onto the shore in Rudy's backyard, carefully climbed out, then carried the drone to the tree. I hoped he hadn't come back home while I was pedaling the little boat across the lake. The door to the yard was sliding glass, and there wasn't a curtain or anything to keep him from seeing what I was doing.

I stood next to the trunk and tossed the drone into the branches. It held for a second, then fell back out, bouncing on the grass as it landed. It ended up taking me four more throws, but it finally caught on a thick limb, about twelve feet off the ground.

Reluctantly, I climbed back into the boat and then pushed off from the shore with my foot. As I slowly glided across the lake, I realized that pedaling one of these boats seemed to involve a set of muscles I seldom used. I was getting sore in places I didn't remember ever being sore before.

It was another twenty minutes of pedaling until I made it back to the clubhouse. Getting out of the boat, I returned the life jacket and stiffly walked back to my car.

I drove up toward the Blue Palms and texted Gabriella that I'd soon be there. Once I pulled into the main entrance, I was a little shocked.

If anything, there were even more television trucks and vans clustered in the parking lots and near the clubhouse than there'd been earlier in the day. Fortunately, Max had given me a special parking pass that let me get to within an easy hike of my room.

I parked and was met by Carson. As he walked me to my room, I asked him how his day was going.

"It's good," he said. "After you head off to the Tropical Paradise, I'm working security at a big banquet they're having for the tournament. Depending on how late you come back, I'll probably still be here."

I was running a little behind, so I quickly got dressed in a flashy outfit consisting of a low-cut plum dress and black sandals with about an inch of heel. I normally don't wear heels at all, so this was something of a fashion statement for me.

As I hurried out the door, Carson easily kept up with me as I power-walked back to my car. I asked him to let Gabriella know I was on my way to the Tropical Paradise. "Roger that," was his only response.

When I got to the Dreamland Cove Bistro, I was shown to a table near the waterfall. The table seemed to be carefully chosen as it was visible from almost anywhere in the restaurant, but it was out of view of the guest rooms or rooftops. There seemed little chance that a sniper could get to us, but our movements during dinner could easily be tracked.

Max arrived a few minutes later. He had a visible escort of two guys in black security polos.

I looked around and it took me a moment to find

Gabriella. She'd positioned herself near the front entrance, keeping a watchful eye over the venue.

"We've spent the last twenty minutes walking through the pools, the pro shop, and the lobby," Max said. "If the Major's anywhere on the grounds tonight, he'll know we're here."

"It's a little strange being seen with you in public like this," I said. "I like it, but is it a good idea? We normally keep everything a secret."

"The Major was able to track us to the Kokopelli Suite last time, but with all the extra security, it won't be possible for him to do that again. It's a risk for you to be seen with me in public, and we'll go back to secrecy mode as soon as possible. But for tonight, I'm hoping the very openness of us having dinner in one of the resort's restaurants will make it seem to the Major like this isn't anything unusual."

"How're your ribs doing?"

"Better. As long as I don't move quickly or twist around too much, I barely feel a thing. Give me another week, and I'll be pretty much back to normal."

The band climbed onto the stage and started plugging in their instruments. I always find the process of a band tuning up and getting ready to perform to be intriguing. As I sat watching this process, I heard Max talking to me.

"Laura," he said. "This is Angelique. I wanted to introduce you. She's new to my security detail, and it's likely you'll be seeing her around."

Oh, crap.

I turned to look up into the face of the woman Sophie had called a skanky bimbo. She was several inches taller than me and outweighed me by at least fifty pounds. Up close, I saw she had the type of hard, muscular body that only comes after years of training.

I stood slowly and held out my hand. My only chance of getting through this was the hope that she wouldn't recognize me.

She held out her hand, and we shook. For a second, everything seemed like it would be okay, but then her eyes narrowed. I could see that she recognized me but was having a hard time placing me.

Suddenly, she sucked in a sharp breath, and I knew she remembered who I was. I knew my only option now was to quickly kill her with kindness.

"Angelique," I said as I continued to warmly shake her hand. "It's so good to meet you. Max has said a lot of nice things about you. I hear you spent several years in the military."

The woman didn't say anything. She only stared down at me with a look of disgust. Her eyes flared with anger while she grunted a noncommittal animal noise. "Pleased to meet you," she finally said through gritted teeth.

At a nod from Max, Angelique moved to a table in the corner. One that was close enough to be able to observe us but not so close it would be overly obvious.

As she walked away, Max looked back and forth between the two of us, confusion on his face. He then looked at me for an explanation.

"It's nothing," I said. "The other day, Sophie saw Angelique having lunch with Milo. She got jealous and called her a nasty skanky bimbo. I was there, and I probably reminded her of the incident."

"Sophie called Angelique a skanky bimbo?" Max said with a laugh. "To her face? And she didn't toss Sophie across the room?"

"No, she just took it. She wasn't happy, but a lot of people were watching, and I don't think she wanted to escalate the situation."

"Huh?" Max grunted. "I didn't know she had that kind of restraint. I may have to move her up to a higher position."

A waitress appeared, and Max ordered two Johnnie Walker Blues and some appetizers.

"What's the plan for tonight?" I asked.

"We're keeping it simple. When you're out here, we'll both be surrounded by an obvious security presence. But whenever you go to the bathroom, there won't be any visible security, and there'll be what appears to be a clear path to the outside. If the Major wants to confront you or even attempt a kidnapping, that'll be where it happens."

"Do you really think he'd try something in the open like this? There's a lot of people here tonight."

"According to Gabriella, it's his preferred way of doing it. He likes to operate in a crowd. In fact, the more crowded, the better."

"I'd think it'd be harder to operate in a bunch of people."

"Not in his case. He's been trained to use the crowd as cover, and without the scar, he's a rather nondescript man. Think about it, how would you describe him? Average height, average build, nothing unusual about him at all, except for the scar."

The drinks came out, followed closely by the appetizers. We started talking about skiing, and I soon forgot the real reason Max and I were on our date. Unfortunately, he soon pulled me back to reality.

"Okay," he said. "Time for you to head off to the bathroom. Keep alert and remember you're being tracked by people you won't be able to see. I don't expect anything to happen this first time around, probably nothing at all tonight, but we need to start somewhere."

I got up and walked down the long hallway to the bathrooms. As Max had said, there wasn't anyone else back here. I also noticed there were several service doors along the hallway.

One seemed to lead to the kitchen, but there were two others that led to unknown destinations. I'd always ignored them whenever I'd been here in the past. But now, they both looked a little menacing.

As I got closer to the first of the two doors, I expected Major Malakov to come charging out with his tranquilizer gun. In my mind, he was firing darts and dragging my limp body out through a dark hallway.

When nothing happened at the first door, I walked to the second. Again, I could imagine him waiting on the other side, ready to spring out and capture me.

Wanting to get this over with as soon as possible, I cleared my throat and scraped my shoe on the floor. There, I thought, if the jerk's waiting for me, he'll know I'm here.

When nothing happened at the second doorway, I walked the remaining steps to the ladies' room. As I entered and made myself comfortable in one of the stalls, I got a creepy feeling that I was being watched. I could envision a room full of security staff watching a big screen image of me sitting on the toilet.

How can I go to the bathroom with a bunch of people watching me?

I eventually got over my hesitation and exited the stall. I made a big deal of washing my hands and even soaped up twice. I wanted to make sure if anyone was actually watching, they'd have no complaints about my personal hygiene.

"Well," Max asked when I returned to the table. "How'd it go?"

"Um, okay, I guess. They aren't actually watching me in the stall, are they?"

"No, no cameras at all in the bathroom. It's one of the limitations of doing this in a public space. If someone found a camera in the ladies' restroom, it would probably end up on the news. But we're closely monitoring who goes in and out, as well as who's in the hallway. We also have cameras covering all possible entrances and exits from the area."

"Okay," I said, feeling a little better about things. "There's nothing going on back there. I guess we'll keep trying. But I hope something breaks loose soon. Doing this for weeks at a time will start to wear on my nerves."

Our dinners arrived, and we dug in. For a while, I was again able to enjoy the fact that Max and I were openly having dinner in a Scottsdale restaurant, just like any other couple.

As we were finishing up, the waitress appeared and asked for our dessert orders. We both had coffee, but then I also indulged in the key lime pie. Max gave me a look when I ordered it.

"Hey," I said. "I warned you about what would happen if you moved me into a resort. I don't often get to indulge like this."

"Do you want to try the bathroom one more time?" Max asked. "If the Major's watching, he'll know this'll be his last chance for the evening."

Thinking about the key lime pie and how upset I'd be if the Major chose this moment to kidnap me, I again went down the creepy hallway and into the bathroom.

Once more, I had the feeling that he would burst through the doors as I walked past them. Even after I'd made it successfully into the bathroom, I halfway expected him to be standing in the stall when I opened the door.

Fortunately, everything was quiet, and I found myself completely alone. About halfway through, the door to the hallway opened. I braced myself but soon realized it was only another woman coming in to use the bathroom.

After what turned out to be another uneventful visit, I walked back to the table and was greeted with my pie. It had loads of whipped cream and a fresh lime wedge.

"Well?" Max asked.

"Not a thing," I said as I squeezed the lime, dripping juice all over the whipped cream. I then forked a piece into my mouth. "Either he's not here, or he's biding his time."

"Well, we knew this wasn't going to be quick. We'll just need to keep it up until we get a response. We'll switch up locations so he doesn't become overly suspicious. But, as far as he knows, we eat dinner together two or three times a week, and this is nothing out of the ordinary."

As we finished up, it was almost time for Max's nine o'clock daily wrap-up meeting. "I'll need to go in a minute," he said. "I'll have Angelique walk you down to your car."

"Um, that's okay," I said. "I'll be good on my own for that."

"Not tonight," Max insisted, using the voice I knew I couldn't argue with. "We've been teasing the Major all through dinner. If he's been watching, walking to your car alone might be more temptation than he can resist."

"Alright, I suppose that makes sense. I'll take Angelique as an escort."

Max waved the big security guard over and asked her to

walk me down to my car. Fortunately, she was a professional about it and didn't seem to be annoyed at the request.

With her leading, we walked through the lobby and out to the valet. She then turned to me. "Do you have your claim ticket?"

"Um, actually, I parked down in the free lot."

Angelique looked down at me like I was some sort of strange alien life form. She then gave me a small smile and an almost imperceptible shake of her head.

"Alright, well, let me know where you're parked. I'll make sure you get to your car safely."

We walked along the side of the valet area to a row of waiting security golf carts. She indicated that I should get in the nearest one, and then we drove down the hill to the public lot.

I directed her through the rows of cars to where I was parked. When we stopped by my car, I swear I heard a barely audible snort of laughter from her.

When I got back to the Blue Palms, the place was still a beehive of activity. Temporary lights and portable generators were scattered throughout the parking lots and clustered near the clubhouse. As I drove through the resort to my building, I heard several bands playing and multiple parties going on simultaneously.

Carson was waiting for me when I parked in the lot near my building. Other than asking how my night had been, he didn't say a lot as he walked me along the sidewalks and then up the stairs to my room.

He went in first, looked around, and then pronounced the space to be clear. As I stepped inside, he turned to look at me.

"Good night," he said. "I'll only be here for another half-hour, then I'll be relieved until tomorrow morning. If you need anything, let us know." He then went outside and closed the door.

I went from the living room back to the bedroom. But even though the suite was beautiful, it wasn't home. I missed having Grandma Peckham and Marlowe to talk to.

I was tired but not exactly ready for bed. I went out to the balcony, sat in one of the chairs, and looked out over the main pool.

A band was playing dance music, and a lively party was in full swing. I briefly thought about going down for a drink and listening to the music, but then I thought about Carson trailing along behind me, so I abandoned the idea.

Instead, I got dressed for bed and called Max. It was almost ten thirty, and I knew he'd be done with his meeting. As always, it gave me a small tingle of excitement when he answered.

"Hey," I said. "I'm about to go to bed and was thinking about you."

"I was thinking about you too. Even though the circumstances are a little unusual, it was nice seeing you tonight. How's everything in the room?"

"The room's great. It's even bigger than my apartment, and it's a lot cleaner. I'm sure I could get used to it, but honestly, I miss Marlowe, and I'd rather be at my place."

"Hopefully, we can clear up everything quickly, and life can return to normal for everyone."

"I'm looking forward to that. When do you want to try to flush out the Major again? Tomorrow night?"

"Tomorrow might be tough, but I'll let you know. Once the golf tournament's over, it should give us some added flexibility. Maybe we can even bring you back over here."

"I'd like that. I seem to feel more at home at the Tropical Paradise than over here."

After I disconnected with Max, I crawled under the covers. I thought the noise from the party outside might keep me awake, but I rolled over and quickly fell asleep.

When I woke up, it took me a few seconds to remember where I was. Fortunately, I hadn't had any more weird dreams during the night.

Per Max's instructions, I ordered room service rather than go down to one of the restaurants for breakfast. Even though I knew there was a security guard posted outside, when there was a knock on the door, I looked through the peephole before I unlocked the deadbolt. I was still feeling a little spooked from the night before, and I wanted to make sure it wasn't the Major pushing the cart.

The TV was turned to the local news, and I watched it as I slowly worked my way through breakfast. Since I'd never eaten at the resort before, I hadn't been sure what to order.

Everything on the menu seemed to be related to golf. I ended up getting what they called the "Three-Man Scramble." This consisted of three eggs, toast, jelly, three pieces of bacon, three sausage links, and a pile of hash browns. They also brought up a carafe of fresh-squeezed orange juice and a big pot of coffee.

By the time I'd finished off the breakfast, I decided that next time I'd only order the basic fruit plate. Resort living was definitely going to make me gain weight.

Even though I hadn't yet come up with a game plan for the day, I took a quick shower and got dressed in a comfortable outfit. I still needed to help track down the Major and get the video of Rudy Rialto. Unfortunately, I only had a vague idea of how I was going to do either of these things.

When I glanced at the clock, it was almost nine. Probably too early to call Sophie on a Sunday morning, but I knew Gina would be awake. Maybe she'd even be available to come along with me.

"Hey, Gina," I said when she answered. As I suspected, she sounded wide awake, but it also sounded like she was in the car. "Are you driving?"

"Hi, Laura. It's good to hear from you. Jet and I drove up to Laughlin yesterday and hung out in a casino most of the night. It was so much fun. I haven't done that since the three of us came up here. That was more than two years ago, even before you broke your leg."

"Are you coming back today?"

"Eventually. We're on our way to Flagstaff. We're going to hike the Lava River Cave. It's an ancient lava tube that goes deep underground and is almost a mile long."

"We did that one in the Girl Scouts," I said. "All I remember about the place was that it was cold, dark, and all of the rocks were black and very sharp."

"Yep, that's the place. Jet loves caves but has never been to this one. It should be fun. What's going on with you?"

"I'm still working on the two assignments, but I'm at a standstill on both. On my missing person, I think I'm close. I'm getting a lot of help from everyone at the resort, but he's proving to be elusive."

"What about the other one? The insurance scam?"

"I threw a drone into a tree in Rudy's backyard. It has a loud beacon on it, so he'll know it's there. The plan is to wait until he's home, position myself so I can get the video, and then I'll turn on the beacon. He seems to be technical, so I'm hoping he'll try to climb the tree to get the drone."

"That sounds like a plan. I'll be back in Scottsdale later tonight. Let me know if you need me for either of the assignments. I'll be glad to help you in between my others."

"Thanks," I said. "At the very least, I may need to pick your brain. If the drone-in-the-tree thing with Rudy doesn't work, I'll be completely out of ideas."

"Okay, I'll be in early. Stop by my cube, and we'll go over what you have. I'm sure we'll be able to come up with a new approach."

I disconnected with Gina and sighed. Before Jet, she was almost always available to help out on the weekends. I was thrilled that she'd found someone, but it was making my job more difficult.

Since Gina wasn't going to be able to help today, I called Sophie. As soon as she answered, I realized it had been a bad idea.

"Wha?" she asked in a half-asleep moan.

"Hey, Sophie," I said in my cheeriest voice. "I need to go to Rudy's house and take the video sometime today. Will you be around later? I'll need some help with this one."

"Um, what time is it now?" she moaned. I then heard her moving around to look at the clock on her phone. "Oh, jeez," she said. "I just went to bed, like an hour and a half ago. Call me later, like about dinnertime."

"Okay," I said. "If you happen to get up earlier, give me a call." But even as I said this, I heard the phone land on her nightstand and disconnect.

Feeling a little down about my lack of progress, I called Max.

"Good morning," he said as he answered. As always, hearing his deep and steady voice immediately cheered me up.

"Hey, cutie," I said. "What are you doing today?"

"Other than keeping an eye out for Major Malakov, the main piece of business is still the golf tournament. Fortunately, that'll wrap up today, and things will start to get back to normal."

"What did you decide about tonight? Do you want to try for the Major again?"

"I discussed that with Gabriella this morning. I hate to delay trying to capture him, but it'll need to wait until tomorrow. The awards ceremony for the tournament is happening tonight at the Blue Palms. Unfortunately, that'll pull away most of the security staff we were using for our project with Major Malakov."

"I understand," I said, feeling a little discouraged about the way the day was turning out. "I might head out later to work on getting a video for an assignment. I guess until then, I'll hang around here. Maybe I'll go down to the tournament."

"If you go anywhere today, it would probably be best if you had someone go with you. I think Carson's on your watch today."

"I know we tried for the Major last night. But I'd really rather not have anyone following me around the golf tournament. That would seem a little weird."

Max seemed to think about it for a moment. "Alright, security is tight around the resort today, so you should be okay. I'll have a VIP tournament pass sent to your room. That'll let you in, and you can visit the hospitality tents."

"What's in the tents?"

"Mostly food and alcohol," he said with a laugh. "They're pretty popular with the fans, and we make good margins on everything."

"Golf, food, and booze? It sounds like a good way to spend the day."

"Well, have fun. If I get a chance, perhaps we can get together later on."

"I'd like that."

Chapter Twelve

As I was finishing up my last cup of coffee, there was a knock at the door. Looking through the peephole, I saw Carson holding up a tournament pass.

"This was just delivered for you," he said as I opened the door and he handed me the VIP pass.

"Thanks," I said as I hung it around my neck. "I'll be down at the tournament for at least an hour or two."

He grunted an acknowledgment, then insisted he walk with me through the resort to the main tournament entrance. Once there, we bypassed the long lines waiting to get in and were soon on the course, along with a crowd of several thousand golf fans.

"I'll be glad to stay with you if you'd like me to," Carson said.

"Thanks, but I think I'll be okay."

"They said you'd say that," he said with a laugh. "But if you want me back, just ask any of the resort security staff, and they'll radio in the request. We're all easy to find, and there must be fifty of us here today. I've never seen so much security at a golf tournament before."

He lowered his voice and leaned closer to me. "They also said you could call Gabriella directly, if you want to. She's running the show today from a security standpoint. She'll make sure the message is relayed back to me."

From the way he talked, I could tell he was a little anxious just mentioning her name.

"Gabriella makes you nervous?" I asked.

"Yeah," he said, still speaking confidentially. "It's weird, I know. She's smokin' hot and has never been anything but nice to me. But honestly, every time I talk to her, she scares the willies out of me."

I thanked him, and he took off towards the main entrance. I walked over to the leaderboard, scanned down the list of players, and looked to see how everyone was doing.

Unfortunately, I don't follow golf all that closely, and the only name I recognized was Phil Mickelson. The only reason I knew anything about him was because he's our local golf legend, having gone to Arizona State and started his amateur career there.

I started walking through the course and tried to see what was happening in the tournament. Unfortunately, all the areas near the tee boxes and the greens were tightly packed with people. I stood along one of the fairways, but all I could see was the occasional golfer walking down the course.

I wandered around until I saw one of the hospitality tents. I showed my VIP pass and went inside. Even though it wasn't even eleven o'clock on a Sunday morning, it was packed with people eating and drinking.

There was a big TV on a stand showing the tournament, and several people were gathered around watching it. Honestly, it seemed to be the best way to catch what was going on outside.

After I'd had a beer and some snacks, I walked back outside and eventually found a spot on one of the fairways that wasn't too crowded with people. From here, both the green and the tee box were too far away to make out a lot of detail.

I could see golfers teeing off and putting on the green, but without being able to actually see the ball, it didn't mean a whole lot. From where I stood, I could watch as the occasional ball flew down the fairway or as one of the pros walked by with their caddies.

I didn't know any of the golfers by looking at them. I could only judge how popular they were by how many people were clapping as they walked past us and by how many people hurried along the sides of the fairway to keep up with them.

In between waiting for the golfers to walk by, I started watching the people. Most of them appeared to be dressed more for the office than for a sporting event, but I guess that's just another aspect of golf I don't understand. I looked across the fairway at the people on that side.

One person seemed odd in that he was looking directly at me. At first, it seemed like a coincidence, but as I watched him, he continued to stare back at me. He was wearing a green golf tournament polo, like he was some sort of official. But something about him wasn't right.

Then it struck me. The man was somewhere in his forties, medium height, and medium build. He didn't exactly look like the Major, but if it wasn't him, then why was the guy staring at me?

I searched his face and saw what could have been the shadow of a scar under his eye, but from this distance, I couldn't tell anything for sure.

He was wearing a bright blue golf cap, which partially obscured his features. Besides, even if there wasn't a scar visible, that still didn't mean anything. It certainly *could* be him.

As he looked back at me, he broke out with a smile. He looked towards the tee box for a moment, then back at me. He put his fingers up to his lips, and I swear he blew me a kiss.

My heart was beating fast, even though I was unsure what I'd just witnessed. The man then turned and started to walk away from the fairway.

Crap.

I knew I needed to follow him, but I was on the wrong side of a fairway that was over four hundred yards from end to end. There was no way I could simply run to the green, cross to the other side, and then double back. There was only one way I had any chance of keeping up with the guy.

Knowing this was probably a bad idea, I quickly walked up to the very edge of the fairway. A rope was strung up at waist level to keep people off the course, and tournament officials were posted every fifty yards or so. I positioned myself between two of the officials, looked both ways along the fairway, and didn't see anyone walking toward us.

Without really thinking about what I was doing, I ducked under the rope and started to run across the grass. It was about thirty yards wide, and I thought I could probably make it in five or six seconds.

As I expected, several people started yelling at me to get off the course, and I could see two of the officials starting to hurry my way. What I didn't expect were the simultaneous calls of "Fore!" by at least ten people on both sides of the fairway.

Shit!

My heart started pounding in a panic. I knew that a very hard ball, hit by a professional golfer, was heading directly at me. I quickly remembered that you weren't supposed to try to look for the ball, since that would only end up with you getting hit in the face.

I briefly debated going back, but I kept going instead. A second later, there was a loud whizzing sound caused by something going extremely fast, passing a few inches from my head.

I had a flashback of standing on the mountain with Max as the sniper's bullets were flying past us. At the sound of the ball, I briefly froze but then pulled myself together and kept going.

As I made it to the far side of the fairway, I turned to see the golf ball land about fifty yards from where I was. It hit once, then bounced with incredible speed towards the green. I was thankful it hadn't hit me. At the speed it was going, it probably would've knocked me unconscious.

I ducked under the rope, and people parted to let the crazy woman through. Scanning the crowd, I saw the man in the blue golf hat walking between the fairways, fifty or sixty yards in front of me. He didn't seem to be avoiding me but was walking quicker than somebody at a golf tournament normally would.

Even as I heard a tournament official trying to get my attention for violating the rules, I took off after the man in the blue hat. He seemed to be heading in the direction of the clubhouse. I tried to keep up by walking fast, but eventually, I was forced to run.

As I followed him, I started to get pissed. He'd blown me the kiss so that I would follow him. I could live with that part. But it was also obvious he'd timed his kiss so that I'd be hit by the ball.

What a jerk.

The man must have looked back to see me coming, or

perhaps he only sensed the pursuit. He seemed to quicken his pace until he was almost running himself.

As I hurried to catch up with him, I reached into my back pocket and pulled out my phone. I knew I needed to call Gabriella to let her know what I was doing.

But what would I tell her? A man who only sort of looked like Major Malakov stared at me and blew me a kiss?

That's okay, I told myself. It's better to call in a false alarm than to get into trouble with no backup.

I'd just managed to unlock the phone and pull up Gabriella's number, when the man suddenly turned and darted inside one of the big white tents that had been erected near the clubhouse. I tried to hit the button to make the call as I ran up to the tent.

Carefully, I stuck my head in the entrance and peered inside. The large space was set up with a podium, a speaker's table, and about seventy-five chairs set up in rows.

Other than the chairs, the tent was completely empty. I saw an open flap on the far side and knew the man must have run through the tent and escaped out the back.

Damn it.

I took two steps into the tent and was about to sprint to the open back flap when a familiar voice called out to me. "Stop where you are. If you don't, I will shoot you full of the sleeping drug."

Panic shot through me, and I had the overwhelming desire to sprint through the opening in the tent, despite the threat of the dart gun. Instead, I stopped and turned toward the voice.

The man in the blue hat was standing ten feet from me, pointing the dart gun at my chest. He had a broad grin on his face.

"Miss Black," he said. "It's good to once again meet you."

With my heart racing in my chest, I looked at the man with the gun. He'd covered his scar again but had also added some subtle features that completely altered his look. Even though I knew this was the assassin we'd been looking for, I still had to closely examine his face to verify the fact.

I knew I had to get him talking. The longer he talked, the more information I'd get and the less danger I'd be in. At least, that was my plan.

I wasn't sure if my call to Gabriella had gone through or not, but if it did, she'd be listening to every word Major Malakov said. She'd then come bursting through the door of the tent with a bunch of security guards to capture him and take him away.

"How are you able to get through resort security?" I asked. "Everyone's looking for you, but this is the second time you've done it."

"I've actually done it several times this week. I would brag that it was entirely due to my finely honed makeup and acting skills, but, to be honest, it's mainly due to the scar. I'll admit, it's become a rather mixed blessing."

"Really?" I asked. "How so?"

"When people think about me, they tend to reduce what I look like to the man with the scar on his face. I've found that if I hide the scar and wear the appropriate clothing, people assume it's not me, even though I match the description in every other aspect."

"Well, I guess it works. You seem to pass through security pretty easily. What are you going to do now? Kidnap me?"

"No, not today. Even with the distraction of the golf

tournament going on around us, security's far too tight at the perimeters for me to remove you from the resort. I could leave with the crowd easily enough, even with them looking for me, but you would be harder to hide. I merely wanted to get to know you."

"Why do you want to know me?"

"Agent Kingfisher and Lieutenant Krovopüskov have been going through elaborate measures to make you appear as an easy target. I wanted to see what makes you so special, other than you're the concubine of Agent Kingfisher."

"There's nothing special about me at all. Why is it important that we talk before you kidnap me?

"If possible, I like to know who I capture. I'm also interested in what personal security you have. As you know, I'm already well acquainted with Lieutenant Krovopüskov, as she worked for me for several years. I trained her to be the perfect killing machine. I only knew Agent Kingfisher by reputation, but I've learned so much about him over the years. I hear he goes by the name Maximilian as of late."

As of late? What?

"Very well," he continued, "that doesn't matter. I hope to have ample opportunity to learn more as I perform torture on him. He was head of the assassination squad the other side sent to eliminate me."

"And why would they want to kill you?" I was still trying to keep him talking for as long as possible. From what he'd said, he wasn't going to take me with him today, but I was getting some good information. Besides, I still hoped Gabriella was listening and would quickly organize a takedown party.

"Well," he said as he looked at his watch. "In the four minutes I estimate we have left, and if you are truly curious,

I'll tell you. Several months before I was shot, my superiors threatened to disband my squad and discharge me from the service. They said I'd become unstable and threatened to have me committed to a mental institution."

"What happened then?"

"I did the only logical thing available to me. I killed everyone up the chain of command who had recommended my discharge."

"I'm guessing that didn't make the rest of the group happy?"

"Far from it. Instead of thanking me for getting rid of incompetent officers, they accused me of murder. Can you believe that? They then assigned members of my own group to hunt me down and eliminate me."

"How did Max, um, Agent Kingfisher, become involved?"

"Once it was clear they meant to take me out, I found it gave me a certain amount of freedom. I used it as an opportunity to eliminate all of the problems we faced, both from our side and from theirs."

"So, I take it neither side was happy with you after that."

"No, I soon had multiple assassins after me."

"And then you were shot?"

"Yes, and the most remarkable thing is that I remember it all very clearly. I knew that Lieutenant Krovopüskov, and at least one other, had been getting closer to tracking me down. For several days, my assassins had been playing an elaborate game of cat and mouse, with me being the mouse."

"You knew they were out there?" I asked.

"Oh yes. I could feel them closing in on me. I'd never been on that side of the hunt before, and I must say it sharpened my senses a great deal."

"Tell me about the day you were shot," I said. "What did it feel like?"

"It was late in the afternoon, and it was a bitterly cold day when I was wounded. I'm not sure which of them pulled the trigger. Over the years, I've come to believe it was Agent Kingfisher. From what I understand, he was the operative in charge."

"It was Gabriella, um, Lieutenant Krovopüskov. She told me the whole story, from her side."

"Really? Was it indeed?" he asked, his eyes sparkled as he thought about it. "Once I have her alone, I'll need to ask her about the details of that day, from her perspective. It will be interesting to learn from her what it was like to think she had killed me. Knowing the Lieutenant, she most likely had some rather depraved private fantasies about it afterward. It will definitely add some spice to our sessions of torture."

Even as he said this, he flushed and began to breathe faster. It reminded me of Gabriella's reaction when she thinks about hurting a man.

"So, she shot you?" I prompted.

"Yes, the force of the impact knocked me backward into some bushes. I know. I should have been killed. It was frankly a miracle that I wasn't. Fortunately, the bullet passed through my face without hitting anything vital."

"That's amazing," I said, truly impressed.

"After several hours, I was found and taken to a makeshift clinic that was run by the patriotic resistance, and the medics there saved my life. I stayed in that clinic for months. I had surgery after surgery. Although, as you can see, the level of care wasn't quite up to what it is in the West. I still have some vivid scars to remind me of the trauma."

The Major then looked down at his watch. "Miss Black. It was a pleasure to visit with you, but now I must go. If my assumptions are correct, I estimate that security will be here in less than two minutes. Don't be sad at our parting. I'm sure we'll meet each other again, no doubt sometime very soon. Now, please turn around and place your nose against the side of the tent. Stay there for at least five minutes, and don't attempt to follow me. I don't want to be forced to injure you in order to make my escape."

I walked to the side of the tent but wasn't going to press my nose against the nasty fabric. Instead, I stood quietly against the wall for about fifteen seconds.

When he didn't yell at me for not following directions, I slowly turned around. The space was empty.

I still had my phone in my hand, so I held it up to look at it. I was disappointed when I saw the call to Gabriella hadn't gone through.

But even as I pushed the button to complete the call, she came rushing in through the front entrance, along with two other security guards. Two beefy men in blue security polos also came in through the back flap.

None of them had made a sound. One second, I was alone in the tent. The next, there were five people surrounding me.

Gabriella was holding her Uzi, and the guards all had collapsible tactical batons out and ready to use. Everyone was scanning the area, looking for Nikolay Malakov.

"He's gone," I said. "He left less than a minute ago. He has on a green tournament polo and a blue golf cap. He's covered up the scar again, and he's done some tricks with makeup to alter his appearance."

Gabriella took a final look around the tent, then signaled

the four goons to go out and look for him, two out the front and two out the back. She then pulled out her phone, which was quietly buzzing.

"You are calling me?"

"I wanted to tell you about Major Malakov."

"Really? It is best to call me before you are taken," she said, a slight smile on her lips. She then used her phone to call in a report.

After she disconnected, she walked over to me. "They will look, but they will not find him. Major Malakov is too good. He easily maneuvered you into being captured in this tent, and he no doubt has his escape route already mapped out. But it will be good exercise for the team to make the attempt."

"He said he went through all of this just to get to know me. He also knows about our attempted deception at the bistro last night."

Gabriella thought about it for a moment, then nodded. "It is understandable he suspected what we were doing last night. Our hope was that in presenting you as easy target, the Major would have been tempted to do something he normally would not do. We now need to alter plan."

"The Major also said he was testing some security assumptions about me, and he seemed to know when you were coming."

"The Major likely believed you were being tracked, and we were actively monitoring you. He took you in order to verify these assumptions. If security quickly showed up at tent, you were being monitored. If no one showed up, you weren't. I imagine he was positioned close enough to see when we arrived. By now, he will have again altered his appearance and will have left the tournament."

Almost as if on cue, one of the security guards came back holding the blue golf cap and the tournament shirt. "These were in a trash can, near one of the exits," he reported.

Gabriella took the items and nodded her head as if she'd expected it. "Gather team at main entrance. I will be there in five minutes."

The man acknowledged the order and left.

"Um, about you actively monitoring me," I said. "How exactly are you doing that? How did you know I was in trouble and the Major was here?"

"I still have tracker on your phone, and I also put microphone in your purse. Please keep both with you at all times when you are not in your room."

"And you didn't tell me about this before now?"

"We have you out there to draw Major Malakov in. How else could we have you walking around without security escort while Major was actively hunting you? I assume you knew."

"Nope, I knew about the phone, but the microphone thing is new. I guess I'll need to watch what I say for the next couple of days."

"Up to you. Nothing you say so far shock me."

"There's one more thing. I let the Major know it was you, rather than Max, who'd shot him."

Gabriella broke out in a huge smile, her face flushed with excitement.

"Really? I was getting into position and didn't hear that. I'm glad he now knows for certain who made him suffer through his years of agony. It is good. I only wish I could've seen his face when you told him."

"He said he was going to ask you how it felt to shoot him. He said he'd do it while he was torturing you. He mentioned something the other day about using a razor. Actually, it sort of seemed to excite him."

The flush on Gabriella's face deepened. "So, he looks forward to performing torture on me? With a razor? Well, I look forward to shooting him again in the face. It's good to once again be on the hunt against worthy opponent."

Carson showed up a few minutes later. He escorted me to one of the VIP tents while Gabriella led the security team in a sweep of the entire resort. It seemed a little strange to sit in a tent full of happy golf fans while there was a maniac killer somewhere on the loose.

After finishing my second beer, I got a call from Max. "Hey," he said. "Gabriella reported what happened. Are you alright?"

"I'm fine. The Major only wanted to talk with me. Gabriella says it's the way he works. He likes to get acquainted with someone before he kidnaps them. He also knows what we were trying to do last night."

"Yes, we'd already suspected as much. Given what happened last night and today, I think it makes sense to hide you away while we figure out a different way to approach the problem."

"Hey, don't stick me in a safe house somewhere while this lunatic is out there trying to kill both of you. Okay, so what we tried last night didn't work, but that just means we'll need to come up with something better for next time."

The phone went quiet for a moment. I could almost hear Max thinking of a way to talk me out of it.

"Let me think about it," he finally said. "I know you want to help, and I think you're remarkably brave. But your safety has to be my top priority."

"I'm not looking forward to having anything to do with this guy, ever again. But stopping Major Malakov before he kills anyone has to be the goal here."

It took Gabriella over an hour to report back. As she'd predicted, the Major had eluded the security team. Either he'd already left the property or had remained but changed his appearance again to something no one could recognize.

It was about halfway through the afternoon, and I'd been with Carson in the VIP tent for a little over two hours. Everyone clustered around the TV was excited because there was a three-way tie for the lead in the tournament. They were apparently going to have some sort of sudden-death playoff to determine the winner.

After everything that had happened with the Major, I wasn't all that interested in golf anymore. I called Gabriella and told her I'd be heading out to work on my assignment for Lenny.

"That's fine," she said. "Make sure you have purse and cell phone with you at all times. Take Carson with you."

"Um," I said. "If it's okay with you, I'd rather not have an escort."

I was having visions of Carson trailing behind me on my assignments for the next week. Besides, I thought, if the Major really wanted to get me, a single security guard wasn't going to do a lot to stop him.

"Take Carson or go back to room. That not from me, it from Max. We are thinking of new plan and he doesn't want you out without visible security until we figure out what to do."

"Fine," I said, knowing I wouldn't win this one. "But only until we get a new game plan."

With Carson in tow, we walked out to my car, and I drove over to the Loop-101 freeway and headed south. In a way, I was a little disappointed when he didn't make any of the usual comments people make about my crappy car.

There was still a couple of hours of sunlight, and I had the fancy time-stamp video camera sitting in the trunk. It was charged up and ready to take the video. With any luck, I could wrap up the assignment in an hour or two.

I drove to Rudy's street and was a little frustrated when his truck wasn't in the driveway. We then drove to the clubhouse parking lot to wait for Rudy to get back home.

As we sat, I explained to Carson what the assignment was all about and how I was going to attempt to get the video of Rudy.

"And you get paid to do this?" Carson asked.

"Yes, but honestly, it's really not the kind of job you can retire on."

"Same with security," he said, shaking his head a little. "But the work's interesting, and they have a good healthcare plan."

We waited for about twenty minutes, and I was ready to drive back to Rudy's when Sophie's ringtone began playing on my phone. When I answered, she sounded like she was awake and in a good mood.

"Hey," I said. "Sorry about waking you up earlier. I didn't realize you'd been out all night."

"Don't worry about it. Actually, I barely remember you even calling."

"Did you do anything fun last night?"

"Went out with the Cougars. We bounced around but ended up in the Living Room Lounge. The usual crowd was there."

"You got back pretty late."

"I know. After the bar closed, Elle and I went over to Pammy's house. She made us martinis, and we talked until Elle, and I fell asleep on her couch. It was a lot of fun."

"More fun than taking home some hot guy?"

"It was different. I don't know, I guess I kinda liked it."

"Good, maybe it'll become a habit?"

"I wouldn't go that far," she said. "One step at a time. What are you doing today? Still want to get the video of Rudy Rialto? I suppose I could drive over and meet you."

"I'm over at Val Vista Lakes right now. Rudy isn't home at the moment, so I'm waiting at the clubhouse for him to come back."

"I'm a little surprised Max is letting you wander around with the psycho killer still on the loose."

"Actually, I'm not alone. I'm with Carson. He's one of the security guys from the Blue Palms."

"Really? Is he cute?"

"Um, I'll tell you about it later," I said. I looked over at Carson, who smiled and shook his head when he heard us talking about him.

"There's one thing," Sophie said. "Tell me it wasn't you I saw running across the golf course while they were trying to do their big golf tournament today."

"Yeah, it was me. But, wait a minute, how do you know about that? It only happened three or four hours ago, and nobody saw it, well, except for the people along the fairway."

"Are you kidding?" she laughed. "They've been running it on the Channel 10 news. I got up about an hour and a half ago, and they must've shown it three times already. The video has an ESPN logo on it, so they're probably also showing it nationally on SportsCenter."

"Why would they care about someone running across a fairway? I know it's not something you're supposed to do, and I almost got hit by a ball, but that doesn't seem to rate a mention on the news."

"Apparently, one of the tournament co-leaders had just hit a great tee shot, and all the cameras were following the ball towards the green when you ran out and came close to getting hit. They have it in slow motion, and it couldn't have missed your head by more than a couple of inches."

I'm on the news? That's just great.

"Are you being serious?" I asked.

"The look on your face as the ball shot by your head was hilarious. It looked like you were about to pee your pants. They didn't identify you by name, or anything, but I could tell who it was. So, what were you doing? Just wanted to play chicken with a speeding golf ball?"

"You're not funny," I said. "I saw Major Malakov in the crowd and had to get across the fairway to chase after him."

"He was at the golf tournament? It figures. Well, did you get him?"

"No, not exactly. But I did end up talking with him."

"No way. You had a chat with him? Like just you and the crazy assassin? That would almost qualify as another shitty day. How'd it go?"

"The guy is seriously disturbed. I hope Max and

Gabriella get him, soon."

"I'm not sure why you always get the nut-bags to chase after. This guy sounds a lot like Carlos the Butcher."

"Unfortunately, I think you're right. Although, this guy somehow seems worse. He believes he's completely justified in what he's doing, and he has skills that'll make him almost impossible to catch. Carlos killed people because he was an asshole. The Major kills people because it's his job, and he likes doing it."

"Just be careful. I don't want to have to head down to the ICU at Tony's clinic again anytime soon."

"You and me both."

"Well, let me know if you need me for the Rudy thing. I need to toss in a load of laundry and head out to the store sometime soon."

"We'll have enough light to shoot the video for about another hour. I'll drive by his place, but if he's not there, we'll need to try again tomorrow."

"Alright," she said. "Let me know."

~~~~~

I drove us over to Rudy's house, but the driveway was still empty. I knew he wouldn't be able to park the big pickup in the garage. If he was home, then his truck was parked somewhere else.

We spent about five minutes driving through the neighborhood, looking to see if Rudy had simply parked his truck on a nearby street. He certainly could have done this if he was hoping to fool anyone, like me, who was actively tracking his movements.

"Well," I said to Carson when it was becoming obvious Rudy wasn't at home, "We can't wait around any longer tonight. Let's call it a day."

I drove us back up Scottsdale Road toward the Blue Palms. Along the way, I called Sophie and told her what was going on.

"It's probably good we aren't doing it tonight," she said. "I'm still at the store, and it would've taken me like forty-five minutes to get down there. Let's plan on doing it tomorrow. I don't have anything scheduled after lunch. See if you can do it then. Lenny's going to be in all day, and the Rudy thing will be a good excuse to get out of the office for a while."

When we got up to the resort, there was still a lot of activity. Fortunately, now that the tournament was over, parking had become much easier. Most of the TV people seemed to be in the process of packing up everything and moving along to the next event.

"Are you the one who'll be staying outside the room tonight?" I asked Carson when we'd parked.

"No, my shift ended about half an hour ago. You'll probably have Angelique tonight."

Great, that's all I need.

"Alright," I said. "Walk me to the room, and we can pick it up again tomorrow."

Chapter Thirteen

Even though I was safely back in my comfortable suite at the resort, I felt restless. It was only eight o'clock and way too early for bed.

I'd already had something to eat, so I wasn't all that hungry. I grabbed a Corona from the refrigerator and turned on the TV.

I was curious after what Sophie had told me, so I switched it to ESPN SportsCenter. Sure enough, after twenty minutes of unrelated stories about football and basketball, they ran the story about me.

As Sophie had described, one of the co-leaders of the tournament had hit a great shot off the tee. The ball was about to land when the cameras caught me running across the fairway. They then went into slow motion as the ball zoomed past my face.

They chose an unfortunate frame to stop the video, to show how close it had been. My lips were pulled back in a grimace, my eyes were wide open with fear, and it did look like I was about to wet my pants.

More than the look on my face, I was upset by the announcers. They didn't seem to worry all that much that I had almost gotten a concussion, or worse. Their only concern was what it would've meant for the tournament if my head had interfered with the shot.

I grabbed another beer and went out to the balcony. The resort was still busy with people but nowhere near as hectic as it'd been the past couple of days.

The pool was still crowded, but instead of a full band, there was now only a man playing a guitar. Still, it made for a pleasant soundtrack to go with the nice evening.

I pulled out my phone and looked at the messages. The detective from Eagle County had called twice more over the last two days. It was probably a good thing I was staying at the resort.

I knew they could track down where I lived using my phone number. I was pretty sure that by now, someone from the Maricopa County sheriff's office had been out to my place, wanting to have a chat with me.

As I stood on the balcony, I looked at a painted steel ladder that was bolted to the wall against one corner. It appeared to be roof access for maintenance, and I hadn't thought anything about it before.

As I drank the beer, it seemed like the ladder could be a point of attack by the Major. The more I brooded on it, the stranger it seemed.

It was odd Gabriella hadn't thought about that. She was normally so thorough when it came to security.

Wanting to make sure there wasn't an easy way for the Major to get to the roof from another access point, I set the empty bottle on the table and started to climb up the ladder.

When I could almost see over the edge, I stopped. I had a crazy vision of the Major sitting on the roof with his dart gun pointing at the top of the ladder, waiting for me to come up. Shaking it off as being unlikely, I continued climbing.

Reaching the point where I could see the roof, I scanned the entire area. I looked for signs of someone being up here, but there was nothing. A couple of air conditioning units were scattered here and there, but they didn't look like they'd make good hiding places for anyone.

Knowing the area was currently clear, I kept climbing the ladder. Within a few seconds, I was standing on the top of the building.

The view of the resort was great. Except for some of the more distant parts of the golf courses, I could pretty much see the whole thing from up here.

As I looked around, I noticed a roof-access door that was probably at the top of a stairwell. I walked over to it and pulled on the handle. It was locked with a deadbolt, and that made me feel a little better about the situation.

I turned back and started walking across the roof toward the ladder when I heard a flurry of activity on the ground level next to the building. It sounded like several people were running along the sidewalks. I walked over to the side of the roof to see what the commotion was.

Without warning, the locked door at the top of the stairwell suddenly burst open. Milo and five security guards ran out onto the roof, two of them with drawn pistols and the rest with collapsible tactical batons. It sounded like several more security men were hurrying to get into position, both in the stairwell and on the sidewalks surrounding the building.

As the guards fanned out across the roof, everyone was searching for something or, as I supposed, someone. After ten or fifteen seconds of not finding who they were looking for, they started calling out "Clear" to each other.

Once it became obvious to everyone that we were the only people on the roof, Milo walked over to me.

"What are you doing up here? You tripped like three alarms, and everyone thinks Major Malakov is on the roof trying to get to you."

"Sorry. No, it's only me. I saw the ladder on my balcony and wanted to make sure no one could use it to get into my room."

He gave me a look and slowly shook his head. "Okay, but I still gotta call it in."

Milo had a security earpiece attached to a curly black cord. He squeezed the microphone button and spoke into it.

"False alarm," he said to whoever was on the other end. "It was, um, a guest." He listened for a moment, then nodded his head and barked out a small laugh. "Right," he said. "I'll escort her back to her room."

The other guards went down the stairway first, and we followed. When we got to the bottom, the security guards dispersed, and Milo walked me up the outside stairs to my room. When we arrived at the door, Angelique was standing there.

"False alarm?" she asked Milo, a small sarcastic smile on her face.

"Yes, Laura was just, um, checking the security arrangements on the roof."

"Good idea," Angelique said, still with the smile. "We might have missed something."

She then used the keycard to open my door. As she did, I had visions of the security chain being attached and Milo needing to go back up to the roof to climb down the ladder to let me in. Fortunately, I hadn't done so yet, and it saved me one more embarrassing thing for the day.

"Are you going to stay put for the night?" Milo asked after he'd searched the suite and pronounced it clear.

"Yes," I said. "I promise."

"Well, if you do change your mind, let Angelique know. She can go with you, and you won't end up giving me another heart attack."

"Fine, I promise, really."

After Milo left, I went back to the refrigerator and grabbed another Corona. I was hoping the maids would restock it when they came in to do up the room the next day. Having a refrigerator full of beer that endlessly refilled itself felt a little like magic.

I went into the bedroom and searched through the closet for something to wear. I briefly held up the negligée I'd brought in case Max would be able to spend the night with me. Seeing how that was looking unlikely for tonight, I instead slipped into one of my ASU Sun Devils T-shirts.

I used about five pillows to make a backstop, then laid on the bed and flipped channels until a little after ten. I knew Max would be done with his meetings for the day, so I called him.

"Hey," I said when he answered, hoping he hadn't yet been told about what had happened on the roof.

"I hear there was some excitement over there tonight," he said. "It's been a busy day for you."

Damn, he already knows.

"Oh, that. It wasn't a big deal. I was checking out the security arrangements and accidentally tripped an alarm. Milo and the guys came over to make sure I was okay."

"I heard, and I'm happy it wasn't anything serious. But I'm glad you called. I'm starting to rethink the idea of using you to help capture the Major."

"But I thought we agreed I'd be perfect to help draw him in."

"I only agreed to let you put yourself in harm's way when I was reasonably certain we could protect you. The events on the golf course today show that the Major is now directly targeting you as a way to get to Gabriella and me. You've gone from being bait to being a prize. I'd rather we pull you away from any more direct involvement."

I was about to get upset and protest that I'd be fine and that I still needed to help, but as I thought about it, I knew Max was probably right.

My contribution was as someone the Major could try to kidnap while I was surrounded by an army of security. If he was going to start targeting me as an individual while I went around the city, trying to do my daily job, then my level of risk had risen several notches.

"Fine," I said. "Maybe you're right. What's the plan?"

"For now, I only want you to lay low and not leave the room without a security escort."

"I can do that. Should I stay here or move to the Tropical Paradise?"

"I think we'll keep you there for the time being. If we need to move you, we have a place in Mesa that should work. It's nice, but it's a little out of the way."

"And you don't think the Major will be able to find me if I move to your safehouse?"

"We don't know. Gabriella says there's no stopping him if he's actively looking for you. But she's in the process of taking some extra precautions."

"What do you think?"

"I listen to Gabriella. She knows him better than I do."

"Alright, let me know how you want to handle things. I'm still working on an assignment for Lenny, but I promise when I leave, I'll take security with me."

When I woke up the following day, I noticed the room was bright with daylight. I hadn't set an alarm the night before, and I saw that it was almost nine. It felt strange to sleep in so late; Marlowe usually wakes me up by seven to be fed.

I ordered the fruit plate and turned on the local news. I was happy they'd moved on from the story of the woman who'd almost gotten brained by a golf ball at the tournament the day before.

When breakfast arrived, I was grateful to see that Carson was back on duty. I wasn't in the mood to deal with Angelique, and I certainly didn't want her to be my security escort for the day.

I munched on the fruit and downed a couple of cups of coffee as I ran around, getting ready for the day. I then called Sophie to see how she was doing.

"Hey," I said when she answered. "What's going on over there?"

"Not a thing," she said. "With Thanksgiving on Thursday, it'll be a short week. Lenny has a couple of existing clients scheduled for meetings, and he'll be in hearings off and on until the court shuts down on Wednesday afternoon. Do you still need me for the Rudy Rialto thing?"

"I think so. I'll position the boat while you take the video. I'll be heading over there in a bit. As soon as I confirm that Rudy's home, I'll give you a call."

~~~~~

When I opened the front door to my room, Carson was patiently waiting for me.

"I'm still working on the Rudy Rialto assignment," I said. "I'm hoping to get it finished today. Are you the one coming with me?"

"Yup, I'm assigned to you all day. Wherever you go, I'm supposed to stick with you."

We walked out to the parking lot and drove over to Rudy's house. As with the night before, Rudy didn't appear to be home.

"Well?" Carson asked. "What's the plan?"

"We're officially on stakeout duty until he shows up."

"Copy that," he said. "Where do you want to go while we wait? Over to the clubhouse again?"

"I was thinking lunch. For some reason, the fruit plate didn't seem to do it for me. Are you hungry?"

"Ma'am, I can always eat."

We got back from lunch at about one-thirty and saw that Rudy was still a no-show. We parked at the clubhouse but drove by Rudy's every half-hour or so.

By four o'clock, I was starting to get discouraged. I knew we only had about an hour and a half of sunlight left.

Carson and I again drove by Rudy's street, and this time, his pickup was in the driveway. With a sense of relief, I pulled out my phone and called Sophie at work.

"Hey," I said when she answered. "Rudy's home, and I'm ready. Can you meet me at the clubhouse at Val Vista Lakes? We're going to use one of the paddleboats to get to where we can see Rudy's backyard. I've got the video camera. It's all charged up, and I need you to take the video."

"Hey, it's almost time for me to go home. I've been dealing with Lenny and his stupid questions all day. You couldn't have done this after lunch?"

"Rudy's home now, and I'd like to get this done today. Otherwise, he might notice there's a drone in his tree and decide to get it down when we aren't around to take the video."

"Fine, I'll shut everything off and be there as quick as I can. Keep in mind I'll be fighting traffic the whole way. You know, after we're done taking the video, I'm going to want dinner. And since this is company business, I'm sure Lenny won't mind paying for it."

Sophie pulled into the Val Vista Lakes clubhouse parking lot at ten minutes to five. I'd already rented a paddleboat and was waiting for her on the dock.

She parked next to my car and got out. Carson was standing next to me, and I made introductions.

"Carson," he said as they shook hands.

"I'm Sophie," she said, giving him elevator eyes and smiling her approval.

"Well," I said to Carson. "We're off. It'll take us twenty minutes to get there, twenty minutes to get back, and hopefully not longer than twenty minutes to get the video. With any luck, we should be done in an hour."

I then gave my keys to Carson, who was going to drive over to Rudy's neighborhood and keep an eye out for us from the street. He got in my car and waited for us to take off.

"Tell me again why I need to come with you?" Sophie

asked as she slipped on her orange life jacket, and we climbed into the small paddleboat. "You don't need two people to take a video. Carson looks like he can handle it. That man is hot."

"Don't forget he works with Milo. Besides, you know how these things work. There's always something that goes wrong. You know how to use the camera and can focus on taking a good video. I'll worry about the boat and anything else that comes up."

"Alright," she said. "Let's see if we can do this without getting shot at, cussed at, or falling into the lake."

We settled into the small plastic boat and started to pedal across the water to Rudy's. The sun was starting to go down, and we both felt the need to hurry before we lost the light.

As our little boat slowly crossed the lake with its friendly splashing sounds, I was glad Sophie was with me and not only for the moral support. My legs were still somewhat sore from the last time I'd gone across the lake. It was nice to have someone else help power the paddles.

Twenty minutes later, we stopped. The sun had dipped below the horizon, and the few clouds in the sky were turning yellow and orange.

We floated about thirty yards offshore, directly across from Rudy's house. After some trial and error, we found a position that would let us see both his backdoor and the area in front of the tree.

One of Rudy's neighbors was outside, grilling chicken and ribs. The aroma wafted over to where we were and made my stomach rumble.

"Oh, that smells so good," Sophie said. "Remember, after we do this, we're going out to dinner. I don't even care if we fall into the lake. After smelling that, I'm thinking barbecue. You don't think Carson's a vegan or anything, do you? He looks like the kind of man who likes eating meat."

"I guess we'll find out. All I've seen him eat so far are salads. But first, let's get this done."

I pulled out my phone and opened the mobile control app. I switched on the drone's camera and hit the record button.

With the video feed going directly into my phone, I used the app to position the camera to look down from the tree into the yard. It had a good view of where Rudy would be when he reached up to get the drone.

Sophie pulled out the video camera, pushed the record button, and held it up to look at the monitor screen. "Okay, I'm ready whenever you are."

"Alright," I said. "I'll start the beacon. Keep an eye out for Rudy. It shouldn't take long for him to show up."

I pushed the button for the location beacon and waited. Ten seconds went by, but nothing happened.

"Are you going to turn it on?" Sophie asked.

"I just did."

"How long does it take for the beeping to start?"

"I don't know. In the office, it happened right away."

"Did you change anything?"

"I don't think so. Let me look."

I studied the settings on the app. It seemed pretty simple, but something wasn't working right. Not knowing what else to do, I shut the phone down and then restarted it.

I first made sure the phone was still recording video from the drone. Then, mentally crossing my fingers, I again pushed the button for the location beacon.

As soon as my finger touched the screen, the drone started to beep. In the office, it sounded noisy, but out here, it was ridiculously shrill.

After three or four beeps, it was obvious that it was way too loud for what we needed.

"Wow," Sophie said. "That sound goes right through you. Can you turn it down a little?"

"I don't know if there's a way to do it," I said as I frantically searched through the app for a volume control.

"Maybe you should turn it off? People in the neighborhood are starting to wonder what's going on."

Sure enough, I looked up from the phone and backdoors were opening up all along Rudy's street. People were coming out and pointing at Rudy's tree.

"Never mind," Sophie said. "He just opened his door."

Rudy stood in his open backdoor, supported by his cane, staring up at his tree. Knowing his neighbors were also looking to see what the problem was, he did his best to slowly slide and limp out to the middle of the yard. He looked up at the beeping drone for almost half a minute, then slowly shuffled back to the house, disappearing inside.

He reappeared thirty seconds later, holding an eight-foot folding ladder in his good hand. He shuffled along with the ladder until he got to the base of the tree, directly below the branch holding the drone. He opened the ladder but seemed a little uncertain whether or not to climb it with his neighbors looking towards both him and his tree.

As he was looking up to examine the drone, he suddenly stiffened, as if he'd had a thought. His head quickly came down, and he started scanning the neighbors' yards, searching for something or someone.

Then, with deliberate slowness, he turned his head

toward the lake. With growing anger on his face, his eyes fixed on Sophie and me.

"Uh oh," Sophie said. "Here it comes."

"You!" he pointed and yelled at us. His voice was loud, even over the sound of the beeping drone. "Think you're both pretty clever, huh? Well, you can tell that bitch from the insurance company that she can kiss my pimply butt. Tell her it won't ever work, no matter what she tries. You won't trick me into doing something I can't medically do. So, you can both just paddle your pretty little asses back to wherever you came from…"

While he was shouting, there was a sudden flash of white feathers as Billie the cockatoo flew out the back door. Apparently, in the excitement, Rudy hadn't closed it all the way, and Billie had seen it as her chance for freedom.

Billie made a beeline for the tree and landed on the same branch as the drone. As she looked around at her new surroundings, the drone let out another loud beep. Billie let out a loud squawk and flapped her wings.

Even from where we were floating, we could see that Rudy's eyes had opened wide, and his face had become very pale. He started talking to Billie in panicked, low tones, even while holding his hands up to encourage her to be calm and not fly away.

He carefully repositioned the ladder under the branch holding both the drone and the bird. He looked over at Sophie, who still had the video camera pointed directly at him, then up at Billie, sitting in the tree. For a moment, he seemed unsure what to do.

The drone let out another obnoxious beep, and then Billie flapped her wings a couple of times. I was guessing she'd never been outside before. With the noise from the drone and the open sky, the experience was clearly new to her.

Even as I thought this, the drone beeped again, and she let out another loud squawk. This time, I could swear she seemed to be talking to the drone.

By this point, Rudy had seen enough. He was likely having visions of his pet of thirty years flying over the lake, never to be seen again. Showing remarkable agility, he quickly climbed the ladder and reached out for Billie.

At first, this seemed to spook the bird. She took a couple of steps on the branch away from Rudy. He then climbed onto the top step of the ladder, something that wasn't recommended, even on a solid floor. Definitely not recommended in the soft grass of a backyard.

Rudy was then forced to stretch out with what had been his bad arm. He reached out so far that I was concerned he'd tip the ladder over.

That would have been a disaster. Not only because Billie would likely fly away, but then Rudy really would be injured, and the insurance company might somehow want to blame me for it.

Fortunately, he was eventually able to support the bird in his hand and lift her off the branch. He then carefully climbed down the ladder, still cradling Billie.

When he was back on solid ground, Rudy looked over at his cane, now lying in the grass. But I could tell from his body language that he knew he'd already blown it.

He scowled in our direction, flipped us the middle finger, and easily walked back into his house, all trace of a limp now gone. He firmly shut the door, and that was that.

"I think you can shut off the drone now," Sophie said. "That sound is starting to tear through my head."

I pressed the button, and the drone shut off. After so much noise and commotion, everything now seemed a little too quiet.

"Did you get the whole thing on video?" I asked.

"Every moment, from when he stepped out of his house until he flipped us the bird."

"Wow," I said as I looked at the files on my phone. "And I have the video from the drone saved on my phone. This whole thing actually worked. I'm impressed. Let's turn the boat around and head back to the clubhouse."

"Now that the thing with Rudy Rialto's over, it's time for dinner," Sophie said. "Are you still up for barbecue? I'm thinking Honey Bear's."

"That sounds perfect. I love that place."

"You know," Sophie said as we both started to pedal the little boat back to the clubhouse. "If you think about it, that went a lot smoother than it usually does."

It turned out Carson wasn't a vegan or even a vegetarian. After a wonderful barbeque dinner, during which we told him all about our adventures with Rudy, Billie, and the drone, Sophie took off for her house, and we drove up to the Blue Palms.

I could sense the resort had changed back from being centered around the golf tournament to focusing on the normal traffic of vacationing Snowbirds. From what I could tell, half of the tourists come to the resorts to golf, while the other half come to drink, lay out by the pool, and party.

"How long are you staying tonight?" I asked Carson as we walked up the broad stairs to my room.

"I'm here until eleven. I pulled a long shift today, so

tomorrow, I start three days off. You'll have Angelique after I go home. What did you do to piss her off? She wouldn't tell me, but it must have been something. She doesn't get emotional about a lot of things."

"Oh, it's nothing. Only a misunderstanding. I'll talk with her, and I'm sure we can straighten everything out."

Carson let me in with his keycard and went through the rooms to make sure the suite was clear. He then went back outside to make himself comfortable on the chair in the alcove.

I turned on the TV and opened the refrigerator. Much to my delight, it was again full of Coronas. Tonight, they'd also left me a bowl full of limes.

I grabbed one and sliced it up in the kitchen. I then popped the top on a cold one and shoved in the lime.

I went out to the balcony, sat in one of the white chairs, and looked out over the pool. There was a band tonight, and a dance party was in full swing. I spent several minutes watching the people dancing next to the water.

I was still in a great mood after getting the video of Rudy, and I would have loved to go down and have a drink at the pool bar, but I didn't want to drag Carson with me. I certainly didn't want Angelique hanging with me as I relaxed and listened to the music.

I texted Max to let him know I'd gotten the video of Rudy and was in my room at the Blue Palms. He texted back to tell me he'd give me a call after his meeting was over.

It had been an eventful day, and I was looking forward to talking with him. I also had every intention of inviting him over to spend the night, and I hoped he could make it.

While I waited, I grabbed another Corona from the magic refrigerator and went into the bedroom. I closed the curtains and got dressed in my negligée.

It certainly wasn't the sexiest one I owned, but it was comfortable, and I knew Max would get the right idea when he saw it. I propped up the pillows, flipped on the local news, and waited for Max to call.

At about ten thirty, *The Love Boat* theme rang out from my phone. Happily, I answered it.

"Hey," I said. "I'm glad you called. Sophie and I got the video of Rudy. It went surprisingly smoothly. I can now be on the Nikolay Malakov thing full-time."

"Laura," Max said. I could tell something was wrong. "It looks like Major Malakov might be near you. We think we have him trapped in the old maintenance barn. I don't know if you remember, but it's the same building where we did the diamond exchange, about a year ago."

"I remember the place," I said. "It's the one that blew up. You have him trapped?"

"Yes, we think so, but nothing's certain. Stay put in your room. Make sure to lock the deadbolt and slip on the security chain. Don't go out until I send you the all-clear."

In the background, someone was shouting at Max.

"Damn," he said. "It looks like we have a fire in the conference center. Laura, I need to go. Stay put, and I'll call you back."

After Max disconnected, my heart sped up, and I started breathing faster. Thinking about Major Malakov being back at the resort amped up my anxiety. I needed to get my pistol and wait until Max gave me the all-clear, but then I wanted to help look for the Major.

I walked into the living room to grab my purse. I also wanted to make sure the chain was on the door. As I did, I saw Major Malakov sitting on my couch. He calmly raised a silenced semi-automatic pistol. It was aimed at the center of my chest. The dart gun rested next to him on the couch.

Crap, this isn't good.

"Miss Black, I told you we would meet again soon. As you can tell, I'm a man of my word. In just a few minutes, we will leave."

"What are you doing here?" I asked, blurting out the first thing I could think of.

"As Lieutenant Krovopüskov may have told you, I love to be the one who controls the situation. Over the years, I've found the best way to cause confusion is to kidnap someone important to my target. It often causes them not to think clearly and to make foolish mistakes. Of course, in this case, I believe Agent Kingfisher's judgment will not be impeded, nor will the Lieutenant's, but it will be an effective way for me to draw them in at a time and place of my choosing."

"Can I at least put on some clothes?" I asked, realizing he was serious about kidnapping me and that I was only dressed in a semi-transparent negligée.

"I think not. We don't have the time, and it would only give you the opportunity to cause trouble."

He then looked at a pair of sandals that were sitting by the door. "Although, you may wish to put on your shoes. We'll be walking across some rough terrain tonight."

"Where're we going? Back in the desert?" Even though I was terrified, I knew I had to keep him talking. My purse was sitting on the kitchen counter, and I knew if someone was listening, they'd be able to tell what was going on.

"Not the desert, but where we're going is rather secluded. I've studied the schedule of the guards, and we have another three minutes before it's safe to leave the room. We'll be spending some time together over the next few days in a small and quite soundproof torture chamber I've constructed, but I'm afraid we won't have much of an opportunity for a quiet chat."

"What do you mean?" I asked quietly. I knew my voice was shaking, but I couldn't help it.

"I have your next week all planned out. It will switch back and forth between sessions of torture and, um, shall we say, abuse. You'll be spending most of your time screaming and crying while I record it all to send to Agent Kingfisher."

His intent to torture and molest me was sinking in, and I started to shake in fear. I said a silent prayer that Gabriella and a handful of security staff would soon burst through the door.

"I know what you're hoping for," he said. "But even though I'm sure your room is actively being monitored, the security staff is currently occupied with more important matters. I've set up a diversion, and the entire security apparatus of this resort now believes that I am holed up in a building on the far side of the resort. Even now, as they are in the process of surrounding the building, they will also receive reports of a fire that has broken out in the lobby of the conference center. I estimate, even in a worst-case scenario, a six-minute response time for them to get to this location."

The Major looked down at his watch. "Alright, time to go. We're going to leave both your purse and your phone here in the room. I'm not sure which one contains your tracking device. Maybe both of them do. But I'm not going to give the Lieutenant a way to find you until I'm ready for her."

The Major raised the dart gun, paused for a moment, and looked me in the eye. "And before things begin to get, um, messy between us, I want you to know that I bear you no personal ill will. You're merely the tool I will use to get to my real targets."

"Thanks," I said, sarcasm dripping off the word.

"I'm now going to give you a mild sedative," he said, waving the dart gun and talking like a doctor about to perform surgery.

"It's the same drug I gave you the other day but at a lower dose. The effects will be similar to being somewhat drunk. You'll still be able to walk, but you'll be disoriented and won't be able to run away. Then we're going to walk out of here."

"What then?" I asked.

"I have a golf cart waiting for us at the bottom of the stairs. We're going to get in it and drive through the resort to a car I have waiting. Now, if you wish, you can stand up and turn around. I'll shoot the dart into your bottom. I've been told that is the least painful part of the body to be shot in."

"And, if I refuse?" I asked.

"Then, I'll shoot the dart into your left breast. If you pull that one out before the drug takes effect, I'll shoot the next one into your right breast. But I honestly don't think you'll enjoy it all that much. The alternative is that I simply shoot you in the face with the pistol and then come up with another plan to get to my targets."

Damn.

I stood up slowly and turned to face the wall. There was a soft *Pop!* and I felt the sharp pinch of the dart. Instinctively, I reached around to yank it out.

The room started to spin, and I began to lose focus. I found the dart and then tried to wrap my fingers around it.

Unfortunately, I couldn't get enough of a grip on the dart to pull it out. To help steady myself, I grabbed the back of a chair with both hands.

The Major walked over and put his hand on my head to keep me from falling over. He paused for ten or fifteen seconds, then reached down and pulled out the dart.

As he did, I tried to take a swing at him, but my arm wasn't properly responding. All I could do was lift my arm a few inches and use my shoulder to try to swing it.

When he saw what I was trying to do, the Major only smiled. "We're now going to walk out the door and then down the stairs. Don't try to fight it, or else I'll give you another dart full of the drug. But that'll make you pass out, and I honestly don't feel like carrying you."

The Major held me tightly by the upper arm and pulled me through the room. He opened the door, and I saw Carson lying in a heap against the corner. I didn't see any blood and hoped he'd be okay.

The night seemed very dark as we walked to the top of the wide staircase. At this point, I was glad the Major was holding me upright.

All I wanted to do was collapse and fall asleep. He held the pistol in his left hand, had his right arm wrapped around me, and had the dart gun slung over his shoulder on a strap.

Stumbling like I was drunk, we started down the first flight of stairs. He had to steady me a couple of times since my legs weren't doing a good job of holding me up.

When we reached the landing for the bottom flight, I was still upright, but my head had started to spin. I think the Major must have misjudged the amount of the drug he'd shot into me.

I feel completely wasted.

We turned the corner and were about halfway down the last flight of stairs when there was a noise. It must have been thirty or forty yards away, coming from the backside of the building.

It was a muffled metal-on-metal sound that caused Major Malakov to pull me to an abrupt stop. He made me stay completely still while he scanned the area, his pistol tracking the path of his eyes. After almost half a minute, the Major determined the area was clear, and he forced me to continue.

There was a Blue Palms maintenance cart parked on the sidewalk, covered with golf tournament stickers. As we walked down the last flight of stairs, the Major angled me toward it.

We were two or three steps from the bottom when I heard a loud *Pop!* It was like someone had opened a big bottle of champagne or set off a firecracker.

In my dazed state, it sounded like it had come from the white three-story building across the lawn. At the same time, I felt something wet splatter against my body.

The Major suddenly released me to grab at his face. I saw that his cheek and now his hand were both covered in blood. I wobbled for a moment and sat backward on the stairs.

When I looked up at the Major, I saw he'd been shot across his cheek, just below the eye that didn't already have a scar. It was bleeding freely, but the wound didn't seem overly deep.

The Major wobbled and shook his head as he tried to get his senses back. He was making a horrible sobbing sound, and the look on his face was one of pure terror.

Being shot in the face must have been bad enough, but I knew it was probably also bringing up a lot of painful memories. He was frantically feeling his cheek with his fingers to determine the extent of his injury.

From three directions, armed security staff converged on us, guns drawn and pointed at the Major. Looking up, I saw two more security goons appear at the top of the stairs. For a terrifying moment, I thought there was about to be a gunfight, with me sitting uncomfortably close to the line of fire.

The Major ignored the three people standing in front of him and instead looked across to the top of the building where the shot had come from. In that instant, I realized it had been Gabriella who'd shot him, and she no doubt currently had her sights centered directly over his heart. Even as I thought this, a red laser spot appeared, centered on the Major's chest.

The Major looked down at the red dot, and I knew he must've come to a similar conclusion about who had targeted him. He slowly shook his head in defeat and dropped both guns. He then stood quietly as the security officers surrounded him, slapped on a set of cuffs, and bundled him into an unmarked white van that seemed to appear out of nowhere.

My head continued to spin as I sat on the lowest step. Between the effects of the drug and the adrenaline from the shooting, the world had gotten woozy.

I started to think that passing out might be a good option. I heard a noise and looked up to see Angelique hovering over me.

It figures.

"Are you injured?" she asked as she bent over me. From her tone, I got the feeling she wouldn't be overly upset if I had been.

She lifted my face in her hands and looked closer at me. "I don't see any wounds. Have you been drinking?"

"I think I'm okay," I said in a drunken slur. I'd been looking and feeling all over my body for wounds. But other than some blood splatter from the Major's face, I thought I was unscathed.

Although, as I thought about it, I might have been drooling a little bit, an effect of the drug. This was partially confirmed when I saw a satisfied smirk on Angelique's face.

"Well," she said. "I suppose it's a good thing you're alright. I probably would've gotten in trouble if you'd been shot."

"Good to know," I said, then passed out.

Chapter Fourteen

When I woke up, I was in bed in my room at the resort, still wearing the negligée from the night before. It was bright daylight outside, and it took me several seconds to realize what had happened.

There was a faint memory of someone talking to me and shining lights in my eyes in the middle of the night. I also remembered Nikolay Malakov and the shooting.

I expected to have a headache and still feel like crap from the drug the Major had shot into me, but instead, I felt pretty good. I experimentally got up and put on a resort robe.

When that went okay, I walked out to the living room. Max and Gabriella were sitting on the balcony, drinking coffee. When they saw I was up, they both came inside.

"Good morning," Max said as he walked up and gave me a hug. "How are you feeling? We had a doctor come in last night to check out both you and Carson. He assured me that you'd both sleep it off and be okay. We described the hangover effects of the drug, and the doctor gave you something to counteract it."

"I feel a lot better than the last time the Major shot us full of drugs," I said. "I wish we could have had it the other day in the desert. That was rough."

"Carson spent the night on the couch and took off about a

half-hour ago. He seemed to be okay, without either the nausea or the headache, so I assumed you'd also be good."

"Plus," Gabriella said, "We heard Nikolay say it was the same drug he used the other day, so we were not as concerned."

"You were listening the whole time he was talking to me?" I asked, starting to get angry. "Wait a minute. Did you know the Major was coming to my room to kidnap me last night? Were you still using me as bait? Maybe you forgot to tell me?"

"Not at all," Max said. "You weren't in the plans last night, other than to keep you out of trouble."

I looked over at Gabriella. "Well?"

"I knew there was possibility Major Malakov would come for you, even though you had what seemed like adequate security. You may not have known it, but in addition to Carson, we had two teams constantly circling your perimeter."

"I never saw them," I admitted.

"When the reports came in that the Major was trapped in building on north side of resort, I suspected it was planned diversion. When report of fire in conference center came in, I knew for sure he would try to kidnap you. We were monitoring audio from your room and were alerted when he was there with you."

"What happened?"

"I took team and positioned myself on roof directly across from your building. We then stationed several armed security staff around your room. They were there as backup plan in case I wasn't able to take him down first. But it was no problem. He came downstairs and presented simple target. I disoriented him with round to the face and security quickly capture him. It was all, how you say, easy peasy, lemon squeezy."

Something had been bothering me, and this seemed like a good time to ask. "You aren't going to get into trouble for not actually killing the Major the first time, are you?"

"No, my old government will not have problem. My original report only listed the Major as cleanly shot and presumed dead. As per protocol, I never listed the kill as confirmed. One look at Major's face will show that my report was accurate. In truth, if what he told you was true, it has been more than dozen years since he cause trouble in Europe or Asia. I do not believe anyone will be overly upset that he is now only captured rather than killed."

"It was pretty amazing how you were able to crease his cheek like that."

"It would have been difficult shot if I'd been far away, but I was less than a hundred yards from target," Gabriella said quietly. "I've been thinking about shooting Major Malakov ever since I learned I did not kill him all those years ago. I wanted to shoot him directly under his right eye. That way, he would have matching scars when he was in his coffin. But Max say no. Only incapacitate and disorient so he could be captured and taken away."

"But, you did a great job grazing his cheek. It staggered him, even though the wound wasn't overly deep. I know you struck fear in his heart. I saw him frantically feeling at the gash on his face. For several seconds, he thought you'd severely injured him. I'm sure he had visions of going through the entire rehabilitation process again."

"I also observed that," Gabriella said with a slightly twisted smile. "It was the effect I'd hoped for. I trust it helped make up for the way he's terrorized you over the past two weeks. For me, I've never had someone come back from the grave so I could kill them again. It was unique opportunity. Yes, hurting him was good, but killing him would've been so much better. That would've been a memory I could have relived, again and again."

"What happened to the Major?" I asked. "Did you already turn him over to the police? What happens next?"

"He's still our guest," Max said. "We have him in the old maintenance barn that we were discussing last night. It seemed like a good place to put him. It's out of the way and secure. I made a phone call to the headquarters of my old unit this morning and talked to the commander. It'll take them a day or two for the paperwork to go through, but it's likely they'll want to take him off our hands."

"Wow," I said. "So, is that it? Do you think this is over?"

"I really do," Max said. "We have no reason to think he was working with anyone else. You're welcome to stay here for a few more days, if you'd like. But with the threat of Major Malakov now over, you can return home any time you'd like."

"Thanks for the offer, it's a beautiful room, but I'd like to get home. Both of my assignments have wrapped up, and I'd like to hang out in the apartment with Marlowe for a few days without worrying about who's going to kidnap or shoot me."

"Before you go home," Max said, "Tony's asked to see you. I think he wants to make sure you're okay and to thank you for helping us with the Major."

"He doesn't need to thank me. I was going to help regardless. I should be the one thanking him for letting me help without needing to sneak around."

Max walked me to my car, and I drove to the Tropical Paradise. I parked in the visitor's lot and was pleased to see security at a more normal level.

I walked through the lobby and up the stairs to the offices. This time, there was only a single guard, now behind the security podium, and both of the glass doors were open.

I walked through the hallways, noticing the noise of the office had returned to normal levels. There was something comforting about that.

When I walked down the executive hallway, I was a little surprised when a strange woman was sitting at Gabriella's desk. She was in her mid-thirties, and I'd seen her around, but I didn't know her name.

"I'm Laura Black," I said as I walked up to her. "I'm here to see Tony."

"Hi, Laura," the woman said. "It's good to meet you. I'm Cheryl. Tony's expecting you." She then reached under the desk and buzzed me into the office.

Tony was seated behind his desk, but he stood and stiffly walked to the center of the room. I gave him a hug, and he gestured that we should sit in his living room group. I took a seat on the couch while he sat in one of the leather chairs.

"I know Gabriella has other things to do today," I said. "But I was a little surprised when she wasn't outside at her desk."

"For the past couple of months, she's been splitting her time between the two of us. With the upcoming changes, she'll be assuming other duties."

"So, you're ready for the handover?"

"I am. Now that this last problem is over, I feel like I'm handing over the organization to Max with a clean slate. I've had a good run, but I'm happy Max is going to be the one in charge. I've been doing this since I was twelve, back in New York, and I could use a break. I can still golf, although I'll walk a bit slower than I used to. It won't be a bad life."

"When is this going to happen?"

"I'm thinking a week or two. We'll have a nice dinner. I'll make a speech introducing Max and he'll make a speech about how he envisions the organization going forward. We'll fill out the forms with Max listed as the new CEO. We'll then issue a standard press release, and that will be that."

"Really? I thought there'd be something, I don't know, more formal."

I then remembered back to the transfer of power during the Black Death. There had been a lot of candles, guns, blood, and threats of death to anyone who talked about the secrets of the group.

Tony gave one of his small chuckles. "No, the time for the old ceremonies has passed. The reality is Scottsdale Land and Resort Management is rapidly becoming a legitimate business. When I first moved out here, I made sure that, legally, both sides were completely separate entities. If one side were to be brought down, the other side would be protected. Over the past few months, I've been actively working to completely sever all internal links between the two sides."

"If that's the case, will Max still run both sides?"

"Perhaps not," Tony said. "But I still need to work out a few more details before I can make any announcements."

I hope Max is okay with that.

"Enough about business," Tony said. "How are you doing? I hear there was another bit of excitement last night."

"Excitement isn't the word I'd use. However, I think that problem is now over."

"I wanted to thank you for your help with this maniac, Major Malakov. It was a little unnerving having a killer loose in my resorts, terrorizing my top guys. He turned out to be quite a nasty piece of work and I'm glad you were here to help out Max and Gabriella."

"It's no problem. Besides, you knew I was going to try to help, with or without permission."

Tony gave out a small laugh. "Yes, I did know that, and I want to do something to thank you for your efforts. I know the last time you did something like this for me, I gave you my old car."

"Yes, you did, and I'm so sorry it was destroyed. I loved that car."

Tony chuckled and gave a dismissive wave of his hand, as if thinking about his old car burning to slag amused him. "We've talked about this before. There's no need to apologize again over something that wasn't under your control."

"Maybe, but I still feel horrible about your car."

"I tell you what. Since I'm out of cars to give you, have Max go out with you and pick something out."

"Seriously? You want to give me a new car?"

"Get whatever you want. I know you won't go crazy on me."

I was so excited. I stood up and gave him another hug. "Thank you so much. After what happened to the last beautiful car you gave me, I'd pretty much given up on the idea of getting a new one, like ever."

"Well, if you want my advice, I wouldn't get rid of your old car yet. You tend to have a rather, um, active lifestyle. If you think you're going to be placing yourself in a harmful situation, I'd take your old car."

I started laughing, mostly because of happiness and also because I knew that my adventure with the Major was really over. I could feel the tension I'd been carrying for the past week and a half draining from my body.

"You've had an exciting week and came through it okay," he said. "It's only made you stronger. I think that calls for a drink. Before you go, will you share a dram of the Balvenie 191 with me? My bottle's almost empty, and I can't think of anyone I'd rather share it with other than you."

"Tony," I said. "It would be my pleasure."

I got to the office the next morning about nine-thirty. The following day was Thanksgiving, and I wanted to finish up quickly and turn in the paperwork for my assignments. I knew I couldn't stick around the office for too long, or Lenny might want to give me another case to work on.

I went up front and dropped off the log sheets for Rudy Rialto. I then went back to my cube to finish up the paperwork on Tony's assignment.

Gina was out for the morning and I supposed it was a good thing. I wasn't sure how much I wanted to tell her about the events of the past couple of days.

When I'd pretty much finished up the report, I went up front to drop everything on Sophie's desk. I then gave her a quick rundown of everything that had happened the previous two days.

"So, let me get this straight," she said, sounding a little put-out. "You were kidnapped, Gabriella shot the crazy assassin, and Tony's buying you a new car? Damn, I should have helped you with that one rather than the thing with Rudy

Rialto. All I got out of that one was dinner. Maybe Tony would have gotten me a new car too."

"But your Volkswagen is still beautiful," I said.

"That's because I take care of it. You won't see any bullet holes or hatchet gouges in my car."

"Shut up, you know that none of that was my fault."

"Well, I hope you take better care of your new car than you did your old one. What kind is he going to give you?"

"I don't know. He told me to pick something out."

"Damn, I'd get a Porsche, the same kind Danica has. You know, something fast."

"I'm not looking for something fast. I need something practical."

"I don't know about that. How many times in your life is someone going to offer to let you pick out any car you want? I'd go for it if I was you."

The door to Lenny's office opened, and he walked out to Sophie's desk. He looked tired but in a good mood.

"Laura," he said, "I'm glad you're here. I got a call from Tony DiCenzo last night. For once, the man seemed like he was in a decent mood. He said you did a good job finding that guy they were all looking for. Based on that, I'm calling the assignment done. I'll need your updated log sheets. I hope you did what we talked about and went overboard with the details about what you did for him. Don't forget, we have a nice retainer waiting to be carved up like a turkey, and I'm going to charge him a boatload. Don't be shy about the hours you spent on this."

"I've been working on it," I said as I handed him the finished report. "The log sheets and summary report for the assignment are right here. I think you'll be happy with the number of hours I put into this."

"Now, about the other assignment you had," Lenny said. "I looked at the videos you and Sophie shot for the Rudy Rialto insurance scam. That was pretty good work. I think the client will be happy. I especially liked the video you got from the drone. It's not time-stamped, but you can see the sweat on Rudy's face as he reaches out to get the bird. I'm still not sure how you managed to set it loose. If you ask me, that seemed a little risky. The bird could have flown away or not landed where you wanted it to, but what the hell, it worked."

Lenny then looked down at Sophie. "I'm also not sure why you had to be there. All Laura had to do was hold the camera up and film the fun."

"I was in a boat," I said. "Too many things could have gone wrong. I didn't want to have to do boat things at the same time I was trying to concentrate on shooting the video."

"Alright," he said, "I was only asking the question. By the way, I took a look at the log sheets and billable hours you turned in on this one. They both seem to be a little light."

"What were you looking for?" I asked.

"We'll need to chew up at least half the retainer on this, or else Brenda Montoya will get pissed," Lenny said. "She's already grumbled about the size of the deposit and I'd like to properly set her expectations on the cost of an investigation. It'll help our cause when the next one rolls around."

"Okay, what do you want me to do?" I asked with a sigh.

"I've already added in a couple of extra hours on my side for legal review. You go ahead and toss in an hour or two for research. Say you were looking up how to train cockatoos how to fly into trees or something like that."

"Fine," I said, knowing it wasn't worth arguing about. "I'll go over everything again. I'll have this on Sophie's desk before I take off."

"Since tomorrow's Thanksgiving, I'm assuming you want the day off?"

"Um, yeah. And since the office is closed on Friday, I was hoping for the entire weekend."

Lenny rolled his eyes as though I'd asked him to give me three months of paid time off. "Alright, take the four-day weekend, you too, Sophie. Better let Gina know as well. At the moment, there's nothing that can't wait until Monday."

The theme to *The Love Boat* started playing on my phone. I excused myself and ducked into the main conference room.

"Good morning," Max said when I answered. "How are you feeling today?"

"I'm doing better. It was great being back at home and sleeping with Marlowe. He was thrilled this morning when I fed him his second breakfast of the day."

"There's something I need to talk with you about. The military's coming to pick up Major Malakov this afternoon, but before he goes, he wants to talk with Gabriella, you, and me."

"All of us, at once? What does he want?"

"I don't know, and it's completely up to you. He's fully restrained, so we won't be in any sort of physical danger. No doubt he'll try to say something nasty to poison our minds. He might even try to say something to turn us against each other. He's a twisted man facing a long prison sentence. Being mean's about the only tool he has left."

"Do you think we should do it? Is this some sort of elaborate plot to get us all together so he can have one last chance of killing us?"

"Gabriella and I are going to listen to what he has to say,

but this one's completely up to you. I can't see how he could physically attack us. I'm sure it'll simply be talk. But I knew you'd want to know about it."

"I'll do it. I think I can take whatever he says. Maybe it will be the final closure I need for this one."

I drove up to the maintenance building on the far side of the resort. The first time I'd been here, there'd been a shootout, and the building had pretty much blown up. The second time, it was to pick up a client, Les Murdock, and by then, it had been completely rebuilt.

As I got closer to the building, there were several security guards visible in the doorway, and a team was patrolling the perimeter. The first guard on the road stopped to ask my name, but then I was waved through. I parked in the dirt parking lot and went in.

As I remembered from before, the large building smelled of gasoline and freshly cut grass. Off to the side of the room were several pieces of golf course maintenance equipment, mainly lawnmowers of one sort or another.

Major Nikolay Malakov sat in the center of the large space, strapped down to what appeared to be a police restraint chair. His face was pale, and he had a large bandage on his face where Gabriella had shot him. Two beefy guards stood to either side.

As I entered, one of the guards knocked on the door to the office. Max came out, followed by Gabriella. Without saying anything, the three of us stood in front of Major Malakov.

Nikolay started laughing as he saw how far away we stood. "You can come closer," he said. "It's not likely that I'll bite, and you can ask the Lieutenant. I've never seen the need to spit on anyone."

"You said you wanted to talk with all of us," Max said.

"We're all here. What did you want to say?"

"I merely wanted to say this. You may have captured me, but I will have my revenge."

"You will need to have your revenge from beyond the grave," Gabriella said. "I think you are going to live in very small concrete box for the rest of your life."

"No, not me," he said, still laughing weakly. "You see, three days ago, I made a phone call."

"You made phone call?" Gabriella asked.

"Yes, to Viktor."

Gabriella froze. All the color suddenly drained from her face.

"Yes," Nikolay said with a smile. "Viktor Pyotrovich Glazkov. I can see from your expression that you know what that means. I told him where you are living and what your new name is, along with my opinions on the best ways to attack you. That man hates you, even more than I do. I really don't blame him, considering everything you did to his organization. As I recall, you even killed his brother."

Max and Gabriella looked at each other. As always, tons of information seemed to flow between them.

"That's right," Nikolay said. "Now you'll need to tell Agent Kingfisher everything you did back then. What you did to Viktor, what you did to his team, and what is likely to happen to you now."

Nikolay then started laughing, as if he was truly enjoying the news he was delivering. "You know how Viktor operates. He won't send in anyone right away. He'll wait until he can study all of your weaknesses. Six months or maybe even a year will go by. You might think he's forgotten about you or has even decided to let you live. Then his team will come in. Although, I imagine Viktor will want to deal with you personally. You're about the only person I know that would make him come out of hiding."

Twenty minutes later, two stern-looking men in suits, along with two uniformed Military Police, came into the room, and everyone made introductions. They congratulated Max on being able to complete the mission, and then the two MPs handcuffed themselves to the Major and escorted him out.

The men in suits were also about to leave when I stopped them. "If I give you the number for the Eagle County Sheriff's office in Colorado, would you give them a call? The Major here assaulted a hotel clerk in Vail about a week ago, and they've been trying to track me down for information about him. If you can let the detectives know that you have him and that he's being held on separate federal charges, they could probably close their case."

"Sure," he said. "I'll be glad to. Do you have the contact information?"

Hoping he'd say that, I pulled out a piece of paper that already had all of the contact information and the case number. "Thanks, it'll pull me out of a huge jam."

"So?" I asked Max. "What happens next?"

Gabriella had taken off as soon as the military left. She was obviously upset, and I felt bad for anyone who did anything today to piss her off. "Is there going to be a trial? Will you have to testify?"

"No, the Major's been on the kill list for over a dozen years. He's an enemy of our country as well as others. I doubt there'll be a trial. I imagine they'll interrogate him until he spills what he knows, then they'll put him somewhere secure and keep him. Probably for the rest of his life."

"So, do you think we've seen the last of him?"

"I hope so," Max said. "He's been a real pain in the ass. I requested that I be kept informed of his whereabouts and any other developments as they come up."

"Do you think they'll tell you?" I asked.

"Hard to say. I'm not in the loop anymore."

"If you were worried about that, why not let Gabriella take him out? It would have solved the problem permanently."

"Ten years ago, I would have and not thought twice about it. But I'm starting to realize that killing isn't always the answer. I've seen too many instances where it only makes the problem worse rather than solving it. Plus, I think we now have a larger problem to worry about."

"Are you talking about this new guy, Viktor?"

"Yes. If what the Major said is true, we may have a team of very angry and determined people coming our way at some point."

"What do you know about him?"

"Not much. I'll need to talk more with Gabriella to get the full story. But I've heard the name before. The guy was a major player. If Viktor now knows where Gabriella is, it could be a serious problem."

"So, nothing's certain then?"

"No, nothing is ever certain. A lot has changed over the years, and Viktor may not have the resources to devote to an operation like this. It's only one more thing for us to worry about."

"Interesting life you have."

"That's true. But now that the golf tournament has finished and the problem with the Major is over, why don't we spend some time together over the next few days? I know you just got back home, but Grandma Peckham probably wouldn't mind taking care of Marlowe again, and you probably haven't even unpacked your suitcase. Why don't you come over to my place tonight and stay for the weekend?"

"Will Tony be alright with us doing that?"

"It was his idea. Sort of to make up for our shortened vacation in Colorado."

"Well, you keep talking about having a house, but all this time, I've halfway assumed you lived at the Tropical Paradise. You really do have a home somewhere in town?"

"I really do. It's not too far from Margaret Sternwood's. What do you say? Thanksgiving is tomorrow. I'll cook you a turkey, assuming we can find one that's not frozen. Then we can go car shopping and hang out for the weekend. I'm sure I'll need to be involved with the business part of the time, but we should still have plenty of time to be together."

Max then bent down and gave me a soft kiss. It had the usual effect of making my heart beat faster and making me tingle all over.

"Actually, spending the weekend with you at your house sounds perfect."

Yes!

As a special bonus,

please enjoy the first chapter of

Scottsdale Silence

the ninth book in the Laura Black

Scottsdale Mystery Series.

Scottsdale Silence

Prologue

"What do you know about Scottsdale General Hospital?" asked the man with the pink stun-gun.

I had awakened to find myself firmly tied to a metal chair in a small cinderblock room with an oil-stained concrete floor. The place had a musty chemical smell.

The face of the man asking the question completely filled my field of view. He was close enough for me to count the pores on his nasty, thin face and smell the tuna fish he'd had for lunch.

His long dark hair was slicked back, and his eyes bugged out of his face, giving him an almost cartoon-like appearance. Another man was behind me, holding my head so I couldn't turn it away.

"I don't know anything about Scottsdale General," I said, slurring my words like a drunk. "Other than the guys there have a weakness for skinny blondes."

My stomach still ached and twitched from the first time he had shocked me. It was making it hard to think clearly.

The man held up the stun-gun for me to look at as he again activated the switch. The smiling cartoon kitty on the front of the bright pink device seemed to be at odds with the pain and torment the weapon was designed to cause.

I watched as an intense white spark popped and flashed

between the two electrodes. The man slowly brought the stun-gun to within an inch or two of my face, just below my left eye.

The snapping noise the thick spark produced was deafening and brought a fresh wave of fear. My cheek soon grew uncomfortably warm as I waited for him to shove the device against me.

"Now then," he calmly said. "Let me ask you again. What do you know about Scottsdale General Hospital?"

At times like this, I wonder why I've decided to stay with the law office. Before this, I'd been a bartender at Greasewood Flat. It was a fun place to work, and the worst thing that ever happened was a drunk guy would sometimes throw up on me.

Since I started working as an investigator, I've been harassed, kidnapped, and tortured. I've been knocked unconscious and threatened with harm more times than I could count.

How did this escalate so quickly? I thought. *I was only taking pictures of naked people having sex.*

Chapter One

I woke up to the sound of a text notification on my phone. I opened one eye, fumbled the phone off my nightstand, and saw a text from Sophie, my best friend and coworker. She pretty much demanded that I come in right away; Lenny, my boss, wanted to see me.

Crap.

I put the phone down and glanced around. The room was in full daylight, but I had no idea what time it was. Honestly, I really didn't care. It had been a long couple of weeks since I'd been able to sleep in.

Marlowe, my overly pampered cat, lifted his head and looked at me, annoyed I'd disturbed him. I put my head back on the pillow and was asleep within seconds.

~~~~

Sometime around ten, I went in through the back security door of the law offices of Halftown, Oeding, Shapiro, and Hopkins, my place of employment. I walked past my cubicle in the back and up to the front reception area.

Sophie was working at her desk. She looked up from her tablet as I came in. Her eyes were bright as she smiled at me.

"You sure took your time getting in here today," she lightly scolded, her smile at odds with her words.

Sophie's parents came up from Mexico about a year before she was born. Although Spanish is her second language, she only has an accent when she thinks it will get her something.

"You're lucky I came in at all," I grumbled. "What are you so happy about?"

"Take a look," she said as she flipped open a newspaper to the society page and pointed.

About halfway down the page was a picture of a beautiful blonde woman with long curly hair, a light tan, and a huge smile. It had likely been taken as a publicity photo since she was wearing a Cardinals cheerleading outfit.

"Isn't this the cheerleader who was out with Snake?"

"Yeah, it is," Sophie said, still smiling. "Would you read the article out loud? I want to hear it one more time."

"Okay," I said as I started reading the copy.

"Cardinals release cheerleader Hayley Reynolds for violating the team's non-fraternization policy.

As we reported last month, Miss Reynolds was seen after the San Francisco game in the VIP room at Nexxus, the popular nightclub in Old Town Scottsdale. She was in the company of several Cardinals players and was seen getting chummy with backup quarterback Snake McCoy. Sources within the team report this wasn't the first instance of her violating team policies. Reynolds had been with the team for the last four seasons. In addition to cheerleading, she's been featured in several local television commercials with Honest George Anson promoting his Phoenix-area auto dealerships."

Sophie started laughing. "I love hearing you read that. It makes me feel warm and happy all over."

"Wow, I'd always heard cheerleaders were discouraged

from dating the players, but I didn't think you could get fired over that."

"I wish I could have been there when they told her the news. I would have loved to see her reaction. I wonder if she only sniffled a little, with maybe a single tear?"

Sophie stuck out her lower lip and pretended to wipe her eye.

"You know," she continued, "I bet she completely lost it and started wailing like a five-year-old. I'm thinking the full waterworks, with big wet sobs, wailing, and lots of snot. It would have been hilarious to watch security escort her from the building." Clearly, she'd been giving this some thought.

"I wonder how Snake feels about his part in getting her fired?" I asked. "I bet he feels pretty bad about it."

"It's his own fault for going out with that nasty bimbo when he could have been with me," Sophie grumbled.

"Have you talked with him since you found out about the cheerleader?"

"Nope, and I'm not going to. He's roadkill and can have that skanky-ass ho all to himself. Although, he might not want her anymore, now that she's back to being an aspiring actress or whatever she was before she became a cheerleader."

I plopped down on one of the red leather wing chairs next to her desk.

Sophie looked at me, concerned. "You look beat. You've got the dark-circles-under-your-eyes thing going on."

"I am beat, and I could use a day or two off. Yesterday was the first day I didn't work since Thanksgiving break. That was like three weeks ago."

"But you got to spend pretty much that entire weekend

with Max."

"I know. Thanksgiving was great. Max told his housekeeper to take the day off, and he cooked me a delicious turkey dinner."

"I'm still surprised Max can cook."

"So was I. There's a lot I don't know about him, at least not yet."

"I'm still a little mad at you since you didn't take any pictures of his house. All you've told me is how beautiful it is, but I already guessed that."

"There isn't a lot to say about it. It's not gigantic like Muffy's. It only has four bedrooms and an office, but everything's so beautiful. He has a great kitchen that looks out over the living room and the big picture windows."

"And you said Max has a huge deck?"

"I think I love his deck best of all. It runs the entire length of the house and overlooks the pool, Paradise Valley, and Camelback Mountain. The weekend was warm enough for us to sit on it every night with a couple of drinks and watch the sun go down. It was wonderful."

"How'd you get along with his housekeeper? Beatrice?"

"She's nice. There's a separate apartment in the back where she lives. She came back the day after Thanksgiving and was with us the rest of the weekend. I guess she's been with Max ever since he bought the house. She told me he never has visitors, and it was good to be able to cook for more than him."

"I'm glad to hear he doesn't have a lot of women over. It's always a creepy feeling when you go to some guy's house, and there's a closet half-full of miscellaneous women's clothes. It makes you wonder."

"Does that happen to you a lot?"

"Sometimes," she said with a shrug. "Hey, when are you getting your new car? I thought it was supposed to be in by now."

"I'm waiting for the dealer to call. It's still listed as 'In Transit' on the website."

"It'll be great for you to ditch your old one. It's halfway fallen apart. Are you going to sell it to a junkyard, or should we ditch it somewhere?"

"I'm thinking about keeping it."

"Seriously? Why would you keep that old P.O.S.?"

"In case I have to do something that could damage my new car. You know, stakeouts and stuff. I don't want the new one to end up looking like the old one. Or ending up like Tony's car."

"Well, good luck with that. I know how you treat your vehicles."

"How's Lenny?" I asked as I nodded my head in the direction of his closed office door. "Did he go out with Elle again?"

"Jeez, it's all I've been hearing about," Sophie said as she rolled her eyes and shook her head. "Yeah, they went out Friday night. Elle went out with the girls on Saturday, but then she and Lenny went out again last night."

"They've been seeing each other for almost two months. Do you think it's turning into a real thing?"

"That's a good question. I wouldn't think anyone could have a relationship with Lenny. I mean, yuck."

"I know. The thought grosses me out as well. I guess we'll find out if it's an actual relationship as time goes on."

"I hope it lasts a while longer. He's been in a relatively good mood since he started dating her."

"You said Lenny wanted to see me? It's not another assignment, I hope. I just finished the last one yesterday morning. I was hoping for at least two or three days off before the next one."

"Sorry. You know how crazy busy it gets this time of year."

"Fine, but please tell me it's not another cheating spouse."

"Well, I can tell you it's not, but it is."

"Jeez, I need to find another job."

"I heard the Cardinals have an opening for a new cheerleader."

"Shut up. Do you have a file for the new one yet?"

"Nope, other than her husband's a doctor over at Scottsdale General, I don't know a lot about it. But the wife will be here in about half an hour, so you can hear everything for yourself."

I sighed and gave Sophie a look.

"Sorry," she said. "Not all of your assignments are going to let you find a lost gold mine or a treasure chest full of antique jewelry. But look at it this way, a doctor will mean a nice house. You'll have lots of big closets to hide in."

"You think you're being funny. But if I have to hide in one more closet, I really might quit."

~~~~

My name is Laura Black. I've been the junior investigator at the law office for a little over three years.

The firm was started back in the eighties with four partners. Since then, the three senior partners have all left the group. One moved to Pensacola, and two of them died.

One met his end in a skiing accident in Colorado. The other one had a heart attack while doing the nasty with a law student intern named Jeanette.

She ended up becoming the publicist for several A-list Hollywood actors, including Stig Stevens. I've actually worked with the woman on an assignment. She seems nice.

The remaining partner, Leonard Shapiro, my boss, has remade the firm into one of the most successful boutique law offices in Scottsdale. To maximize his profits, Lenny prefers keeping to high-profile criminal, civil, and family law cases.

The more desperate and hopeless the case looks, the more he likes it. Anxious clients don't ask up front how much everything will cost.

~~~~

The door to the street opened, and the client came in. She was a pleasant-looking woman, somewhere in her mid-forties, with short brunette hair and subtle makeup.

She was dressed in designer labels and had a high-end bag but otherwise didn't go out of her way to display her wealth. The only jewelry she wore was a wedding set, but the center stone must have been close to three carats.

"I'm Jessica Palmer," she said as she walked up to Sophie's desk. "I have an appointment with Leonard Shapiro."

We made introductions, and then Sophie went into Lenny's office to let him know the client had arrived. She came out a few seconds later. "Mr. Shapiro can see you now."

The three of us went into the office. The client took the chair directly in front of Lenny's oversized desk while I sat to the side. Sophie took the chair near the door, in case she had to answer the phone or greet someone coming in off the street.

We really need to get someone in to help Sophie run the office.

"Mrs. Palmer," Lenny said. "Thank you for coming in. How can I help you?"

"It's like I explained to you on the phone," she said, her voice was a little shaky. "I believe my husband, Michael, is having an affair. If it's true, I'd like to divorce him."

Lenny looked her over and turned to Sophie. "Would you make me a Beam on the rocks? Mrs. Palmer, would you like a cocktail or perhaps a glass of wine?"

The client blew out a breath. "It's early, but thank you. A glass of wine might help."

Sophie got up and poured the drinks. By now, I was used to not being offered one. In fact, if Lenny did give us a drink at one of these client meetings, I'd be a little worried.

Sophie placed Lenny's Jim Beam on his desk and handed Mrs. Palmer a glass of chilled pinot grigio. Our client took a couple of sips and it seemed to relax her.

"Mrs. Palmer," Lenny said. "Go ahead and tell us what's going on and what you'd like us to do." He was using his concerned lawyer's voice. I'm sure he practices it in front of a mirror.

Our client took a deep breath and started speaking. "My husband, Michael, is head of surgery for Scottsdale General Hospital."

"Would that be the main hospital campus on North Hayden Road?" Lenny asked, making notes on a yellow legal pad with his black Montblanc pen.

"That's right. Three or four times a month, when my

husband comes home from work, he seems distant, almost angry. When I ask him about it, he always says it's nothing. If I press him, he'll say he had a hard case in surgery, that sort of thing. But this has been going on for several months, and I'm starting to become concerned."

"When did you start to suspect he was having an affair?"

"It was a couple of weeks ago, right after Thanksgiving. He came home in a foul mood. When I asked him about it, he snapped at me. He said everything was fine, but he'd had a long and crappy day at work."

"What did you do then?" Lenny asked.

"All of the surgeons are scheduled through a central office. I happen to know someone who works there. I called her the next day to find out if he'd had a tough case or if he'd maybe worked on something unusual the day before."

"What did she tell you?"

Our client's voice became quiet, and she looked down at her hands in her lap. "She said he hadn't been scheduled for anything past noon. In fact, he'd listed himself as unavailable every Tuesday and Thursday afternoon for the entire month of December."

"Did your friend see that as unusual?" Lenny asked.

"Not really," she said with a laugh. "Several of the surgeons there have standing times off during the week. Most of them use the time to play golf."

"Did she say how long he's been taking Tuesday and Thursday afternoons off?"

"He's been doing it since early in the summer. That makes it almost six months."

"I take it he told you he'd been working on all of these days?"

"Yes, like I said, whenever I'd ask him what was wrong, he'd blame some difficult case that day. He'd then sit in his den and watch television until he decided to come to bed."

"What would you like us to do?" Lenny asked.

"I'd like to find out for sure. If he's started seeing someone new, I'd like to start divorce proceedings, right away. We have two boys in their early teens, and I'd like custody."

"Is there a prenup involved?" he asked.

"No, back when he proposed to me, he said he wanted one. But I refused."

It's always at this point I hope Lenny will suggest marriage counseling. Whatever problems couples are having in their marriage, there might still be a chance they could work things out if they could openly talk to each other about it.

Instead, Lenny's lips curled up in a smile. Looking at him, I could almost hear the sound of an old-fashioned cash register bell ringing.

"Very well," he said, again using his lawyer's voice. "Not having a prenup will simplify things and help us out considerably."

Our client visibly relaxed and took a big sip of her wine.

"Sophie will have some paperwork for you to complete," Lenny continued. "We'll also need a twenty-thousand-dollar retainer to get started. After that's squared away, we'll get right on it."

Jessica seemed a little put out by the retainer's high-dollar amount. She raised an eyebrow, sucked in a breath, and was about to say something, but instead, she let out a deep sigh and took another long sip of her wine.

Our new client stood, and Sophie walked to the wet bar to refill her glass. They both then went out to work on the paperwork while Lenny asked me to stay behind.

As they left, I marveled at how, once again, Lenny had judged precisely how much the client would be willing to pay. He'd then pushed it to the limit.

"Twenty thousand seems a little high for a couple of days of surveillance," I said, not being able to help myself.

"Really?" he asked, surprised. "I had been about to ask for twenty-five. But I decided to pull myself back a bit. It's pretty obvious what's going on with the husband. Plus, I had Sophie check out her finances."

"And?"

"She comes from a wealthy family, and her husband pulls down almost a million a year as head of surgery at the hospital. They have two kids in their early teens so the divorce will drag out for at least a year. Maybe more, depending on how hard he wants to fight it. I can easily see pulling another twenty-five or thirty thousand from her before this is over."

Hearing this was disheartening. Sometimes, I really do hate my job.

"Look," Lenny said, speaking slowly as if to a child. "This one should be simple. Tomorrow's Tuesday. The guy's going to be in the hospital all morning. Sometime around noon, he's going to take off. He's a doctor, so he'll likely be driving something flashy. Even I could tail someone like that. Follow him around and figure out if he's nailing some broad. If he is, take some pictures."

"Yeah," I grumbled. "More pictures of naked people having sex."

"Why are you complaining?" he asked, genuinely

confused. "It's like I keep telling you. You've got the eye for it. Some of your pictures lately have been quality work. As good as anything you can find on the internet."

"Eeeewww."

"Hey, if you don't like your job, you could always go back to bartending. You said you enjoyed doing that."

"Fine, I didn't say I wouldn't do it."

I went out to reception in time to see Sophie run the client's credit card. The signed paperwork was already sitting on her desk.

"Jessica," I said. "Do you have a few minutes? I'd like to get some basic information from you."

She said she did, and we went into the conference room. After about thirty minutes, I had everything I needed for my day of surveillance.

~~~~

Gina, Sophie, and I walked down the street for tacos and a Corona. The weather was a little cool, but several heaters were scattered in the seating area to keep the chill off. After my last assignment, which kept me busy for so long, it was great to catch up with them.

"What's going on with you and Jet?" I asked Gina. "You've been dating him for over a month already."

"It's been almost two months," she said, smiling. "We get along so well. As soon as I get a few days off, we're planning on going up to Page. I want to take him hiking up Antelope Canyon. He's also never seen Horseshoe Bend. I thought we'd get there for the sunrise."

"I went up there with my family when I was a kid," Sophie said. "It was a freaking long drive from California, but my parents let me spit into the Grand Canyon, so that was pretty cool."

"In the movies, John Wayne threw a beer bottle into the canyon from there," I said.

"They'd probably arrest you if you tried to do something like that now," Sophie said.

"What about you?" I asked Sophie. "How is it having only one boyfriend at a time?"

"It's harder than I thought it would be," she said. "Don't get me wrong, Milo's a great guy and everything. But when I go out with the cougars, and all of those hot guys start buying me drinks? It's been a challenge not to go home with at least one or two of them."

"Here's to taking home hot guys from the bar," Gina said as she held up her beer.

"Hot guys from the bar," we both said as we lifted our beers and clinked our glasses together.

~~~~

We went back to the office, and I was thinking about going home when Lenny popped his head out and walked to reception.

"I'm glad you're all here," he said. "There's something I want to ask you about."

From his tone, we knew what he wanted to talk about. I heard Sophie moan, and I looked at Gina. I knew they both felt as uncomfortable as I did.

Ever since Lenny started dating Elle, he's been asking embarrassing personal questions about dating and relationships. The only reason we kept humoring him was that we were the ones who had nudged him into dating Elle in the first place.

As usual, Lenny ignored our moans and sideways glances.

"I've been dating Elle for almost two months, and it's been great," he said. "But all we ever seem to do is go out to dinner and then head to her place. I want to ask her to go somewhere with me, like maybe for the entire weekend. I was thinking Vegas."

"That seems reasonable," Gina said, clearly relieved the question wasn't about a disgusting personal hygiene issue. "How can we help?"

"Every time I bring up the idea of doing something more involved than a dinner date, she shuts me down. I don't know if I'm being too subtle or somehow asking wrong."

"I don't know if there's a wrong way to ask someone out," I said. "Tell her you think it would be fun if you spent the weekend together and offer to take her to Las Vegas."

"I could do that," Lenny said. "But I've been thinking…"

Sophie barked out a short laugh. She then quickly tried to hide it by pretending to cough.

"Anyway," Lenny continued as he looked down at Sophie. "I was thinking maybe the reason she doesn't want to do anything more than an evening at a time with me is that she doesn't know how I really feel about her."

I started to get a bad feeling about where this was going. "And how do you feel about her?" I asked.

"I'm in love," he said, a big stupid smile on his face. "I'm thinking about asking her to marry me."

"No!" we all shouted at once.

Sophie started to laugh nervously, and I could tell Gina was getting annoyed, so I stepped in.

"Um," I said. "You've only been going out for seven or eight weeks. Perhaps you should give it some time, like maybe six months or even a year, before you tell Elle you love her. It's the sort of thing that can spook a woman if you hit her with it too soon."

"Really?" Lenny asked. He seemed genuinely perplexed. "I thought all you gals liked it when men fell in love with you?"

"We do," Gina said in her motherly tone. "But it's best if it's felt on both sides before you start voicing it. Otherwise, it can quickly sour the relationship."

"You're serious?" Lenny asked. "That seems to fly in the face of what I see whenever I watch a movie on the Hallmark channel. The women there seem to fall in love after three or four dates. But, hey, I'll take your word on it."

~~~~

I stayed in the office long enough to finish catching up with both Gina and Sophie. I then drove back to my place to enjoy my last few hours of freedom before things started getting busy again.

As I walked down the hallway to my apartment, I heard the TV playing in Grandma Peckham's apartment. I hadn't talked to her for a few days, so I knocked.

I had to knock a couple of times, but I eventually heard the TV volume go down. A moment later, Grandma opened the door. Today, she was wearing her pink jogging suit.

"Why, Laura," she said in her always cheerful voice. "Come in, dear. How have you been? We haven't had a chance to do more than say hello in the hallway since you spent the weekend at your new boyfriend's house."

"I know. It's been busy at the office."

"It's the Snowbirds," Grandma said as she shook her head. "Every year, there seems to be more of them. It's getting to the point where I'm nervous even driving down to the store. Having one old lady driving down the street doesn't seem to be a problem. Young people have such good reflexes. But when everyone on the street is a senior, it can make driving a challenge."

"How's the wedding going? It's in a little under two weeks."

"Well, it's mostly going okay."

"What part's not going well?"

"Honestly, I'm starting to worry something's going to go wrong with the ceremony."

"I suppose all brides get nervous before the wedding. I'm sure things will go smoothly."

"Oh, I'm not worried about getting married," Grandma said. "It's my wedding planner."

"I didn't know you had a wedding planner. I thought your granddaughter Megan was doing all of that."

"She's been helpful, but if you remember, we took over a wedding they were going to have at the Scottsdale Barrington for New Year's Eve. I also inherited their wedding planner."

"You said the other couple canceled, and you were able to use their caterer, their flowers, and their photographer. I know it saved you a lot since you could use the deposits they'd already paid."

"Yes, I'm saving a great deal, but I've been hearing nothing but horror stories about the wedding planner. She seems nice, but when I talked to the people at the Barrington, they said her weddings over the past few months have mostly been disasters."

"That doesn't sound good. What kinds of things have happened?"

"Photographers not being on time, limos not showing up, and one where the minister was over an hour late. The worst one I heard was when the caterer tried to serve prime rib at a vegetarian wedding."

"Wow. Any of those would be enough to ruin the day."

"Honestly, I think that's why the other couple canceled. They didn't want to risk their wedding."

"Most of those issues seem like bad luck as much as anything else. Have you talked with your wedding planner about it?"

"I did. She's not sure why the problems keep happening. She seems as angry and bewildered as anyone about the whole thing."

"How can I help?"

"Well," she said. "I was thinking. You're a detective, would you talk with her? Maybe you could find out what's wrong."

"You know I'm not a detective. I'm only an investigator at a law firm."

"Oh, I know, but it's pretty much the same thing."

I let out a sigh to show Grandma how I felt about getting put in the middle of something like this. She only looked at me with her little old lady smile.

"Okay, fine," I said. "I guess you can consider this part of your wedding present."

"Thank you, dear. I knew you'd want to help."

"Have you and Grandpa Bob decided where you're going to live? I know you'd considered moving over to his place."

"We'd talked about me going over there. We even talked about getting a place in Sun City. But I think he's moving over here. My place is a little bigger, plus my furniture is so much nicer. And honestly, I don't want to pack everything up."

"That's great news," I said. "I was really hating the idea of you moving away."

About the Author

Halfway through a successful career in technical writing, marketing, and sales, along with having four beautiful children, author B A Trimmer veered into fiction. Combining a love of the desert, derived from many years of living in Arizona, with an appreciation of the modern romantic detective story, the Laura Black Scottsdale Series was born.

Comments and questions are always welcome.

E-mail the author at LauraBlackScottsdale@gmail.com
Follow at www.facebook.com/ScottsdaleSeries/
Twitter: @BATrimmerAuthor